SHEM FLEENOR

Letters Not Sent

1848 Publishing Company

New York City

ISBN: 978-1-951231-08-8

Table of Contents

CHAPTER ONE

The Lower East Side of Manhattan, July 1936

Even drunk, Zapata Abrahams usually had terrible
difficulty falling asleep. Part of the reason for his incessant
insomnia was his inability to find any semblance of
relaxation or rest on the tiny, rickety, lumpy and musty
brown couch in the cramped one-bedroom apartment on
Broome Street in lower Manhattan that his family was
barely able to pay rent to live in. The biggest reason for
Zapata's perpetual restlessness was, however, primarily a
result of the clinical angst and anxiety his father radiated
since returning from the bloody and mud filled French
trenches after "The Great War," eighteen years earlier. His
father came back from war a shell of who the son had
fondly remembered. The trauma that transformed Leopold
in France seemed to creep closer to doom each passing day
during the Roaring Twenties and especially during the
Great Depression. Even though Leopold left France, the
war never left Zapata's father.

Zapata, now twenty-three years of age, was but a
knee-high toddler when his father first left for the mustard-
gas filled trenches of the Western Front. Zapata fondly
remembered his father as far more hopeful, ambitious and
attentive before being drafted into the Expeditionary Force
and sent to confront der Kaiser's highly industrialized war
machine comprised of conscripted peasants with canons,
machineguns and automatic rifles at their disposal. Leopold
had even, Zapata remembered, sometimes scraped together
enough cash to take his only child to Yankees games or to
Coney Island to ride the B&B Carousel at Luna Park.

Zapata often reminisced of his father's sense of hope and belief in the American system and way of life before the war. Leopold had long dreamt of buying a farm so he would not have to suffer the stuffy and nauseating indignity of the A-train twice a day to and from the Meatpacking District where he slaughtered pigs twelve hours a day, six days a week. Leopold was actually initially glad to have been drafted into the Expeditionary Force because he mistakenly believed it would better position him to buy a glorious plot of earth beyond the confines of the soul crushing city if, that is, he was lucky enough to survive the war.

Any naïve delusions Leopold suffered that the war would be something other than horrendous was, however, quickly disabused by the reality and carnage of trench warfare. By the time Leopold returned to New York after suffering sixteen months in the closest thing humans had to hell, his feet had been amputated just above the ankles due to a particularly virulent and aggressive case of gout in both limbs. The loss of his feet was but the most obvious casualty Leopold suffered but, arguably, the least severe of his injuries. In reality, the complete abandonment of hope, ambition and optimism was equally as tragic as the loss of his limbs. Terrifyingly crippling dreams grew so constant during the dog days of the Great Depression that Leopold simply stopped going to bed altogether for fear he might likely harm – maybe even kill – Sara, his devoted wife, during the night. Most nights Leopold thus sat quiet and listless in his secondhand and dilapidated wheelchair, which was parked next to the couch which his son had so much difficulty sleeping in. Most nights Leopold gazed sorrowfully and silently out the window and radiated resentment and despair-laced tension that prohibited Zapata from getting rest.

Zapata often tossed and turned wide awake at night lamenting the quick and steady decline of his father's mental health, which was already evident at the July Fourth fireworks at the Statue of Liberty not long after returning to the city after sixteen long months of killing der Kaiser's Huns in a war he never believed was morally justified to begin with. His father glared at Lady Liberty as if he wanted to knock her over into the Hudson River. In Leopold's mind, the so called "Great War" was, despite Woodrow Wilson's quixotic assertion that it was a "fight to preserve Democracy," a vicious meat grinder where working class men were systemically sent to die or forfeit limbs and sanity so that European aristocrats who had precipitated the war could bolster the last vestiges of the feudalism that underwrote their sociopolitical entitlements. "Women, never mind millions of negroes, couldn't vote," Leopold explained to his young son while the fireworks filled the night sky above Lady Liberty's crown, "some fucking democracy."

Ever since returning from the war with a belly full of rage and a head full of terror Leopold had great difficulty seeing any inkling of good in people, including his only child and his patient, faithful and dutiful wife. Leopold's cynicism was further informed by his ancestors' long history of confronting exploitation. They, along with all other Iberian Jews who refused to convert to Catholicism, had been chased out of Spain during the

Inquisition in the fifteenth century. Most recently, Leopold, his wife, and his son were forced to move from a grand apartment in Baychester so that some New Dealers could build a new highway and shopping center in the Bronx. The federal government compensated Leopold just enough to lease a shabby one-bedroom apartment on Broome Street. Being relocated from the home his dearly departed mother and father had built with their own hands after fleeing Prussia during the Pogroms of the late-nineteenth century, and where he had subsequently lived most of his life, was the final straw that shattered what little was left of Leopold's tattered spirit.

Though he grew more bitter with each setting of the summer sun in 1936, Leopold was especially careful to keep his ideas to himself so as to not be painted with a proverbial red brush of "Bolshevism," and thusly outed as an "anti-American radical," which in the decades after "The Great War" could quite literally cost a Jew born in what used to be Prussia his family, freedom, political identity, or even life. He had thus kept his despair and depression bottled up as best as he could. He had flirted with political activism in the 1920s. His service in the Expeditionary Force and the fact that he had sacrificed limbs in "The Great War" provided him a modicum of moral authority many of the leftist ideologues lacked. But after seeing firsthand the brutal mistreatment of veterans during the bonus march on the Washington Mall in the summer of 1932, he came to see political activism as a waste of time and energy in the United States. "We've been colonized by the American empire as much as the damn Philippines and Puerto Ricans," he often lamented in the months and years after General MacArthur violently crushed the peaceful gathering of vets desperate for their pensions and ultimately to survive the onset of the Great Depression by being paid the money they earned by risking life and limb on the Western Front during "The Great War." After MacArthur's violent quelling of the Bonus Marchers' protest, Leopold seemed to grow more and more reconciled to the notion that fighting a hegemonic power like the American empire was a futile endeavor. He thus receded from political activism and gradually went deeper and deeper into his own despair.

So many restless nights since the summer of 1932 Leopold had sat wide awake in his wheelchair stewing, smoking his corncob pipe, clutching his pearl-handled chrome revolver, and gazing blankly out of the second-story window of the living room at the lower Manhattan night as taxis whizzed by Broome Street. Such was the case on this particular night.

Zapata quickly removed the musty and faded gray pillow from his face. His weary, bloodshot and suspicious eyes darted towards the front door of the apartment as the sound of rain-soaked wingtips click clacked up the wooden stairs and into the dark and dank hallway outside the cramped and dingy apartment.

"Is someone visiting?" Sara, Zapata's mother, called from the bedroom as her feet slid into her aged and scuffed house slippers.

Zapata sat up quickly to listen more intently. A thunderous banging on the door startled him. He cautiously crept towards the door and peaked through the peephole.

"Open up," a surly man holding a Federal Bureau of Investigation badge in front of the peephole demanded, "we know you're in there." Zapata nervously glanced back at his father. Leopold, however, stared blankly out the window, unaware of the agents outside the apartment. Zapata cautiously creaked the door ajar. Three of J. Edgar Hoover's G-men burst into the apartment.

"What's this about?" Zapata fumed. His startled and worried mother, who was wearing a stained white housedress, hurried out of the bedroom and into the living room. She flicked the kitchen light on and squinted at the agents who had forced their way into her humble home. Agent Robinson, the biggest of the three, aimed his pistol at Leopold's head. Leopold, meanwhile, continued to gaze out the window, unfazed by the agents' intrusion.

"I'm sorry, but we don't have any money," Sara's voice quivered. "But we do have a Victrola that works alright. Please, just take it and whatever else you want and go."

"This isn't a shakedown, lady," Krewson, the grizzled G-man donning the dark-blue fedora said. "We gotta take your husband in."

"He's armed," Robinson, who was donning a black raincoat cautioned his partner while glancing at the pistol in Leopold's hand.

The agents' eyes had finally adjusted to the dimness of the apartment. A beam of streetlight from outside the window Leopold sat next to reflected off the chrome barrel of the revolver in his lap. The trio of agents trained their weapons on Leopold, who continued to gaze disconsolately outside at the rain falling to the slick concrete on Broome Street.

"Drop your weapon!" the third G-man, Agent Muska, demanded in a thick East Brooklyn accent.

"He's done nothing wrong," Sara pleaded as her trepidation transformed into anger. "He's a war hero, for god's sake."

"A war hero?" Krewson sneered. "The hell he is. He's a goddamn terrorist."

"Terrorist?" Sara chortled in shocked horror at the absurdity of the assertion. "He can't even walk. He gave his feet for this godforsaken empire."

"You watch your mouth when talking about my country," Robinson snarled as he pointed at Leopold. "He's a card-carrying member of the Communist League."

"The Communist League?" Sara retorted bewilderedly. "He's been to a meeting, maybe two, at the most, since Black Tuesday, but that hardly makes him a member of the Communist Party. Besides, he hardly ever speaks. He's surely no activist. And even if he was, being a Communist is not illegal; not yet, anyway."

"Well then," Robinson grunted snidely, "if he's no Commie then he won't have any qualms about coming with us to answer a few questions."

"What questions?" Sara demanded. "He's practically a shut-in, for God's sake. All he ever does anymore is listen to the radio and stare out that damn window."

"We uncovered another plot to bomb the J.P. Morgan office," Muska explained. "Your husband has been implicated by an informant."

"An informant?" Zapata chimed in as he glanced at his father sitting stock still and gazing plaintively out the window. "A goddamn rat will say anything when being questioned if he thinks it might get him off the hook."

"Well, if your father really the paragon of innocence you say he is, he'll have no problem doing his civic duty by coming with us and answering some questions about his whereabouts and associates," Krewson said. "If he's as innocent as you say he is, we'll have him back by morning."

"This is such a preposterous violation of our civil rights," Sara said as she scowled defiantly. "My husband has been very ill. He's not fit for this nonsense. This government has put him through far more than enough already. Please, I beg you, just leave us be." She motioned towards the door to usher the intruders towards the exit. Leopold suddenly and deftly caressed the barrel of his pistol against his thigh, which alerted the agents.

"Drop your goddamn weapon! That's an order, not a request!" Robinson demanded. Leopold placed the gun barrel under his chin and calmly squeezed the trigger.

Naples, Italy, July 1936

Whitewall tires skidded to a halt on the slick cobblestone street, which was lined with rickety apartment buildings that had been haphazardly erected shortly after Garibaldi died. A cadre of men, each donning the black shirt, trousers, and boots synonymous with Benito Mussolini's National Fascist Party, rushed out of each egress of a shiny new black Mercedes Benz. The first from the car pushed open a rusting metal door leading into the dark, dank and musty foyer of one of the apartment buildings. His wide-eyed compatriots rushed in after him.

Three stories up, twenty-one white wax candles flickered atop the sweet-smelling chocolate and buttercream birthday cake Maria's mother, Bianca, had baked earlier in the day. Bianca, who was thirty-nine years old, and Maria's father, Giuseppe, who had recently turned forty, both looked much more proximate to being elderly than to youthfully exuberant. They had aged a lifetime in the fourteen years since Mussolini rose to power.

Maria, wearing a yellow ribbon in her unwashed raven hair, had a thoughtful though reserved and somewhat embarrassed half-smile on her face as she blew out the candles in one swift, stiff breath. Her weary eyes scanned the trails of smoke wafting towards the warped wooden ceiling overhead. Her parents applauded as Maria bowed appreciatively and leaned back in her creaking chair next to the small coffee-stained wooden dining room table in the quaint and dimly lit two-bedroom apartment, which was just a few blocks from the docks stained with seagull feces that lined the Port of Naples.

The foghorns of ships entering and departing the port used to be a soothing sound that sometimes aided in Maria falling asleep. Giuseppe had, however, recently been nominated to be a spokesman for the local textile workers union. The foghorns thus mollified Maria's insomnia less each passing night, especially since the sound was increasingly a glaring reminder of the many boys she had gone to school and church with all her life being shipped across the Mediterranean Sea to wage a savage war against Ethiopians, the last African holdouts to be conquered and colonized by European imperialists.

"What did you wish for?" Bianca asked her daughter while cutting a piece of cake and placing it onto a bright blue plate. Maria's weary eyes scanned from the window across the small square table towards her mother.

"I just wish for one good night sleep," Maria said hesitantly while sighing, hoping for an unattainable miracle. A sudden gust of wind wafted through the third story living room window.

The soft tranquility of the moment shared between Maria and her parents quickly dissipated as the steady and hollow sound of heavy and shiny black leather boots marching lockstep up the narrow and fragile wooden staircase outside the cramped apartment grew nearer and nearer. Giuseppe's face flushed white. He, long dreading an inevitable incursion by Mussolini's men, reflexively rushed into the dingy bedroom he shared with his wife to retrieve a rusting cigar tin stuffed with billfolds and passports. He dumped the money, birth certificates, and passports on the bedspread that Maria's mother had sewed for the couple as a wedding present two decades earlier.

A clenched fist wrapped in a black leather glove pounded the door in the dark hallway outside the apartment. The flickering yellow light over the stormtroopers added an extra layer of menace to their appearance.

The barrage of banging filled the dark and cramped hallway outside the apartment but sounded hollow inside it. Giuseppe pulled open the drawer of the nightstand nestled next to the bed. He snatched the antique Rotazione pistol he had acquired earlier in the week at a pawn shop down by the port. He then shoved the money and documents back into the cigar tin and raced into the dining area while his shaking hands clumsily shoved chrome bullets into the revolver.

The shiny black fist banged the door once more. "Open the door," the first stormtrooper demanded. Maria glanced nervously at her mother's flushed white face. "Here, take this," Giuseppe whispered pleadingly while shoving the tin stuffed with money and documents under his wife's trembling arm. "It's all we've got." He peaked out the living room window and surveyed the cobblestone street below. There was no sign of Blackshirts at street level. The sound filled the interior of the apartment, reverberating in Maria's sweat soaked spine. "Hurry!"

Giuseppe pleaded. "Go down the fire escape fast!" Bianca and Maria stood stock still, paralyzed by fear and confusion. "Go!" Giuseppe demanded as he shepherded them towards the dim and cramped hallway leading towards the fire escape outside the parents' room.

"Go where?" Bianca worried. "Both of our parents are dead and your brothers have already been arrested by the Blackshirts."

"America, just like we talked about. Now is the time," his voice quivered. "There's enough money for you both to get there. Catch the next ship you can get on. Now go!"

"Please papa," Maria pleaded as her fear transformed into anguish, "We can't go without you."

"Open the door immediately," one of the Blackshirts demanded while signaling towards his compadre with the ax to move closer to the front of the line. "We will break it down," the menacing man added.

"We will be together soon enough," Giuseppe promised, "now hurry!"

Bianca clenched tightly to Maria's quivering hand and led her daughter into the smaller of the two bedrooms, ushering her onto the jerry-built wooden and rain slicked fire escape leading to the cobblestone below. One of Maria's scuffed white and black saddle shoes came untied, which slightly slowed her ability to descend the ladder. Maria, however, finally managed to navigate the fire escape to the slick cobblestone below. "Hurry mama, please," she begged. Her worrisome and tired eyes scanned upwards as her mother, who was clutching the cigar tin full of cash and documents under her arm, had a great deal of difficulty traversing the ladder. Exhausted and terrified, Bianca momentarily ceased descending the ladder in the hope of catching her breath. She was then stunned stiff by the sound of the front door of the apartment being battered off its hinges by the ax wielding Blackshirt. "Drop the pistol," the man in charge demanded.

Giuseppe tried to fire the gun. But it was an inoperable antique passed off as authentic by the desperate and dishonest pawnbroker who had sold it to him. Giuseppe was then manhandled and pinned to the hardwood floor. His forehead was split open on the corner of the dining room table. The buttercream cake fell onto the floor next to his face and intermingled with his crimson blood. A wide-eyed Blackshirt cautiously entered the bedroom with his gun drawn. He cautiously crept towards the open window and pushed the cream-colored curtain aside with the barrel of his pistol. His nervous eyes peaked out of the window and scanned downwards towards the street. Bianca, who was petrified stiff on the fire-escape ladder ten feet below, glowered up at him. "Hurry mama, please, don't be afraid," Maria pleaded while stumbling nervously into a gutter full of mud. The nervous Blackshirt cautiously aimed his pistol at Bianca's forehead. Her wide and terrified eyes beamed up at him pleadingly. "Come back up here," he demanded. "Please, I don't want to shoot you."

Bianca instinctively descended a few more rungs of the slippery ladder as the Blackshirt cocked the hammer of his pistol. She fumbled the tin, which plummeted two-and-a-half stories to the cobblestone next to Maria. The impact of the collision between the tin and sidewalk caused the top of the receptacle to pop open. A few bills fluttered away in the wind whipping up from the port. Maria scrambled to shove the cash back into the tin and pushed her passport into the pocket of her black Sunday-best dress, which she had worn to mass each week since she was sixteen.

"Halt," the young fascist demanded while aiming his pistol down at Bianca; her aching arms quaked. "I will shoot you, so help me God!" his unnerved voice cracked. Bianca's left shoe slid from her foot and splattered in the mud puddle next to Maria. Bianca grew so terrified and tired that she finally let go of the ladder and fell two stories to the cobblestone below. Her right femur shattered on impact. She gnashed her teeth, winced, and wailed agonizingly. But fear, adrenalin, and endorphins permitted her to drag herself up from the muddy gutter and to her feet. She tried to run, but her leg gave out after a single excruciating step. She collapsed face first to the wet cobblestone. Inside the apartment building, the young Blackshirt raced down three flights of creaking wooden steps and out into the street. "Halt!" he demanded while aiming his pistol at Bianca, who was writhing agonizingly in the gutter.

"Go!" Bianca begged her daughter. "I'll find you."

Maria hesitated a moment and then scurried around the nearest street corner leading down the hill towards the port. The angry and determined Blackshirt chasing her aimed his pistol. "Stop or I'll shoot," he snarled. Maria rounded another corner leading into a narrow and trash filled alleyway, narrowly avoiding a gun blast that shattered a shard of concrete just inches from her head.

Bianca used every ounce of strength and courage left in her enervated and aching body and soul to climb up out of the gutter. She hopped on one leg in the direction of her daughter's would-be captor, who violently tackled her. Bianca fought as hard as she could but was quickly subdued. Both she and her assailant were covered in mud by the time he was able to handcuff her and shove her into the backseat of the glimmering Mercedes. Maria, who was grief stricken and terrified, sobbed uncontrollably as she hurried down the steep hill leading towards the port. The cigar tin full of cash was held tightly under her arm. Disgruntled fisherman lining the dock feared the hollow PUM, PUM, PUM, PUM, PUM sound of her scuffed shoes smacking atop the boardwalk as she ran towards the rows of ships would frighten the fish away. They gesticulated violently as they hurled crude insults and insinuations at her. But Maria did not dare look back for fear of being yet another of thousands of Il Duce's desaparecidos.

Miami, Florida, July 1936

Stono Turner was born in Snellville, Georgia, the same day D.W. Griffiths *Birth of a Nation* was privately screened for President Woodrow Wilson at the White House. Stono's father, Odysseus, was a longtime sharecropper. Despite his lack of formal education, Odysseus, who claimed to have been a great-grandson of Nat Turner, was an especially eloquent and outspoken member of the local chapter of the newly formed United Negro Improvement Association.

In 1917, not long after Stono turned three years old, his father was lynched by a mob outside of Waycross for neglecting, or perhaps refusing, to step from the pristine sidewalk into the muddy gutter as a Confederate Veteran donning a long white beard and gingerly leaning on a cane slowly shuffled by. Stono, who was named after a 1739 South Carolina slave revolt, felt perpetual dread and terror as a young boy growing up in the Deep South, a place where life was always precariously hanging in the balance. He was thus especially excited when, at the age of eight, his mother, who was a housekeeper scraping out a living check to check, told him they were moving to a new resort city named Miami in Florida. "The Magic City," as Miami was incessantly referred to in mass marketing, seemed like a transcendent consumerist utopia in ads Stono had seen of the burgeoning metropolis on billboards, movies, and on the side of bus-stop benches. Ads for Miami popularized the notion that the further south tourists went in the state of Florida, the more sophisticated and cosmopolitan its citizens were.

Stono was thus especially dismayed to find Miami as atavistic as the rest of the former Confederate States of America. His first week in Miami, for example, Stono was assaulted by six white high school boys and made bedridden for more than a month for swimming at a beach that prohibited black sunbathers. From that day on, he carried the switchblade bequeathed by his father in his sock as a layer of potential protection from the white terrorists who sometimes got their kicks by tormenting and abusing black boys.

Early in 1936 Stono's mother fell victim to a respiratory infection and died, leaving the twenty-two-year-old to fend for himself. Public services in the black sections of Miami, especially "Colored Town" and Lemon City, were nearly non-existent until after World War II. As such, maladies amongst "The Magic City's" black population were far more common than amongst whites. And as a housekeeper struggling to pay her bills, she could not afford time off to seek treatment or attempt to recuperate. She also had no medical insurance and thus treatment was a luxury she could not afford. A cold thus turned into bronchitis, which turned into pneumonia. Unable to afford a funeral, Stono buried his mother himself in a hole her alone dug out by the Miccosukee Indian reservation. Though dejected, the son had little time to properly mourn his mother. He was too busy confronting the Great Depression in a virulently Jim Crow city.

Stono worked upwards to eighty hours a week driving a cab to all corners of Dade and Broward County, which, thanks to Henry Flagler's Florida East Coast Railway and Juan Trippe's Pan Am Airways, had quickly become a prime vacation destination for northern tourists eager to escape the filth, grime, crime, mass immigration, and racial intermingling increasingly common to industrialized cities north of the Mason-Dixon Line.

Stono had only just dropped off an elderly Jewish couple visiting Miami from Astoria, Queens, at Carl Fisher's gaudy hot pink Flamingo Hotel on Miami Beach.

The pair was happily visiting "The Magic City" for the first time. The husband, an insurance salesman, was nearing retirement age and considering buying a cute two-bedroom pastel bungalow three blocks from the pristine and gleaming beaches of Biscayne Bay. The kindly couple gave Stono a two-dollar tip as gratuity for job well done upon arrival at the hotel. They were apparently naïve of the fact that Miami was a closed shop town, even amongst cabbies. Black cabbies had been barred from chauffeuring anyone but other black folks around town since the job-starved vets had come back from France in 1918. Stono was, however – unlike lots of Yankee tourists to Miami – aware of the risk of running afoul of Dade County's white supremacists, many of whom had few qualms about violently enforcing Jim Crow. The local police were some of the most prominent members of the John B. Gordon Local 24 branch of the Klan. They were infamous amongst Miami's black residents for setting up checkpoints at both ends of the causeway connecting Miami Beach to the mainland to harass black cabbies and often impound their cars for simply attempting the gain entrance to the barrier island, which was exclusively inhabited by white families.

Stono was thus particularly distressed to see the lights of a Ford sedan, which had been tracking him since he crossed over to the mainland from Collins Causeway, pursue him beyond the city limits of Miami as he sped towards Liberty City. The headlights in his rearview mirror grew big as manhole covers as he sped his ageing Buick onto the Tamiami Trail on the outskirts out of town.

Stono's scuffed taupe Keds pinned the gas pedal to the floorboard of the cab. A big billow of dirt kicked up behind the car. The near-bald back tires caused the Buick to fishtail slightly on the dirt road, which was built adjacent to a newly laid line of railroad track leading out towards Liberty City, which was one of the few parts of Dade County where white folks who were fearful of "black infestation" and subsequent diminishing of property values, permitted African Americans to reside without the constant, though still occasional, threat of lynch terror.

The Ford, which had a V-8 engine, finally caught up to Stono's cab as Miami's meager skyline began to shrink beyond the dusk horizon behind them. The eldest passenger in the Ford, a particularly mean son-of-a-bitch in his mid-fifties, leaned out of the window and displayed a shiny Sherriff's badge in one hand and a pistol in the other. He demanded that Stono, "pull over to the side!"

Stono quickly calculated his chances of making it safely to Liberty City by ditching his car somewhere and running home through the pine forest and swamps adjacent his neighborhood. He, however, calculated that the Sheriff would be able to track him home due to his license plate. Stono thus let out a deep and anguished sigh as his scuffed right Ked mashed the brake pedal. The Buick skid to a stop by the side of the road next to the railroad tracks. The Ford lurched to a halt on the swamp-side of the road just as thick pellets of rain began to fall out of the sky.

Two burley men, each wearing gas stained grey overalls, and each with grease-stained hands clutching shiny American-made revolvers, along with a man donning a midnight blue Dade County Sheriff's Department Deputy uniform, approached the cab as quickly as caution permitted. A wave of terror crashed into Stono. His heart pounded as though it were trying to burst out of his ribcage. But the fear reflexively piqued the sense of rebellious outrage he had inherited from his father. "What the hell ya'll want?" Stono asked insolently, knowing damn well what the men wanted: to terrorize him to the point that he would cease to chauffer white folks around town.

"Look here, nigger," the deputy said while spitting out a mouthful of red chewing tobacco residue on the yellow dirt road underfoot, "we warned you last month that if you didn't stop picking up goddamn Yankees, there'd be all kinds of hell to pay."

"What am I supposed to do?" Stono sneered, momentarily reflecting back on the hundreds of hours he spent as a janitor at Booker T. Washington Vocational School in order to save enough money to buy his cab. "I can't make no money if I don't pick up no goddamn Yankees. I gotta make a living, just like ya'll do."

"You know goddamn well Miami is a closed shop, which means no cotton' pickin' nigger drivers are allowed in the white parts of town," the smaller of the two cabbies sneered. "There's plenty of other work for ya'll coons. Why don't you try bell hoppin' at Flagler's Royal Palm? They got all kinds of nigger-loving Yankees and kikes stayin' there."

"I got an even better idea," Stono said defiantly. "How about ya'll fascist crackers pull your heads out your ass? You ignorant crackers is the reason the damn capitalists can dictate the price of labor. If ya'll crackers ever read a book every once in a while, you might side with us niggers against capitalists like Flager, Collins, and Fisher. Us workin' folks, black and white, could have us a bigger slice of the pie if ya'll crackers didn't have your heads so far up your asses." Odysseus would have been proud.

The deputy cocked his Smith & Wesson and placed it against Stono's sweat-soaked forehead. "Get out of the car, you Bolshevik lovin' nigger," he seethed.

"Go ahead and kill me, massa," Stono defied. "If I can't drive no white folks from the train station to hotels and back, you practically starvin' me to death anyhow. I can't take this terrorism no more. Go on ahead and kill me."

"We will gladly oblige," the bigger cabbie said, smiling. "We ain't strung up none these uppity niggers since before Black Tuesday."

"Yeah," the deputy said matter-of-factly, "the coons down here been pretty good bout stayin' in their place. But they been gettin' awful uppity now that that nigger lover Roosevelt and his horse-faced wife are in office. We might need to start settin' some examples with some good ole fashioned necktie parties."

The smaller of the two cabbies fired a few rounds of ammo into the engine block of Stono's cab, then two more into the front tires for good measure. The two cabbies then yanked Stono out of his Buick and manhandled him into the backseat of the idling Ford.

The two cabbies hunkered down in the front seat of the cab. The deputy sat down next to Stono in the backseat, sure to keep the pistol cocked and aimed at the captive's head. The V-8 fired up and rumbled along the dirt road adjacent to the railroad tracks. Stono was more disheartened than he was afraid as he peered out the back window at the inoperable Buick that he spent his lifesavings on in the hopes of climbing out of poverty.

The Ford sped adjacent the new FEC extension, the tracks of which had been laid just a year earlier, leading towards Homestead. The speedometer was pinned to fifty-miles-per-hour. A bulb of sweat slid out from under the deputy's hat and rolled into his eye. He winced slightly and wiped another bead from his brow with the barrel of his pistol just as the Ford took a sharp right turn west over the railroad tracks. The car momentarily caught air as it raced over the railroad crossing. The force of the car speeding over the tracks and landing so abruptly caused the pistol to misfire, splattering the deputy's brains all over roof of the cabin.

The flash of fire, clattering sound of the shot, and gruesome sight of the deputy's pink brain matter drenching the ceiling of the cabin startled the driver to the point that the car skidded and careened off the muddy dirt road and into a pine tree adjacent the swamp. The driver was nearly decapitated as his head went through the front windshield. The dazed cabbie in the passenger seat was severely concussed, but miraculously survived the collision. The force of the crash caused a bit of vertigo in Stono, who was out of sorts to the point of nausea as he fumbled to pry the door of the car open. He shook his head, which was ringing from a concussion. His eyes darted around the backseat of the cab. The Deputy's head was half-mush. Stono vomited and then cranked down the window and climbed out of the car and into the muddy ditch. He stumbled while trying to crawl out of the ditch to the dirt road. He fell back into the knee-high swamp water. A seven-foot-long alligator on a nearby bank of the swamp ducked under the murky water, which somewhat sobered Stono. He frantically trudged his way out of the swamp and up the ditch to the road. He ran as fast as his injuries would permit towards his disabled Buick. The muddled sound of a train's foghorn momentarily startled him. He rightly feared he would be blamed for the death of his kidnappers and ultimately sent to the electric chair.

The struggling cabbie clinging to survival in the front passenger seat grabbed a pistol from the glove box, stumbled from the car and meandered after Stono. The dazed and somewhat confused cabbie haphazardly fired a shot, which grazed Stono's right leg. The brunt of the force knocked Stono into the embankment separating the road from the railroad tracks. He slid back into the swamp. Though hobbled, covered in mud and terrified, adrenalin propelled him. He climbed back out of the swamp, up the ditch, and then hobbled quickly as he could towards the tracks leading towards the Buick.

The cabbie chased after Stono and fired another a round. The bullet missed Stono by an inch. But the percussion sound frightened him, so he hit the deck, which allowed the cabbie to gain ground on his prey. Stono finally climbed to his feet. His face was covered in mud. He tackled the cabbie atop the tracks as a train traveling seventy-miles-per-hour hurled towards them. The conductor sounded the foghorn, but, given that the tracks were so slick, did not dare pull the break lever for fear of derailing and crashing the locomotive into the swamp, thereby losing millions of dollars' worth of building supplies and agricultural products, which would have surely cost him his job.

Stono feared his head would be turned to mush if he did not break free from his assailant's grasp. He struggled to pry the pistol from the cabbie's sweat and rain-saturated hand. The cabbie desperately fired off four more rounds, but none of the shots hit Stono. He tried firing again, but the gun was finally empty of ammo. The cabbie let loose of the revolver and put all his energy into choking Stono, who was able to retrieve his father's switchblade from his sock. The memory of being assailed by six boys at the all-white beach when Stono was eight flashed in his mind as he jammed the chrome blade into the cabbie's kidney. The cabbie's grip on Stono's throat loosened the moment the stainless steel lodged in the man's flesh. The cabbie slid back down the embankment and into knee-high swamp water. Stono barely avoided being mashed under the locomotive. He stumbled on the rocks by the railroad tracks and fell on his backside and peered into the swamp as the cabbie pleaded for help as the gator fast approached its prey. The conductor, who assumed he had narrowly missed killing one of many hobos who congregated around the railroads during the Great Depression, paid very little mind to Stono or the cabbie. He certainly did not care to explain the situation to law enforcement or to jeopardize his employment with the FEC by making an unscheduled stop. He thus simply adjusted his rearview mirror slightly, took a long hit from his Marlboro and then sounded the train's foghorn.

City of London, England, July 1936

Twenty-five-hundred kilometers from Moscow, a young, dashing, rebellious, and fair-haired Englishman named Albion Edwards IV, who was in his final year of undergraduate studies at Oxford University, hurried excitedly into his father's office in the City of London, the United Kingdom's version of Wall Street. The idealistic lad had been fired with zeal as a result of the recent outbreak of war between the fascists, Popular Front, and anarchists in Spain. Despite (or perhaps because of) the fact that he attended one of the most unabashedly pacifist institutions the world had ever created, Albion, ever the rebel, felt especially compelled to join the fray in Spain.

He felt like he were floating on air as he exited the cedar-paneled elevator en route to his father's corner office overlooking the River Thames winding through the heart of the financial district.

"I'm terribly sorry, m'boy," the surly white-haired secretary sitting dutifully at her desk outside Mr. Edwards' office said in a refined accent, "you can't go in there just now. Your father is in the midst of a very important meeting."

Unbowed, Albion ignored the secretary and quickly entered his father's smoke-filled office to find him haranguing an underling just a few years Albion's senior. Edwards III, donning a navy blue and pinstripe three-piece suit, was bewildered by the sudden intrusion. He placed his spectacles onto the bridge of his pointy nose in order to make absolutely certain that his son, who he had not seen or spoken to in months, was not, in fact, a hallucination.

"What's the meaning of this interruption, Albion?"

"I need to speak with you immediately."

"Can't this wait?" Albion's father said as he placed his spectacles gently atop his ornately designed handmade mahogany desk made of wood harvested in the Congo. "I'd be happier to ring you at your dorm after the conclusion of the workday, if you like. Now," he motioned towards the exit with his hand, "if you'll please excuse me."

"No," Albion said defiantly as he glanced down at the befuddled and disgruntled underling gazing up at him confusedly. "I've got a ship to catch at sunset and am desperate to speak with you in person and in private, if you please, before I depart."

"Well then, alright, I suppose," Albion's father quietly huffed as he reluctantly signaled for his underling to excuse himself from the darkened office. "You've got five minutes, but not a second longer," he grunted while glancing down at the golden pocket watch hand made in the Swiss Alps.

"I'm going to Spain," Albion gushed excitedly, his eyes lit with mischief. A massive grin commandeered his face.

"Spain?" his father blurted. "But they're having a nasty Civil War at the moment, aren't they?"

"Yes sir, that's the reason I'm going," Albion explained. "I've volunteered to cover the war for *Cherwell*."

"*Cherwell?* his father asked bemusedly. "What in the bloody hell is a *Cherwell*?"

"It is Oxford's student newspaper."

"A student newspaper is funding a correspondent from Spanish lines?"

"No sir," Albion explained, "I'm funding the trip with my trust fund."

"How can you – my only son – be foolish enough to risk your savings and quite possibly your life in such a foolhardy manner?" He sneered as if his son had passed gas. "Even that silly pacifist fool Neville Chamberlain has the good sense not to get involved in this bloody mess. Besides, England, and this very firm for that matter, are heavily invested in an incredibly profitable ore mining operation outside Guernica. The coup, in other words, is rather beneficial for us, for you, in fact. Franco will put down those foolish leftists and their ridiculous utopianism, and business will be better than ever once proper order is restored. Besides, the country in the process of industrializing and so we stand to make a very pretty penny indeed on real estate speculation alone, never mind raw materials. Spain is, you see, merely suffering growing pangs because it is in the difficult process of industrializing. But their suffering is our gain, you see. We have a chance to get in on the ground floor. You see, son, going to Spain is an altogether foolhardy proposition indeed. I know you are young and fancy yourself as somewhat of an idealist, what with all the nonsense your literature and political science classes fill your young mind with. I also know the restlessness a lad in his final year of undergraduate studies feels. Believe me, I do. But I forbid you from going to Spain until the conflict there has been settled. It's far too dangerous, m'boy. Tell you what, I will send you to Spain next summer as graduation present once all that nastiness between Franco and those silly idealists is settled. Now, it was nice of you to drop in," Albion's father said while glancing at his watch. I will have your mother call you this weekend, if you like."

"I am going," Albion defiantly declared. "I've already bought a ticket and packed my steamer trunk. Spain is a bold investment in my future. When the war is over, I'll have a bonnie portfolio and would stand a decent chance of landing a job with *The Guardian*, or *Telegraph*, maybe even *The New York Times* or *Le Monde* as a foreign correspondent."

His father sighed and rolled his eyes, unimpressed at the prospects. "I thought the plan was to work in finance," he reminded his son. "There's very little money in reporting stories. I've not paid tens of thousands of dollars for you to attend Eton and Oxford, never mind an army of tutors, so that you might squander my largesse in order for you to engage in idle navel gazing and writing tripe about things that really don't matter much at all to our ilk."

"Perhaps there's not much money or prestige in being a journalist," Albion admitted. "But there is honor and dignity in the profession. Journalists are essential to any democratic society. Besides, I don't give a toss about money. I want a life defined by honor, valor and adventure."

"You've grown more than a bit quixotic and perhaps terribly daft up at Oxford, haven't you m'boy?" his father sneered insultingly as he plucked a cigarette from the gold and engraved case nestled in the pocket of his navy blue and pinstripe waistcoat.

"Maybe so," Albion conceded, "but I'd rather be foolhardily daft and living for pride of purpose than slowly dying as a rich, miserable and sexless old coot who cares about nothing but profit margins and bottom lines." Albion turned on the heel of his scuffed wingtips and strode confidently out of his father's office feeling, for the first time in his life, truly liberated.

"Now hang on just a minute!" his father raised his voice, "who told you I was sexless?"

The secretary and underling outside their employer's office shared a quizzical glance as Albion walked confidently past the window overlooking the River

Thames. His proud and confident smile belied the fear he felt as the elevators doors slid shut.

Tarragona, Spain, July 1936

Azure Sanchez, a sixteen-year-old girl with a head full of flowing garnet hair, had just returned from hunting hares in the forest adjacent to the tiny farm and quaint cottage in which she lived with her mother and father outside of Tarragona, Spain. She wore the same baby blue dress she had worn to church the day before. It was covered in mud and the hem had been torn slightly while hunting rabbits that morning. Her barefooted and nearly dehydrated mother and father toiled diligently in the field full of thorny cotton stalks. The scorching midsummer sun was high in the sky. Azure's father, Xavier, gently plucked cotton buds with machine-like precision and efficiency and then placed them into the massive burlap sack his wife's aching and sun spotted arms held aloft. The pair of peasant farmers, Xavier and his wife, Pilar, made a dynamic team.

Xavier, upon seeing his daughter approach the barn across the field with the spoils of her hunt, smiled softly and doffed his sweat soaked cap. Pilar, who had quarreled with her daughter the previous evening because of Azure sneaking out of mass before communion, did not exude the warmth her husband did for their daughter. Pilar was, however, glad at the prospect of enjoying a bit of protein – a luxury – the hare would provide. Pilar set the burlap sack by her side. She then bent down and took a quick swig of water from her leather canteen. She then picked up the sickle her husband sometimes used to separate cotton buds from the vine and offered it to him. "My hands are too sore to use it today," he said softly as his weary eyes gazed down at his arthritic and sun spotted hands. "I'm afraid I'm all thumbs these days." His eyes expressed deep sorrow because his sore hands would mean a longer workday for both he and his wife.

"It's nothing," she sighed and dropped the sickle in the red earth next to her dirt covered feet and lifted the burlap sack towards her husband. He winced due to his already shredded thumb being pricked by yet another thorn. Pilar's back ached nearly as much as her heart. She had, in recent weeks, grown increasingly dismayed that Azure seemed to be rapidly drifting away from the Church. The older and wiser Azure became, the more she questioned the existence of God and necessity of priests. Her sense of universal righteousness was also increasingly challenged by news about the fascist coup that had transpired the previous month. The Leftist Popular Front that had advocated land reform and promised to diminish the large landowners'— including the Catholic Church's – control over the peasant farmers who harvested the landowners' crops and thereby underwrote their wealth, political power and social privilege, had been challenged by an overthrow launched by Francisco Franco, an aristocratic general who was backed by the monarchy and the Church. Azure had long dreamed of getting an education or factory job in some fancy, modern and industrialized city such as Madrid, Valencia or Barcelona. But the coup not only restored the pre-1933 social and cultural status quo that had existed since the rise of Spain's monarchy in the Dark Ages, it had also ensured that Azure's future would be agonizingly similar to the subsistence existence her elders had always known. She thus feared she would be a slave to her landowners until her dying breath. She had grown desperate and suicidal in the month since the coup, which caused greater tension between she and her devout mother, who feared the unknown almost as much as she feared her God.

A beam of sunlight shined through a gap in the worn and weathered wood of the barn's loft, illuminating Azure's gaunt and stoic face as she lit a candle. She cautiously ascended the dark and rickety staircase towards the loft of the barn where bales of cotton were stacked like cordwood. She had not eaten protein in more than a week and was thus especially desperate to skin the meager hare and boil a nice sunset meal to nourish her famished parents, who had been toiling since long before sunrise.

A quick guest of wind suddenly blew out the candle. A tremor of terror churned in Azure's starving belly as the rumbling sound of a diesel engine under the hood of a jet-black Rolls Royce could suddenly be detected fast approaching the farm. She cautiously peaked out of a crack in the façade of the loft. The sight of dust billowing up on the horizon caused her to reflexively drop the blood-soaked hare on the dusty wooden floor of the loft beneath her calloused and dirt-covered bare feet. She white-knuckled the barrel of her rifle as she crept on her belly towards a breach in the side of the barn overlooking the cotton field. Azure's worried almond-shaped brown eyes squinted through a three-inch crack in a plank and scanned the cotton field below.

The rumbling V-8 engine shook the ground beneath Xavier and Pilar's feet. They reluctantly stopped toiling the cotton stalks and held their hands nervously over their respective brows to protect their eyes from the glare provided by the late-afternoon sun sinking beyond the sprawling amber horizon. Their weary and sun-stroked faces betrayed a dreadful anticipation as the cloud of dust grew nearer and nearer and the sound of the grumbling engine grew louder and louder. Pilar and Azure shared a quick and portentous glance as the dust covered Rolls Royce skid to a stop three-car lengths from the barn where Azure was hiding.

Xavier's trembling hand wiped sweat and dirt from his stress-striped and sun-spotted forehead with his soiled handkerchief. He slowly approached the dust-covered Rolls, followed closely by Pilar, whose reddened face was colored with dread. Azure's mother placed the half-full burlap sack of cotton on the ground and slunk nervously behind her husband as he humbly approached the moneyed men in their midst.

Two confident young men, neither of whom was older than thirty years of age, and both of whom donned the powder-blue shirt, khaki trousers, and slick-black riding boots synonymous with the Falange, swaggered out of the car and fast approached the farmers. Their sense of dashing supremacy seemed particularly stark in contrast to the ragged, exhausted, aging, malnourished and disheveled peasants who apprehensively approached the luxury sedan with their heads bowed and eyes cast towards the red earth below their feet.

"Senor Martinez," Xavier said softly and pleasantly, nearly genuflecting, as he subserviently wringed his cap between his hands. "I have not had the good fortune of seeing you since your father passed away," he hesitantly continued. "I'm so very sorry for your loss. You and your mother have my deepest condolences." Xavier glanced nervously over his shoulder towards the breach in the loft of the barn, sensing his daughter's anxiety.

"I appreciate your condolences, Senor Sanchez," the elder of the two fascists said as he ran his forefinger over his slick black moustache. "I will gladly pass along your condolences to my mother, who, as you might imagine, is still despaired." Martinez scanned the fields behind the peasant farmers. "How are things for your wife and daughter of late?"

"The famine has been a terrible ordeal," Xavier's voice trembled, "but we have, by the grace of God, found a way to manage."

"Praise be," the other Falange chortled somewhat sarcastically while scanning the peasants' earth stained and calloused bare feet."

"To what do we owe the pleasure of your visit?" Xavier hesitantly asked.

"I'm terribly sorry to be the bearer of bad news," Martinez said bluntly while gazing beyond Xavier at the late-afternoon sunshine soaking into the pastoral farmland sprawling toward the horizon. "My father always thought that you and your wife were fine tenants of his land. You helped him earn a profit far more many seasons than not. He also believed you both were, although illiterate and backward in many ways, fine Christians and thus worthy of his patronage." Martinez forced a toothless grin. "But," Martinez continued, "you see, the world is changing very fast. Spain is, praise be to God, finally, under General Franco's guidance and vision, industrializing. Farming, you see, is no longer as sustainable a business model as it once was. Our profits, as you have noted as a result of the famine this summer, are dependent on the cycles of the season, weather patterns, pestilence and the will of God. My father, he was old fashioned. But I am taking this land into the future." Martinez gazed upon the farmland with a hardly veiled disdain. "I have decided to build a luxurious resort and golf course here. He smiled, beaming with a pride seldom seen outside hospital delivery rooms. Martinez, seemingly unaware, or perhaps simply ambivalent to how dire such news would be to Xavier and Pilar, brimmed with the kind of glee that only easy riches can illicit in a man of such immense wealth.

"A golf course and resort?" Xavier's words were soaked with trepidation as they tumbled from his mouth. His confounded eyes confusedly scanned the idyllic blue, green, gold and amber landscape as a warm and soft summer breeze gently swayed the cotton stalks.

"Yes," Martinez said haughtily. "These fields will soon comprise a five-star resort with eighteen holes for playing golf and two Olympic-sized swimming pools. This land will go from being peopled by peasants to some of

Europe's most moneyed leisure seekers. It'll be nothing short of a modern marvel by the time the dust settles."

One man's marvel is, however, another man's tragedy. "Golf?" Xavier, who had never heard of the game, muttered despondently. "But what about us? My wife and child? Where will we go? My ancestors have cared for and tended to this land since long before you were even born. It is surely as much our land as it is yours."

"This is, according to the deed in my safe, my land and my land alone," Martinez sneered as he glared down at the suddenly terrified and bewildered peasant farmers. I alone will decide what to do with it."

"What about us?" Pilar pleaded. "All we know is this land, these fields. It's everything to us."

"There is an exodus of peasants from the countryside to the cities in search of factory work," Martinez said while diffidently shrugging his shoulders. "Perhaps you might consider going to Madrid or Valencia along with much of the rest of Spain's godforsaken rabble. But whatever you do, don't go to Barcelona. Those people are savages. They'll turn you into atheist anarchist homosexuals by Christmastime."

"Madrid or Valencia?" Xavier defiantly chortled at the sheer absurdity of the suggestion. He rubbed his blistered and bruised hand across his sweat-soaked forehead. "Factory work? All I know is farming, tending these fields—our fields." His weary, frightened and bloodshot eyes lovingly beheld the amber waves of grain and fluffy white cotton leading all the way to the horizon. "I know nothing about any factory in any city. All I know is these fields. I'm not leaving this land. You'd have to kill me first."

"That could certainly be arranged," Martinez smiled wryly while rolling his intense brown eyes. "I, however, suggest that you stay until after harvest to get your affairs in order and figure out what is next for you and your family. I, very graciously, will give you until a week after the end of harvest season to vacate the premises. That gives you ample time to find new employment and lodging."

Pilar, now overcome with grief, fear, and despair at the prospect of being separated from the land she had known a lifetime, crossed herself with her hand from forehead to navel, then shoulder to shoulder, and dropped to her knees. She sobbed and prayed inconsolably. Xavier grabbed Martinez at the cuff of his neatly starched powder-blue sleeve and pleaded, "Please, I beg you to reconsider. Your father, for all his faults, would never do something so dishonorable."

"How dare you display such insolence to my father and I, after all we've done for you and your family. You'd not even exist if not for my father allowing you to tend his fields all these years. You only have a family in the first place because of my father's largesse and patronage." Martinez pried his sleeve free from Xavier's desperate grasp and shoved him to the earth next to Pilar, who continued to cry and plead to her god for mercy. "Stop crying!" Martinez demanded. "God can't help you. This is *my* land." He cast his arm out at all he surveyed. "You are *my* tenants on *my* land. As far as you are concerned, *I* am your God." He smirked as his Falangist compatriot chuckled at the site of the groveling peasants. "I hereby decree that you and your pathetic fucking family be cast off my land within one week of the end of harvest season. If you find the terms of my graciousness unsuitable, I'd be very happy to see to it that your cottage is razed and you are evicted before the next sun sets beyond the horizon; *my* horizon."

Brokenhearted Azure began whimpering ever so quietly the moment her father began to clutch at the collar of his burlap shirt and gasp for air. He staggered onto his feet momentarily, then dropped suddenly to his knees, and then face-first into the dirt next to his wailing and terrified wife. Xavier desperately clutched at Martinez's shiny black knee-high riding boots, then suddenly, after a deep gasp of air had fled his body, went completely limp and lost consciousness. Pilar struggled to pry her husband over onto his back. The sun beat down on Xavier's dirt and sweat-drenched face. Pilar tried to wipe his face clean, but her hands were as soiled as was his face. Tears streamed down her cheeks. Martinez cast his index finger ominously down at Pilar. "You have three weeks to vacate this property or I will have you removed under the full authority of the law provided to me as the owner of this land." Pilar was so grief stricken that she could not quite process what she had been told. She stammered inaudibly as she glared up at the landowner, who seemed to eclipse the sun sinking behind his head and shoulders. The second Falangist finally broke his silence.

"We can't just leave the bitch here," he said.

"Why the hell not?" Martinez demanded. "She's my peasant. I can do whatever the hell I want with her."

"What if she goes to the newspapers?" Martinez's compatriot warned. "It would be a headache we don't need."

Martinez nodded his head in reluctant agreement. He rolled his eyes, shrugged his shoulders, and unceremoniously removed his gun from his holster, then planted a slug in Pilar's brain. She fell back into the dirt. Her lifeless eyes stared blankly up at Martinez a long tense moment. Her concave and bloody skull fell into her dead husband's lap. Crimson blood and pink brain matter oozed from her head, soaking the dirt and burlap sack half-full of cotton. "There," Martinez said emotionlessly while holstering his revolver, "problem solved. You happy?"

"Just one less peasant," the younger Falangist shrugged indifferently as he began to make his way back towards the Rolls Royce. A sudden and deafening clattering sound filled the fields. A pigeon flew frantically from the loft and out of the barn. Azure had fired a round of buckshot at the murderer as he a sauntered nonchalantly towards the sedan. A shard of burning hot lead grazed Martinez's neck. His compatriot, however, took a direct hit of buckshot to the chest. He wheezed and whined as blood flowed from a large cavity. Azure hunkered frightened behind a full burlap sack of cotton tucked in the corner of the loft. Martinez meanwhile struggled to haul his blood-covered and fast dying compatriot into the back seat of the car. Blood soaked into the leather seats. Martinez then scrambled to climb into the driver's seat, cowering as low as he could, but still able to look over the steering wheel. Azure then fired another round at the car, shattering the rear window. The Rolls' V-8 engine roared like a snarling dragon as it rumbled away from the cottage and barn, kicking up yellow dust, red dirt, and diesel fumes in its wake as it raced away

After the dust had settled and Azure could no longer hear the rumbling of the sedan's V-8 engine, she carefully tucked her antique rifle and a few rounds of shells in a burlap sack full of cotton in the barn loft. She ran as fast as she could through the forest adjacent the cottage towards the village. She finally came upon the church, which was by far the tallest structure in the village and nestled on the quaint and ancient town square of Tarragona. She knew the Franco regime and the Catholic Church had close ties. But she, perhaps naïvely, trusted Father Ramon, who had baptized her, to provide guidance in the midst of such an unholy calamity.

"What is the matter, my child?" the elderly nun who taught Azure to read the previous winter asked as she approached the nave from across the village square.

"Please," Azure panted as a drop of sweat slipped from her eyebrow, "I need to see Father Ramon; there has been a terrible accident."

"Well," the nun bemused, "he is taking confession for the next hour, but I think he is currently without any parishioner."

Azure nodded and then ran as fast as she could inside the nave. She came upon the small oaken confessional. "Bless me Father, for I have sinned," she panted while crossing her chest.

"How have you sinned, my child?"

"I just…" she hesitated. "I think… I think I just shot… I think I killed a man."

Father Ramon's eyes went wide as windows. He gasped, sat more upright and alert and peered through the screen at Azure trying to catch her breath. Her face was claret and saturated with beads of sweat. Bulbous tears streamed down her sun-blistered cheeks.

"Azure, is that you, my child?"

"Yes, Father."

"Did you just say you killed a man?" He asked disbelievingly.

"Yes, Father, I believe so." She began to sob as the gravity of the situation begun to pile up on her like dirt atop a grave. "You see, Senor Martinez's son came to evict my family from our land. He killed my mother. I tried to kill him. But I think I killed the man with him."

"Dios Mio," a deep disbelieving sigh escaped Father's Ramon as he creaked back in his bench and nervously rubbed his forehead, running his dehydrated hand across his desiccated and pale scalp. "Senor Martinez owns that land, my child," Father Ramon said matter-of-factly. "You are his tenants. He can do with it as he pleases. That's the law of the land. You must turn yourself in to the authorities, my child, and face justice for this grievous sin."

"But, Father," her voice seemed to harden, "Senor Martinez murdered my mother. Wouldn't a truly righteous God be on my side?"

A long, tense and heavy pause hung thick in the supposedly sacred space between Maria and priest. "I'm sorry child, but your mother is a tenant on Senor Martinez's land. Her life is as much his as it is her own."

"But that is not righteous or just, father," she boldened. "How in the hell can God's will be so unjust? If God gave everyone, including peasants, free will, how can my mother's life be worth less than Senor Martinez?"

"I know that God's will can be mysterious to us lowly humans, my child. But you must obey it, no matter how baffling it may seem at times. It's imprudent for mere mortals, especially peasants, to question the will and logic of the almighty God. Now, you have certainly sinned in the eyes of the Lord. And only the almighty God and He alone can make sense of all this. Don't be afraid, my child. I will escort you to the constable and ensure that you receive a fair hearing in the courts."

Azure's anguish and fear was suddenly replaced by furor. "To hell with God," Azure fumed. "To hell with you too."

"I know you are angry my child," Father Ramon gasped, gobstruck, "but you must confess to your blasphemy before we go to the constable."

A tense and heavy moment of silence lingered. Father Ramon nervously peeked through the screen. But the confessional had been vacated.

Azure ran as fast as she could from the nave, past the elderly and curious nun, then across the village square, and into the thick forest leading towards the farm.

Dusk had descended over the farm. Azure blew out the candle the instant she detected the sound of the Rolls Royce's V-8 engine roaring in the dark distance. She quickly tucked her knapsack under her arm and raced from the front doorway of the cottage and into barn to retrieve the rifle. She hurried into the barn and quickly, though cautiously, navigated the narrow and flimsy staircase leading to the loft. Her fingers were wide as her hands searched for the rifle concealed in one of the burlap sacks full of cotton.

Martinez, Father Ramon, and a chubby constable with a noticeable limp in his stride arrived. Trouble locating her firearm slowed Azure, who had shoved all she could fit into a small knapsack while getting set to flee into the forest and ultimately the unknown. She was terrified to be forced to leave the farm, fields, and her parents, which was all she had ever known of the world. But staying, she was sure, would lead to her inevitable death by firing squad or the gallows.

Martinez, who neck was bandaged with gauze, crept into the cottage with his pistol drawn. He frantically ransacked the inside of the cottage in the hopes of finding clues to Azure's whereabouts.

By the time Azure was finally able to retrieve the rifle from the burlap sack filled with cotton and load it with rounds of buckshot, Father Ramon, who was followed closely by the limping constable clutching a rifle of his own, was cautiously ascending the dark and rickety staircase towards Azure's hiding spot in the corner of the loft behind a burlap sack full of cotton.

"Come my child," Father Ramon whispered as he ascended the steps. "I won't let them harm you. We can work all this out. I will speak on your behalf. You have my word."

Azure held her breath and clutched her rifle tight against her chest; her heart thumped like a rabbit's. She was trapped and fully conscious of the fact that she was embroiled in a life or death situation. 'It's either them or me,' she thought to herself as Father Ramon crept closer up the stairs towards the loft. "It's not going to be me," She blurted as she pulled the trigger. The brunt of buckshot blast forced the priest and constable to tumble down the stairs. Both men fell flat on their backs. They writhed in agony and gasped for air. Azure raced down the wobbly steps and hurtled them. She then ran headlong into the cotton field towards the adjacent forest.

The percussion of the gun blast alerted Martinez, who hurried out of the dilapidated cottage. The full moon hung low in the early evening summer sky and thus provided just enough illumination for Martinez to locate and track Azure in the shoulder-high cotton stalks. Though sedated with barbiturates as a means of alleviating the pain in his gunshot wound, he chased her with the focus and intensity of a greyhound after a hare. He wildly fired six shots from his pistol into the stalks of cotton, but none got near her.

She haphazardly flung the rifle over her shoulder and squeezed the trigger. The gun, however, misfired badly, disabling the weapon and dazing her. The sound of the misfiring rifle startled and scattered the vultures feeding on her parents' corpses nearby. Her hands were suddenly blistered, scalding hot and covered in black soot. The gun blast was so loud and close to her head, her ears rang like a church chime after Sunday service. Her eyes were bleary and full of gunpowder and tears as she stumbled towards the backend of the cotton field near the forest leading to Tarragona.

Martinez finally caught her and violently tackled her into a pool of dry blood, just steps from where her mother was murdered. Azure, whose head ached and eyes burned, struggled to break free from her assailant's grasp. She dug her soot-covered thumb into the gossamer gauze barely protecting his neck wound. He tried to fire another shot from his pistol, but the chamber was empty, so he smashed her square in her jaw with the handle. Her head swooned and bottom lip bled profusely. He then bit into her cheek with the ferocity of an alligator. She screeched while clawing the bloodstained earth into her hands. Her eyes were soaked with gunpowder, tears and dirt. She could hardly see beyond five feet. Death seemed to beckon.

But as her hands clawed, scraped, and dug into the red dirt under her body as she tried to wriggle free from his grasp, she suddenly felt a wood handle and curved-metal blade beneath her thumb and forefinger. In one swift motion, she thrust the sickle her father used to harvest cotton into Martinez's side, just below his ribcage. Hot crimson blood flowed from his body, mingling with the blood of Azure's parents in the soil. He gasped for air and finally let loose of Azure. He then pulled himself onto his haunches and he struggled to breathe. His eyes were wide with horror as they stared the yawning abyss of death square in the face. His trembling, dirt and blood-soaked hands clutched at the gauze which was coming unraveled from around his neck wound.

Azure – panting, out of breath, and bewildered – struggled to climb to her feet. She coughed and wheezed violently while stumbling through the thorny cotton field towards the black and forbidding forest. Martinez lost consciousness and plopped onto the ground face first. She hoped he was dead. She took one last and longing look at her rapidly decomposing parents and whispered a disconsolate prayer for some mystical power to redeem their souls in the hopes that she might one day see them again. He gargled on blood. She thrust one last plow of the siècle into his back and then stood over him feeling a sense of power and justice she had never known before. She winced in agony as her blistered hands quickly searched his pockets. She finally pried car keys from his pocket, then raced towards the barn. She could hear Father Ramon pleading for help. For a moment, she hesitated, wanting to offer him some kind of aid. But she knew that if Martinez were, by chance, still alive, he would surely murder her, so she raced towards the sedan as fast as her weary and aching legs could carry her.

She jumped into the driver's seat. Her nervous, blistered and soot-covered hands fumbled with the keys as she tried to force them into the ignition. She had seen a person start a car in a talkie that had been projected at the Church one Sunday after mass when she was a child but had never even dreamed of driving a car before. It thus took her a few tense moments to figure out how to ignite the engine, turn on the headlights, and put the car in drive. The crisp, cold and dry breeze coming suddenly coming from the air conditioner vents on the dashboard startled her at first. But the cool relief slightly soothed her blistered hands. Hopped up on terror and adrenalin, she finally mashed the gas pedal with all the might she could summon in her famished and exhausted body. The car rolled through the cottonfield like a tank. But she finally figured out how to tame the behemoth of an automobile just enough to steer it onto the nearby dirt road leading towards the new highway between Tarragona and Barcelona that Franco's Army had built in order to move the heavy artillery supplied by Adolf Hitler's regime in the hopes of crushing the particularly recalcitrant resistance in Catalonia and the Basque region.

Berlin, Germany, July 1936

The Fuhrer, dressed in a black tuxedo, was absconding from a rendition of Wagner's *Siegfried*. He descended the steps of the Staatsoper im Schiller Theater, which was next door to the Reichstag, Germany's parliament building. He was followed closely and somewhat sheepishly by a small retinue, which included his young lover, Eva Braun. She donned a gaudy cream-colored sequin ball gown replete with a lace veil braided into her bobbed hair. A bowling-pin shaped aid stuffed into a khaki suit with a mop of grease-slicked black hair atop his head hurried up the marble steps from the strasse towards the retinue. "Have you heard, mein führer?" the aid gleefully blurted, hardly able to conceal his excitement. "There's been a coup in Spain! Franco has done it! The Nationalists will be drinking coffee on Gran Via within weeks!" Hitler stopped dead in his tracks, turned on his heel, and gazed methodically at the marble steps under foot. He gnawed slightly on the edge of his forefinger, deeply contemplating a move in a chess game.

"What about Il Duce?" Hitler asked.

"Mussolini is supplying thousands of men!" the aid beamed.

"Fantastic!" Hitler clasped the palms of his hands together like a child who'd just received the Christmas gift he'd been aching for since summer. "Tell Franco I will supply any hardware he needs—tanks, planes, munitions. I'll match whatever manpower he supplies." Hitler's eyes gazed at the shining lights of the Reichstag, "just think what crushing the Leftists in Spain will mean to our industry, our economy!" His eyes lit up like Roman candles. "Franco's Spain will make a wonderful trade partner. Together, Franco, Il Duce, and the German people comprise an unbreakable power. Our Thousand Year Reich is far more than a mere pipe dream now; it's our destiny."

"The latest polls, unfortunately, indicate that the vast majority of Germans are desperate to avoid another military conflict," the aid hesitantly said. "Restoring the economy is the primary concern of most people. How shall we market this to the German masses, mein führer?"

Hitler squinted long and hard at the twinkling lights of the Reichstag reflecting off his freshly polished black wingtips. "We will convince the masses that Germany will both redeem its pride and restore its economy through militarism, beginning with our unwavering support of Franco."

"Very good, mein führer," the aid beamed excitedly.

"We'll call our partnership with Franco and Il Duce, 'Operation Magic Fire,'" Hitler said as he spread his hands wide, like an advertising agent pitching a tagline to shareholders.

"It's wonderful, my love," Ava Braun said softly while tucking a windswept and bobbed curl behind her ear. "I love the homage to *Siegfried*. The German people are so blessed to have such a visionary and intrepid leader." Hitler nodded appreciatively, agreeing with his lover's sentiment, and then quickly descended a few steps as the retinue followed closely behind.

"France and England will surely be forced to respond," the aid calculated as he hurried to catch up to the group.

"I'm not so sure about that," Hitler seemed somewhat disappointed and vexed. "Chamberlain and Daladier are fucking cowards. They don't have the stomach for another war, especially since they know we are far superior intellectually, militarily and have a far more triumphant will and spirit for warfare. The Brits and French are stupid, but not so stupid to calculate that losing a war to us will destroy their economies and topple their fledgling empires, which German reparations underwrite. Both Daladier and Chamberlain know that losing to us will make vassal states of their empires. They won't readily risk that. But if we can somehow get Stalin into Spain too France and England won't be able to stand idly by. And then we might get our desired rematch with Britain and France." The aid and Hitler both simultaneously and methodically nodded in agreement. "If we can get Russia into the fray," Hitler optimistically added, "those pussyfooting will have no option but to intervene." Hitler grinned gleefully, "then," he said, "we will finally be able to fulfill our destinies as masters of the universe. Our Reich will reign for more than a thousand years."

"Excellent, mein führer," the aid said as he flashed the fascist salute to his demigod before hurriedly waddling down the steps towards to the Reichstag. "I'll send word to Franco and Mussolini at once."

Hitler excitedly clutched Eva Braun's tiny hand wrapped in an ivory-colored silken glove and gently kissed it. Eva, feeling as though she was the soon-to-be queen of the universe, blushed and grinned. "I never love you more than when you have that belligerent look of war in your eyes," she smiled seductively as she gently bit her lower lip with her top incisors.

Moscow, The Soviet Union, July 1936

Josef Stalin was shaken awake from a Vodka-induced stupor by a small, elderly woman with ghost-grey hair, paper-thin skin, and glasses as thick as mason jars resting at the bridge of a large pink nose that was home to a large and hairy mole. Flakes of crusted snot and pirogue were embedded in Stalin's bushy moustache; fresh drool saturated his chin. He reeked so acerbically of vinegar, urine, weeks of unwashed sweat, stale vodka and vomit that the unfortunate aid tasked with waking the Soviet Premier did very her best to not allow air to infiltrate her nasal passages. She finally roused Stalin awake. He gasped for air, as if escaping from a nightmare in which he was trapped inside a disabled U-boat pinned to the bottom of the Baltic Sea. "What? What the hell is it?" he demanded while wiping viscous and sticky drool from his chin with his hand, which was the size of a baby polar bear paw.

"I'm terribly sorry to wake you, Premier Stalin," the aid's voice quivered. "I, however, felt it imperative though equally regrettable to have to inform you that I have dire news from Spain."

"Spain?" his beady and bloodshot eyes stared into the aid's flinching soul. She shuttered slightly.

"Franco's Nationalists and the Falange launched a coup to topple to Republic," her eyes darted towards the stained hardwood floor. "They are backed by the Catholic clergy, too"

"And why exactly is this bad news?" Stalin asked while rubbing his tobacco stained fingers through his unwashed graying hair.

"Franco's coup was, you see, not entirely successful," the aid proceeded with caution. "The Nationalists are in control of much of the South. But the Republicans successfully repelled the coup in Madrid, Barcelona, and the Basque region. Anarchist labor unions have the balance of power in Catalonia and parts of Madrid. The Republicans and Popular Front therefore have an advantage because the vast majority of the population, including most of the peasantry and industrial workers, support the Republic. Even a few of the more idealist clergy have sided against Franco and the Nationalists, sir."

"I'm confused," Stalin yawned. "Isn't that a good thing? If the vast majority of the people are against the coup, the coup should be relatively short-lived. Franco is a bourgeois pencil pusher. What do I care if he is defeated?"

"Well, you see, sir," the aid nervously proceeded to explain, "our intelligence agency advised that Franco and the Nationalists are heavily supplied with Moorish mercenaries, and Mussolini is backing Franco with several more thousand troops, many of whom have battle experience from the invasion and occupation of Ethiopia. Franco also made a radio announcement declaring that they will not cease until they have taken the country back and not until after the traditional economic and political status quo has been restored—total victory."

"I see," Stalin said somewhat bewilderedly as he stroked his moustache. "If Mussolini is involved, Hitler, I wager, will be too." The aid nodded ominously, presaging an impending apocalypse comparable to "The Great War." Stalin suddenly became seething, which especially frightened the aid, who knew all too well how sadistically unpredictable the premier could be when he was angry. She thus instinctively crept a few feet towards the exit of Stalin's quarters.

"Those damned anarchists and bloody Trotskyites in Spain are responsible for this calamity," Stalin fumed. "Those fucking idiots just couldn't just leave well enough alone! They pushed too far too fast! What did they expect would happen by taking land from aristocrats and the Church and handing it over to peasants? What did those idealistic idiots think would happen by encouraging workers to appropriate the means of production, and offering free daycare for children? What did they think was going to happen if they tried to abolish private property and legalize divorce? Those fucking fools with their pie-in-the-sky utopianism! Don't they realize the shit storm they've created for me, for Russia? We can't afford another 'Great War,' lest the whites, or worse yet, the Trotskyites, take control of the Kremlin. We'll have to build dozens of new gulags and thousands more miles of rail lines into Siberia because of those damned Spanish anarchists! We've only just dealt with the Ukrainians! Now we have to deal with Hitler and the Trotskyites in the same fucking war! The entire balance of power in Europe will fall to the axis powers if Hitler wins Franco's war."

"What do you, in your infinite wisdom, suggest we do about the coup in Spain?" the aid asked ever so cautiously. "Surely there is too much riding on it to stay on the sidelines."

Stalin tore the cork from an unopened bottle of vodka with his teeth and glared at the elderly aid as though he wanted to bury her alive. "Roosevelt and the Americans have finally recognized us and given the regime legitimacy. We have to respond or else we stand to lose our credibility on the world stage. We have to make it seem as though we support the Spanish Republic in their fight against the fascists, or we could easily lose any ounce of moral authority we might be able to pry from the Americans, British, and French. But job one, above all else, is destroying those damned Trotskyites, wherever they exist. No matter what, we have to obliterate the Trotskyites. Then and only then can we defeat Hitler once and for all! Find the oldest tanks and munitions you can. I don't care if they are taken from museums. We have to create the illusion that we support the Republic, but by no means are we to support the Trotskyites or anarchists. Let the Leftists and Nationalists kill each other on by one. Let Hitler and Mussolini have their fun for a while. Let their men die in Spanish trenches. Once Spain is but a pile of ash, blood, steel and bodies, we will take out Hitler and the rest of those Nazi cocksuckers."

"As you wish, sir," the aided forced a nervous and toothless grin as she hurried towards the door. "I'll alert the generals and inform them of your orders." Stalin dumped a gulp of vodka down his throat and flopped back onto his leather couch and pulled a large cigar from his front shirt pocket. He lit it, took a deep drag, let out a lung full of smoke and gazed out at the window at a torrential rainstorm falling hard on Red Square's cobblestones.

CHAPTER TWO

New York City, November 1936

Zapata's mother, Sara, succumbed to grief and voluntarily, against Zapata's wishes, was admitted to a solarium up state, just outside Ithaca, three weeks after witnessing her husband's suicide. A week after being admitted, she died of a heart attack. Though the doctor said it was "highly unlikely," Zapata knew in his soul that the cause of death was as much heartbreak as heart disease. In the days after his mother's death, Zapata's solace knew no limit. He teetered on the brink of mental and emotional breakdown. But, unfortunately, in the midst of a Great Depression there was a dearth of time for him to sulk, never mind take the requisite time to heel especially the deep and bitter emotional and psychological wounds he was suffering and enduring. He had to figure out a way to eke out a living and scrape by, lest he perish as well.

He was, it initially seemed, fortunate to have landed a job laboring at the Domino Sugar factory, which was a sprawling complex just a short walk across the Williamsburg Bridge from the Lower East Side. Sugar had become a hot commodity among the aristocratic class during the 1500s, and the consumer fetish had helped fuel the African slave trade long into the nineteenth century. By the 1930s, sugar was popular amongst all classes, especially the poor. One of the few ways that members of exploited classes could purchase a modicum of momentary satisfaction and respite from the harsh realities of the Great Depression was by drinking a bottle of Coca-Cola, eating an ice cream cone, or sprinkling some Domino on cornflakes. One of the few booming industries amongst the lower classes in the Depression era – other than the escapism provided by motion pictures and the radio – was sugary products. Zapata thus felt himself – despite the recent tragedies to befall his family – relatively lucky to have landed what seemed to be a relatively secure job in a booming industry. As grueling as it was to heave forty-pound bales full of sugar to and from the loading knock for hours on end in the middle of the night could be, the physical travail was cake compared to the anguish of having so suddenly lost his mother and father. He did not much mind how difficult and backbreaking the labor was, since the physical demands of the job permitted him a degree of respite from the grief that stalked him in his quiet moments.

He happened to meet Maria atop the Williamsburg Bridge one morning after working the nightshift. The sun was just rising over Brooklyn. Maria's misty and melancholy eyes gazed across the East River at the lights of the bridge and the Lower East Side of Manhattan twinkling atop the water. Her shoulders slumped forward. Tears streamed down her icy-pink cheeks. Instinct told Zapata to leave her be and to mind his own business. But an overwhelming angst, which seemed justified in light of his parents' recent deaths – especially his father's suicide – consumed him. He thus doubled back and nervously asked, "Is something the matter?"

She ignored the question, but nervously and surreptitiously wiped a tear from her cheek with her shivering hand wrapped inside a tattered brown mitten. An awkward silence wafted through the air two elderly Hasidic men en route to morning prayers at the synagogue on Houston Street wearing heavy black shoes shuffled atop the ice and salt covered sidewalk behind them. "Would you like a cup of coffee?" Zapata whispered to Maria. "Maybe some pancakes too? I know a nice little place on Canal Street open this early."

"I'm sorry," Maria said coldly in a broken Italian accent. "Please just leave me be."

"Sorry. But I can't do that," Zapata sighed while glancing over at the neon-yellow and white Domino Sugar factory sign reflecting off the glassy brown surface of the East River. "I've been working all night and now I have a powerful desire for pancakes and black coffee. But as much as I want pancakes and coffee, I hate eating alone. I would feel very lucky if you would do me the honor of dining with me. Come on, I'm paying." Maria studied at Zapata's face, trying to decipher if he could be trusted. The deep sorrow mixed with anticipation in his longing and tired brown eyes softened Maria's jading soul ever so slightly. Plus, she was excruciatingly hungry and the promise of a free meal made him seem, under the circumstances, worth the risk.

"My name is Zapata." He held out his hand. She reluctantly clasped onto it. "My name is Maria." She forced a beleaguered smiled.

Zapata, somewhat awkwardly, held tight to Maria's hand the whole way down the bridge and a few blocks more to a small café on Broome Street. They shared a piping hot pot of Ethiopian coffee and a stack of blueberry pancakes and scrambled eggs. The warmth of the café, enticing aromas, soft candle lighting inside, mixed with the first full rays of the morning sun shining through the plate-glass window had the effect of soothing their souls ever so slightly; enough so that they opened up to each other as though they were longtime friends enjoying a long overdue reunion rather than strangers just getting to know each other.

They, for both good and ill, certainly had lots in common. Like Zapata, Maria had been tragically separated from her parents. Her mother and father were, like Zapata, a laborer. Her father was an organizer at a textile factory in Naples. The fascist Blackshirts were devout enemies of the labor unions, particularly the militant textile workers Giuseppe was elected to be a spokesman for. Mussolini considered unions an impediment to profit and thus a menace. Il Duce was particularly determined to purge Italy of unions by disposing of union leaders one-by-one, if necessary. Mussolini and his Blackshirts had systemically imprisoned, disappeared, or simply murdered tens of thousands who the fascists deemed potential impediments to his reconstitution of the Roman Empire throughout the Mediterranean and Northern Africa. He had grown particularly sadistic to enemies, both real and imagined, since the 1935 invasion of Ethiopia – the last African nation to be colonized by Europeans.

"I'm afraid they're likely are dead," Maria confided as she began to cry. "If they're not already dead, they will surely not survive Il Duce's reign of terror." Bulbous tears streamed down her face. "I was forced to flee or else suffer a similar fate. I've lived at a boardinghouse on Avenue A since I arrived here three months ago. I hate it there. The family I rent from lie, cheat and steal. And the oldest son— he's seventeen—is sweet on me and never gives me a moment of piece, even when I'm in the bath."

Zapata's heart ached as much for Maria as for his own sorrow. He did not know what to do ease her pain. He thus did the one thing he could think of: he grabbed her hand as it reached for her cup of coffee. He looked deep into her teary eyes, gazing into her soul and promised: "I will help you in any way I can. We can be in this together, if you need me to be." Though it was seemingly a shallow gesture or platitude from one stranger to another, at such a heightened moment of fear, anguish, and despair in both their lives, and at a time when nothing seemed certain but more economic turmoil and social despair, his assertion warmed and comforted her similar to when she was a child and her mother would wrap her in a warm wool blanket on a cold winter night. Though terribly frightened and filled with a sense of angst, depression and fear, she wanted that moment—that feeling of fleeting belonging, warmth and security—to endure a lifetime.

The feeling of vulnerability to Zapata quickly frightened Maria, who was suffering from post-traumatic stress disorder, which seemed to trigger bi-polarity. She pulled his hand from Zapata's and used it to lift her coffee cup and take a quick sip. "Thank you for your time and for breakfast," she reluctantly said and gently wiped a drop of coffee from her bottom lip. "I need to get to the factory."

"Factory?" Zapata asked nervously, sensing a change in energy between them.

"The cabana wear factory on Bowery," she let out a deep anguished sigh. "I work the day shift."

"Well, uh," Zapata feared he was being blown off, "May I walk with you a while?" he meekly anticipated her response.

"No, thank you," she said hesitantly and as graciously as possible in the hopes of not disappointing him too terribly much, especially in light of the fact that he'd been so kind to her. "The other girls will be a bother about it if they see us together."

"I see." His heart sank and he tried to force a toothless grin as he plopped a sugar cube into his coffee. "Well," his chest tightened, "will I ever get to see you again?" He gazed across the table as she wiggled her tiny and desiccated hands into her shabby brown mittens.

"I suppose I could perhaps meet you here tomorrow morning after your shift and before mine, if you like," she said softly and a bit reluctantly.

Zapata's body language beamed joyfully for the first time since long before his father left for France with the Expeditionary Force. "Tomorrow it is."

"Thank you… for everything," Maria's eyes twinkled slightly as Zapata gently shook her hand. She hurried from the warm and softly lit café into the blistering cold and grey city outside. She hurried into a narrow alleyway, a shortcut to Canal Street. A modest grin slightly cracked the façade of anguished despair her being had been lugging since the fateful day in Naples when her parents were visited by Il Duce's Blackshirts.

CHAPTER THREE

City College of New York, Harlem, December 1936

Zapata and a cohort of undergraduate students sat in a small semi-circle around Dr. Benjamin, a 38-years-old assistant history professor with chiseled facial features and thinning brown hair who had not yet earned tenure. The class was concluding a spirited debate on the merits of nonviolence and whether the democratically elected Spanish Republic was justified in waging warfare against fascists, especially in light of how outmanned and outgunned the Republic was in contrast to the Nationalists.

"Even if the Popular Front is justified in defending itself," Bethany, a pretty and smart young Jewish girl from Riverdale said, "violence just leads to more violence. Maybe if the Popular Front hadn't fought back the Soviets wouldn't have backed them. If the Soviets hadn't backed them, maybe England, France, and the U.S. would have. As is, fighting the fascists is a suicide mission. The Republic doesn't possess the resources or manpower as the Nationalists, so they are ultimately sealing the fate of democracy in Spain and setting workers of the world back in the process."

"It might be a suicide mission to fight Franco, Hitler and Il Duce's forces," Zapata said, "but I agree with the adage: 'it's better to die on your feet than live on your knees.' Besides, French and British companies have too much invested in Spain to support a leftist appropriation of resources and redistribution of land. Even Texaco – an American corporation – is making money hand-over-fist selling oil to Franco. I admire the Republicans' willingness to fight, especially considering that nobody thinks they can win. Nobody thought the American, French, Haitian, or Russian revolutionaries could topple the monarchies, but history was on their side, so it was inevitable they'd win. So maybe the Republic and democracy will survive in Spain. Maybe history is on their side."

"What about your daughter and wife?" Professor Benjamin prodded Zapata. "Is there *really* any honor in leaving a wife and child behind so you can go fight and possibly die for high-minded idealism or 'being on the right side of history'?"

Zapata gazed contemplatively a moment at the laces of his sugar-crusted workboats and thought long and hard a moment. "I have to ask myself," he finally explained, "'what kind of world do I want my wife and child to live in?' More than that, I have to ask myself, 'do I want to be the kind of husband and father who would sacrifice his ideals for the comfort and security of only my wife and child, a comfort and security made possible by widespread social inequity and injustice throughout the world?' To be honest, I'm not sure what the right answer. Maybe there's not a right answer."

"That's the point of these discussions," Benjamin smiled. "They are designed to get you to ask the right questions. Never mind answer. To hell with answers! There are no easy answers to incredibly complex questions. It's essential to understand that each person has to decide for him or herself what is right or wrong, to cut through all the noise, all the dogma, all the propaganda and tap into his or her own aura, their own soul."

"But isn't that also the case for the fascists?" Bethany asked. "The fascists actually believe they are right, too."

"That's a good point," Professor Benjamin agreed. "You've honed in on a key point to keep in mind: all people, regardless of their race, class, gender, ethnicity, religion, or creed, or whatever are shaped by their own personal experiences in the context of their culture—by *their* history. Identity and decisions are not made in a vacuum. In some sense, we don't even actually make conscious decisions a lot of the time; decisions are often dictated by the circumstances—the moment—in which we find ourselves. An animal backed into a corner is far more prone to violence than an animal running free through a forest."

"But humans are not animals!" Bethany refuted. "Humans paint, we create, we love. By your understanding and logic of humans, pugnacious and homicidal warmongers like Hitler, Mussolini, and Franco are, in fact, the animals backed into a corner by Jews, Ethiopians, labor unions, and the Poplar Front. But that notion is a false consciousness a homicidal maniac use to justify aggression, oppression, and genocide."

"I agree," Benjamin smiled coyly. "Those of us who genuinely value high-minded ideals such liberty, fraternity, equality, the redeeming value of art, science, truth, and beauty are by no means animalistic, not as much as fascists who subscribe to Social Darwinism. But Franco launched a coup because he perceives humans to be animals. He believes he was backed into a corner by the Popular Front's eagerness to strip the conservatives of the political and economic privilege and power they believe to be their birthright. The genuine divide amongst humans is not so much between liberals and conservatives or capital versus labor. The real divide is between those who believe humans are spiritual beings guided by the ideals of the Enlightenment versus those like Franco, Mussolini, and Hitler, who think the Enlightenment is quixotic bullshit and that humans are essentially animals perpetually locked in a battle of survival of the fittest. The debate over whether humans are spiritual being or animals perhaps has no beginning or end and ultimately says more each particular person's conception of humans than about whether or not humans are animals or not."

"That's what it is so important to not let those who think of humans as animals struggling for existence in a jungle to debase those of us who see humans as spiritual beings in search of true enlightenment drag us down to their debased spiritual and intellectual conception of reality."

"That appears to be a contradiction from your earlier statement about violence being justified so long as you are on the 'right side of history,'" Benjamin grinned and rubbed his hand through his thinning brown hair.

"I suppose you're right," Zapata smiled humbly and graciously. "Engaging in violence inevitably debases spiritual beings into animals."

"And," Bethany added, "if history is truly on your side than non-violence is perhaps the only way to ensure history remains on your side. I admire the Haitian, French, American and Russian Revolutions. But none of those places is the social utopia imagined by enlightened thinkers. Perhaps their recourse to violence turned those nations into the same brand of oppression the revolutionaries fought against in the first place."

"It's a paradox," Benjamin said, "that's why good questions are so much more valuable in the humanities than what might appear to be right answers."

Bethany nodded agreeably as one of her classmates, a young Hasidic sitting next to the window toward the back of the room, shoved his notebook into a burlap bag. Benjamin, sensing unrest as a result of class winding to a close, pulled a silver pocket-watch from the breast pocket of his heather gray waistcoat and glanced at the time. "Before you go," his voice rose a level above the rustling hum of undergraduates anxious to get to their next class. "We have a chance to ask some fascists what they think tomorrow."

"Tomorrow?" Bethany asked, somewhat puzzled.

"Tomorrow's seminar is cancelled so that we all can go see a group of Silver Shirts speak at the Roseland Ballroom."

"The Silver Shirts?" Bethany sighed and rolled her eyes. "Do we have to?"

"I'm afraid so," Benjamin said somewhat reservedly. "They are being hosted by the chancellor of the college. He has requested that all liberal arts majors attend. Feel free to ask whatever you want. Don't pull any punches if you feel the need to sock it to them." Benjamin stood and pushed his notebook into his faded leather tote bag as the undergrads shuffled out of the classroom into a long hallway leading out towards Convent Avenue.

Union Square

A bitter early winter wind whipped through the middle of Union Square on a particularly bleak, cold, and gray December dusk. Zapata, Maria, and their newborn baby girl, Versailles, who was bundled tightly in a royal blue papoose, navigated the mass of people assembled on the square. They waded through fevered rabble rousers of every stripe—anarchists, communists, Democrats, Republicans, Silver Shirts, and end-of-days evangelicals— all soap boxing, all professing that they and they alone had the tonic to save society from economic depression, despair, and decay, and that those who disagreed with them were naively wrongheaded, if not merchants of evil and hell bound.

Zapata mostly tuned them out. But on this particular occasion – in light of having just left a debate about the merits of violence, non-violence, and whether the war in Spain was a revolution pitting labor versus capital –a steely-eyed recruiter for the International Brigades, a small and middle-aged man with a thick French accent, bushy handlebar moustache, and dark blue bags under his sleep-deprived gray eyes—was especially resonant to Zapata.

Maria, however, was far too exhausted to pay the rabble-rousers any mind at all. She had been toiling in the cabana wear factory since just after dawn and was simply too damned knackered to find any interest in anything but a bite to eat, followed quickly by a warm blanket and sleep.

"I'm not sure how long I can keep doing this," Maria sighed sorrowfully. "Versailles keeps me up half the night and daycare takes half my wages. I can feel my soul being crushed more and more each day. I wish you didn't work the nightshift because I could really use help with her throughout the night. Sometimes she'll cry a quarter-hour before I can even lug myself out of bed. The neighbors bang on the wall and scream profanity. Now they glare at me as I pass them in the hall."

"I'm sorry, mi amore," Zapata said as he gently nestled his arm around his wife's shoulders and kissed her forehead, which was bundled in the knit black beret he gave her on the fifth night of Hanukkah. "You know I can't work the dayshift. Those positions are reserved for friends of management—those unaffiliated with the unions. Besides, I need to finish school. Once I get my degree, I can find a nice white-collar job and we can move out to Huntington and buy that little farmhouse you've been dreaming of. Just think of how great it'll be to grow our own food, to milk our own cow. Versailles will adore living on a farm – all the wide-open spaces to play and explore. We've just got to persevere a little while longer."

"I'm not sure I can endure another three more years like this," she said disconsolately. "We can't afford to keep

Versailles in daycare another three more years, and I'll burn out long before then."

"What do you want me to do?" Zapata said frustrated. "I didn't create the capitalist system or this goddamn Great Depression. I'm doing the best I can."

"I know. I'm sorry," she said. "I'm just exhausted and think I might also be suffering from a bit of postpartum depression. I don't mean to take my frustration out on you. You're right; I need to be a bit more patient. We'll find a way." Her scuffed work boots stopped suddenly at the A-train subway station entrance on 14th Street and Broadway. She softly kissed her husband's icy and unshaven cheek. She then walked towards the staircase descending under Broadway.

"Where are you going?" he asked. "Don't you want to get dinner before I have to head across the river to the factory?"

"Not tonight," she lamented. "I'm too tired. Besides, we can't afford for both of us to eat out. I'll heat a bit of broth in the potbelly at home." She and Versailles disappeared into the dank and dark of the subway station below the street. Zapata, whose empty stomach snarled, lingered a while longer on the square. He bought a soothingly warm bag of boiled peanuts from a vendor on the corner of Broadway and Fourteenth and then wandered back over to where the International Brigades advocates was baring his soul and whipping a small cadre into something less than a frenzied revolutionary movement.

"Many of you men cannot find work!" The recruiter bemoaned in a broken French accent, frantically shaking his fist over his head as he'd seen Vladimir Lenin do in old newsreels. "Those of you who do have jobs are almost certainly making a slave wage while those hogs down on Wall Street make more money than you can even imagine. And how do those swine 'earn' their riches and consolidate their political power? I'll tell you how: off the sweat of your backs, from the blood of your hands! It's nothing short of criminal! I know how powerless you lot feel. I've been down and out too, believe you me. We've all fallen victim to this godforsaken Great Depression at one time or another. It ruins more families and lives each day. But make no mistake, brothers and sisters—capitalism, the so-called 'invisible hand of the market,' is by no means some mystical force of nature. This Great and terrible Depression is no tidal wave, earthquake, or hurricane. It is manmade by those damned Wall Street bankers in league with war mongering fascists like Adolf Hitler, Benito Mussolini, and Francisco Franco. The inevitable revolution that Karl Marx prophesied nearly one hundred years ago is now in its opening stages; the curtain has just been drawn. *The* Revolution to end all revolutions has begun in earnest in the cities and haciendas of Spain. This is our chance, brothers and sisters, once and for all to finally strike a fatal blow against the menace of capitalism and to finally put the means of production and balance of political power firmly and definitively in the hands of the workers of the world forever more. The Republic of Spain's fight against the fascist menace is the cause of working men and women all over the world. Joining the International Brigades is the workingman's glorious moment in history to strike a crushing blow against fascism, Wall Street, and ultimately the rapacious capitalist system responsible for workers' oppression and subjugation. The International Brigades is your chance to end the Great Depression, to end your seemingly endless toil, suffering, sorrow, struggle and sacrifice. Join the International Brigades brethren. Change the course of your life, your family's lives, and the course of human history forever! You men who can hear my voice, this is your chance to lay claim to your manhood!"

Zapata's frigid and stiff fingers dug deep into the brown, warm and salty peanut bag for the last morsel in the bottom corner. He dropped the bag of husks in the trashcan next to him and gobbled the last peanut. He then tightened his crimson plaid scarf and turned his coat collar up to protect his throat from the frigid early winter wind whipping east from the Hudson River along Fourteenth Street. His tired eyes glanced up at the clock at the south end of the square. The oratory caused him to lose track of time. He rushed east across Union Square and then down the subway station steps under the street bound for the L-Train that'd escort him under the East River to the Bedford Avenue stop.

Williamsburg, Brooklyn

Frigid winter winds whipped off the East River, making Kent Avenue feel like the inside of an icebox. But the men huddled around the furnaces inside refinery at the Domino Sugar factory in Williamsburg perspired profusely. A bead of sweat dripped from Zapata's nose and mixed in with some sugar crystals. Stono, who had arrived in

Brooklyn a month and a half earlier after riding the rails from Miami up the east coast, felt especially lucky to find work as a refiner, even though it was a particularly hot, grueling, and tiresome twelve-hour shift six days a week. He also made much less money refining and lugging bales of sugar out to the loading docks lining the East River than he had made as a cabbie in Miami. Though overworked and underpaid, Stono's quality of life was modestly improved due to the fact that he didn't have to confront the pervasive terror of constantly looking over his shoulder for fear of being lynched.

Rogers, the nightshift foreman, was a surly man with slick gray hair, steely blue eyes and a voice deeper than a canyon. He had a particularly short fuse, especially towards the black workers who had fled the Deep South. Many black laborers in the northern industrial centers of the United States during the Great Depression were often snared in a kind of catch-22 with management because, although they could often be hired for much cheaper than a worker of European ancestry, and tended to work more diligently and with less complaint. They were also sometimes used as strikebreakers against ethnic white unions, they were concomitantly resented by many of the migrants from Europe for the very reasons management appreciated them. The foreman at Domino, however, had worked his way up from laborer to middle management. He considered himself as much a member of the workforce as an employer. He thus shared many of the ethnic white workers' sense of animosity towards black workers like Stono who had migrated to the north from the south, thereby placing even greater pressure on an already overstressed industrial labor market. Rogers was indicative of most middle managers: he needed black labor because it was cheap and easily replaceable, but resented needing black labor because it helped disprove the notion that whites ethnic laborer were superior workers.

Zapata, unlike Rogers, genuinely liked and respected Stono. He and Stono shared an enthusiasm for Jazz. Zapata especially admired Stono's indefatigable work-rate and his ability to ignore the onslaught of snide comments lobbed at him on a daily basis by many of the workers, especially those who belonged to the American Federation of Labor, which barred all but white men from joining. The AFL tended to be far more nativist and atavistic than the International Workers of the World, which hurt both groups ability to collectively bargain with management. Both Stono and Zapata were brethren in the IWW, which, unlike the AFL, permitted workers of all races, nationalities, genders, and creeds to join the union. The "Wobblies," as IWW members were often referred, was also vital to getting the Wagner Act passed in 1935, which promised workers basic human rights when dealing with management. The Act, however, was also a kind of powder keg because it signaled a sea change in the government's relation to workers. All through American history, the federal government dogmatically supported management in squabbles with labor. But the Wagner Act put the federal government in labor's corner to a degree unseen in the country's history. The unintended consequence of the Act, however, was that management grew increasingly hostile and antagonistic to labor. Any threat of working-class dissidence was often taken as a declaration of war and thus elicited harsh overreactions on behalf of managers. But management's hostility could also, in theory, add more cohesion and solidarity amongst workers. The massive influx of immigrants to the United States up to the 1924 Immigration Act also meant that by the mid-1930s, workers who had been born in foreign lands but had come of age in American cities gradually came to see themselves less in racial and ethnic terms, and more in economic terms. In other words, Zapata and Stono saw themselves as workers and consumers oppressed by capitalism, more so than the "kike" or "nigger" that members of the AFL often reduced them to. The melting pot of America, in short, enabled Zapata to intermingle, marry, and have a child with a Catholic-turned-anarchist from Italy. All this seemingly portentous melting together of various races, creeds, and genders into one cohesive labor union seemed both toxic and dangerous to the mostly Protestant Anglo-Americans who owned the vast majority of America's corporations—companies such as Ford, Singer, General Motors, Dodge, General Electric, IBM, Texaco, United Fruit, Dow, DuPont, United Fruit, and Domino Sugar. The tension between the AFL and IWW, and both organization's tension with management, played itself out on the factory floors and sometimes in the streets on a daily basis during the especially contentious 1930s, a moment in history when it seemed as though the capitalist system could collapse completely at any moment.

Stono, who had worked nearly twelve hours straight hauling forty-pound bales of sugar from the factory floor down to the loading dock, slipped and fell down the stairs, which ripped open a bag and scattered crystals across the cold concrete floor. "Goddamn it!" the bleary-eyed foreman rushed over and grabbed Stono by the arm, trying to pull him brusquely to his feet. "You clumsy nigger!"

Stono yanked his arm free from the foreman's grasp and brushed some crystals from the front of his trousers. He was visibly upset, but shrewdly tried to ignore the slight. "I'm sorry, boss," Stono said conciliatorily. "I slipped in some sweat. That's all. It won't happen again."

"I'm docking the cost of that goddamn bag from your check this week," the foreman grunted while pointing down at the mound of sugar seeping from the puncture in the bale.

Zapata, whose gray overalls were covered in sweat and congealed sugar, hurried from a nearby refining vat to Stono, who was struggling at the bottom of the steps to get the sugar back into the bale. "Give him a break, Rogers," Zapata pleaded. "It was an honest mistake. Besides, it's not like management can't afford to lose one lousy bale of crystals now and again."

"Don't speak for management," the foreman grunted. "Don't you dare speak for me, buddy. These bales of sugar are worth more to us than this clumsy nigger is." He wagged his finger at Stono, who had a glum look of despair on his bashful face. "He just cost us money and it's coming out of his share, by god."

"That's bullshit," Zapata said. "Management needs us workers as much as we need you."

"The hell we do," the foreman said snidely. "There's not one man here that can't be replaced in twenty minutes. I know fifty men standing on a breadline this very moment that'd kill for this job."

"Bullshit," Zapata said. "Think of the time and financial burden of having to train a new workforce. Alone, we are 'replaceable.' But as long as we workers are united, you are at our mercy. You can't fire us willy-nilly without incurring great cost to Domino. If you cost the company money, you're more replaceable than us. You don't want to lose that pretty little Victorian on Ditmas Avenue, do you? You think your pretty little wife would stand by her man if you had no job or house?"

"Are you threatening me, boy?" the foreman sneered.

"It's no threat," Stono said nervously. "He's just trying to make you see that management need us much as we need y'all."

"It's not a threat. It's a promise," Zapata grinned as he turned and walked towards the big brown loading dock doors leading out of the factory into the cold and gray street. "Come on men," Zapata hollered. "We're walking out. Let's show management what we're made of, what we're worth to these bastards." He glared at Rogers. "We'll be outside until you realize how valuable we are to this operation."

Fourteen Wobblies stopped working and, in a show of solidarity, followed Zapata and Stono from the warm interior of the factory and onto frigid Kent Avenue. Zapata was a bit dismayed because he, perhaps naively, believed more men would offer their support by following him and Stono to the street. The members of the AFL were, however, more conservative and cautious and not willing to risk their livelihoods, especially this close to Christmas and the New Year. Some AFL members thought of their families and the terribly frightening difficulty and insecurity of finding new employment opportunities in the middle of a Great Depression. They, and even a half-dozen Wobblies, balked. The foreman, meanwhile, raced up the stairs and into his office, grabbed his phone and dialed as fast as the rotary phone would permit. "We've got another walkout," he hollered into the receiver. "It's those goddamn Wobblies again!"

The sun was just peaking beyond the Brooklyn horizon by the time Stono, Zapata, and the other twelve Wobblies made their way out to the Kent Avenue. What none of dissidents realized when they walked out, however, was that management had been preparing for a work stoppage—a costly burden that was more and more common since the Wagner Act passed. What the Wobblies suspected but could not prove was that management was actually trying to incite walkouts by doing petty things like making Stono pay for the bag of sugar so that the unionists could be replaced with cheaper and more pliant non-unionized workers. Not long after the Wagner Act passed, management hired a Goon Squad to squelch workers' dissidence. By the time the Wobblies that walked out had lit their cigarettes, the New York City Red Squad, which was an arm of the NYPD, and Domino Sugar's very own

Pinkerton-like Goon Squad arrived in diesel-powered open bed trucks ready for war. Many of them wielded batons and Louisville Sluggers that were already stained with the blood of workers who had tried to back capitalists into a corner by inciting work stoppages.

Zapata, Stono, and the rest of the Wobblies assembled on Kent Avenue were outnumbered by a 6-to-1 ratio. Most of the Wobblies felt an innate internal conflict over whether to fight, and almost surely endure savage and emasculating beatings, or take flight. They were caught in a vicious catch-22 between swallowing their pride to plead for management's forgiveness and go back inside to finish their shifts, or else fight and certainly lose their jobs, and their sense of manhood. The men thus, against their best judgment, hunkered and decided to stay and fight a battle they knew they could not win. "Better to die on our feet," Zapata declared, "then to die on our knees!"

The Red Squad, Goon Squad, and unionists collided in the middle of Kent Avenue. It was a quick ordeal that left a few members of law enforcement and the majority of the dozen unionists badly battered and bloody. The factory workers all spent the night in jail. The cops, conversely, except for the one hospitalized after being punched square in the jaw by Stono, all spent the night tucked into their own beds. Though the cops and factory workers should have perhaps had a common affinity for the other due to similar pay scales, the psychological wage provided to law enforcement by fighting for elites' economic and political privilege created a kind of false consciousness that ideologically divided the bluecoats and the blue-collar factory workers similar to the way race and gender does. The battle between the cops and Wobblies outside the factory on Kent Avenue, along with scores of other conflicts between cops and blue-collar workers all across the nation during the Great Depression, seemed to especially illuminate railroad tycoon Jay Gould's assertion that he and other financiers could simply "hire one half of the working class to kill the other."

The battered, bruised and wounded Wobblies were denied medical treatment. Some of them had life-threatening injuries and faced a night of terror and peril in the congested holding cell where they were penned like farm animals. The few Wobblies able to avoid serious injury during the confrontation, including Stono and Zapata, quietly commiserated. Stono, feeling as though he had nothing left to lose, was especially bitter and defiant. But Zapata, the father and husband who was responsible for two lives beside his own, was frightened and suffering severe regret pangs.

"I fucked up," Zapata bemoaned. "We should have just let it go. They have all the power and we are lucky to have had jobs at all."

"Come on, man," Stono seethed. "They can take our blood, they can take our jobs, but we can't let them take our pride too. A man is nothing without a sense of pride."

"That's not the point," Zapata wheezed while clutching his rib. "I can't let them to take my family from me." "I'm nothing without my wife and little girl."

The click clacking sound of heels from scuffed wingtips on the concrete floor outside the cell quickly approached.

"Abrahams?" the cop called out like a town crier. Zapata dragged himself up slowly from the wobbly wooden bench he and Stono sat. He clutched his bruised ribs, winced and shuffled meanderingly to the front of the holding cell. "You've been bailed out," the cop said somewhat bemusedly.

"Really?" Zapata was surprised. "By who?"

"How the hell should I know?" the surly cop muttered while shrugging his burly shoulders and unlocking the cell.

"Hopefully the charges will be dropped," Zapata said glumly as he looked down at Stono and gently patted his friend on his aching shoulder. "If not, I'll see you at the hearing."

"Ain't going to no trial," Stono said flatly. "I got other plans."

"What plans?" Zapata was equal parts curious and confused.

Stono dug his swollen right hand into the front pocket of his tattered blue overalls, revealing a worn business card. His quivering hand held it aloft for Zapata to see. "I'm gonna call this here International Brigade recruiter I met on Union Square a while back to bail me out of here. I'm gonna go to Spain," he whispered. "We're already at war here. Hell, we might as well go to Spain where we might at least have a fighting chance, and get paid for it too."

"Alright," the cop said impatiently as he eased the gate of the holding cell open just wide enough for Zapata to creep through the egress. "Let's go, Pinko," he said snidely while motioning down the long dark hallway leading towards the stairs.

Maria was bundled in a plaid wool blanket. It, however, did little to diminish the biting wind ripping up the street from the East River. She was shivering while gazing up the concrete steps outside the precinct and clutching Versailles tight to her bosom. As warm and caring as she was to her daughter, she was equally cold to her husband as he finally limped out of the double doors of the precinct and down the steps to the street. His forehead had a terrible lump on it; a stream of dry blood was crusted to his cheek. He winced a bit from a sharp pain in his sternum as he leaned over to give Versailles a peck on her tiny, cold and runny nose. He leaned in nervously to kiss Maria too, but she pulled away with a disgruntled expression pasted to her frigid face.

"How could you be so foolish?" She seethed while trying to fight back anger-laced tears. "How are we supposed to afford a lawyer for you if Domino presses charges? I had to sell the potbelly just to bail you out!"

"What choice did I have?" he grunted defensively. "The foreman was abusive to Stono. I'm part of a union, a brotherhood. If one of us is oppressed, we're all oppressed. The only strength we have is our numbers—our solidarity."

"What about solidarity with your family?" she blurted. "What will we do if you lose your job? How will we eat, pay rent? Survive! What the hell will we do if you are convicted and sent to prison? What then?"

He grimaced as he gently slid his arm over her shoulders and pulled her close. "Don't worry, my love. I'll apologize to management. The foreman can be reasoned with, I think. He's not a bad man. He used to be a workingman before he was promoted to foreman. So deep down, he knows management needs labor to make capital as much as we need capital to work. They need us as much as we need them. Besides, if I'm fired from the factory, I will find a job somewhere else."

"How can you be so naïve? So daft?" she blurted coldly while rolling her eyes and shrugging her husband's arm from her. "We're in the middle of a Great Depression! Management is constantly seeking to replace unionized workers. You're not skilled labor, so you're as replaceable as toilet paper."

"You should speak kindlier of me and the men," he said. "Your father was, like me, not ashamed of being a workingman."

"My father didn't suffer from the same delusions you seem to," she said as she stopped dead in her tracks and looked long and hard at her husband. "And look where my father is now; disappeared by Il Duce. I won't suffer through that again, not ever. I'll die first."

"You won't suffer," Zapata said reassuringly. "I promise. What happened to your parents can't happen here. For all its faults, America isn't Italy."

"That billy club that cut open your face and put that lump on your head must have knocked all the sense out of you," she said coldly as she glared. "Did you forget what happened to your own father? Did you forget that I just bailed you out of jail and you're almost certainly going to be unemployed by tomorrow? You really think what happened to my father and yours can't happen to you too? How can you be so stupid? You have a family to consider! Do you want what happened to me and you happen to Versailles too? Do you want her to suffer the fate of losing her parents and being orphaned?" Zapata felt terribly emasculated as he sulked down into the subway station beneath the sidewalk. "Where are you going?" she asked bemusedly.

"City College." His disconsolate voice was monotone. "I can't afford to fail my history class any more than I can afford to lose my job at the factory," he mumbled under his breath, "not if we ever want to move out to Long Island and start that farm we've been dreaming about." A wave of disheartened discontent seemed to swallow him as he leaned on the handrail for support and limped down the stairs into the dark tunnel without looking back at his wife and child. Maria watched him disappear into the cold dark tunnel.

CHAPTER FOUR

Harlem, December 1936

Zapata was more than slightly concussed after the battle with the Red Squad and Goons on Kent Avenue, which surely contributed to him forgetting that class was scheduled to meet at the Roseland Ballroom for the Silver Shirt presentation. The Silver Shirts were an American-made paramilitary fascist organization inspired by Adolf Hitler's anti-Semitic rhetoric and meteoric rise to power. The Silver Shirts, who planned to discuss the supposed merits of Franco's coup and the "Jewish Problem" in Europe and the United States, were invited to speak by the chancellor of City College, an archconservative Catholic who was personal friends with both J. Edgar Hoover and Father Charles Edward Coughlin. Hoover was head of the FBI, a devout "red hunter" anti-Bolshevist who was also a seething anti-Semitic. Coughlin hated Jews even more than Hoover. He was also a shamelessly outspoken proponent of Hitler and Mussolini, both of whom were backed by the Vatican, which perceived genocidal maniacs to be a lesser form of evil than Jews, who Christians widely considered to be "Christ killers." Nearly thirty million Bible thumping Americans enjoyed Father Coughlin's wildly popular radio show, which was ominous of Fox News, every Sunday. After the 1936 presidential election, he falsely accused President Franklin Roosevelt of "leaning toward international socialism on the Spanish question," and increasingly perpetuated the notion that Adolf Hitler, Benito Mussolini, and Francisco Franco's brand of fascism was a necessary tonic to communism. He claimed that

Jewish bankers were behind the Russian Revolution, and that Bolshevism was a conspiracy to subvert Christianity around the world.

The audience that had assembled in the ballroom that chilly early winter afternoon – especially Professor Benjamin, whose elderly grandparents were recently relocated to a ghetto outside Warsaw – was charged with electric tension by the time Zapata staggered in the back door. Nearly every time the Silver Shirts' fair-haired leader, William Dudley Pelley, tried to elucidate or elaborate a point, half the audience, many of whom were Benjamin's students, booed, hissed and harangued him. Zapata, who had yet to dress his wounds from the early morning fight outside Domino, limped to the front of the ballroom and slunk into a rickety wooden foldout chair between Bethany and Benjamin, both of whom gave Zapata a long glance as if to say, 'what the hell happened to you?' Zapata slowly shook his head and shrugged his shoulders slightly as if to reply, 'don't ask.'

Pelley pushed a bit of blond hair and sweat from his forehead as he entered the portion of his presentation where he justified imperialism on the grounds of scientific racism. "Humanity has always been divided into castes," he bellowed as half the audience booed. "There have always been brainworkers and mudsills. The most historically successful brainworkers are those with Teutonic and Saxon blood. The natural order for darkies has always been manual labor in service of more civilized Anglo and Teutonic races. These are historical facts!" he said as he banged his fist atop the sturdy maple podium. "In that sense," Pelley continued his diatribe, "we are not merely justified by natural order, but by natural law to invade lands peopled by inferior species and extract resources and labor that mudsills would inevitably squander." Half the room cheered. The other half jeered.

"What about the Jews?" Bethany demanded.

"What about them?" Pelley pondered.

"How are you any more civilized than a Jew?" Bethany seethed.

"The natural order dictates that Jews are meant to be laborers," Pelley said matter-of-factly. "They did a fine job building the Pyramids for the Pharaohs of Ancient Egypt. But it is an abomination for Jews to be bankers and politicians. Let Jews be bankers and panics, depressions, and wars are simply inevitable. The Jew's place is at the bottom of the universal caste system. That is God's law. It is an abomination having Jews doing brainwork, plain and simple; it can only lead to disaster and despair for the whole world. Jewish bankers caused the 'Great War' and cost millions of Europeans and 116,000 Americans their lives. They also caused the Great Depression, which is currently causing widespread suffering and despair all around world."

Bethany reached under her seat and plopped a backpack into her lap. She dug her fist deep down into the book bag and then hurled a large brown egg at Pelley. Gooey yoke splattered across his furrowed forehead and stuck in his bushy blond mustache and bangs. Pelley was so flabbergasted, stunned and appalled by the assault that he took a long and what seemed to be thought filled pause to process what had happened. He staggered and finally flopped into a chair ten-or-so feet behind the podium. He wiped his eyes with a snot-crusted handkerchief. He then leapt suddenly from the stage and charged directly at Bethany like a skewed Brahmin bull in pursuit of a matador donning red. Zapata – who was still wired with angst and anger from his fight with the Red Squad and Domino Goons, and panged from the spat with his wife outside the precinct – instinctively clenched his fist and struck Pelley squarely in his face. Pelley clutched his broken nose, which was profusely gushing crimson blood. He dropped to the floor and writhed in agony. Blood stained his silver shirt.

A riot nearly ensued between the cadre of Silver Shirts, who were supported by some slack-jawed and atavistic rabble-rousers, versus Benjamin's history classes, and some other unaffiliated leftists assembled in the ballroom. Chancellor Cunningham hurried up onto the stage and pleaded for calm and order. "Dr. Benjamin," Cunningham hollered into the chrome microphone, "you get your students out of here this instant, or so help me God, I will expel every last one of them."

Benjamin was equal parts proud and disappointed in Bethany and Zapata as he half-heartedly ushered his classes out of the building. Cunningham stayed in the ballroom a moment where he pleaded for Pelley's forgiveness. He finally raced out of the ballroom and eventually caught up with the class as they walked near the subway station on Convent Avenue. "I need to speak with all three of you in my office at once!" He wagged his fist at Benjamin, Zapata, and Bethany. The rest of the students quickly dispersed. The trio caught in Cunningham's proverbial crosshairs meanwhile reluctantly followed the fuming chancellor into the building and down a long corridor leading towards his corner office overlooking Amsterdam Avenue.

"How dare you cause such a disgusting spectacle to an invited speaker," Cunningham seethed as he slammed the door and then slumped into the leather chair at the business end of his oak desk. He glared at the anxious and angst filled trio huddled together on the vinyl couch pushed up against the wall from his desk.

"How dare you invite such vitriolic hate and warmongers, sir," Bethany said defiantly.

"Listen and listen good, young lady," Cunningham seethed snidely, "this is the United States of America. We, unlike those Bolshevik bastards you seem so fond of, are free to speak our minds. You may vociferously disagree with what other folks think or say, but you, under no circumstances, have the right to accost them. This is not a vaudeville performance or the Old Country, by God. This is America. People are free to speak their minds without fear of being assaulted."

Bethany put all her energy into not giving Cunningham the satisfaction of seeing her cry after he placed her on academic probation. Zapata, who had thrown the punch that broke Pelley's nose, was expelled—

"effective immediately"—and told he'd be "lucky if charges were not pressed."

"If Zapata is expelled," Professor Benjamin warned, "I'll tender my resignation."

"Wonderful!" Cunningham smiled. "I'm delighted to accept your resignation. Clear out your office immediately."

Bethany's bottom lip quivered and she began to sob. As the first person in her family to attend college, she was particularly fearful she'd disappoint her immigrant parents who each worked fifty hours a week. She was equally sorrowful because she felt largely responsible for Professor Benjamin and Zapata's fate. She respected and admired immensely and thought it unfair that they'd not have been adversely affected had she simply not hurled the egg at Pelley.

Thick icy pellets of rain dropped heavily from the sky onto Amsterdam Avenue outside Cunningham's office as the trio slinked out of Cunningham's office. Bethany pled for forgiveness. Zapata assured her that he was solely responsible for his actions.

"It just felt like the right thing to do," he explained.

Benjamin tried comforting Bethany by assuring her that "things would inevitably work out, one way or the other. They always do." They each took turns shaking hands and giving each other hugs, and then went their separate ways: Bethany towards the Bronx, Benjamin to Queens, and Zapata downtown.

Despite Benjamin's words of wisdom, a chilling and sober sickness sunk into the pit of Zapata's belly on the A- train downtown. "How will I ever explain this to Maria?" he muttered repeatedly. The elderly woman in the seat across from him nervously wondered if he was a madman before surreptitiously moving to the other end of the car.

A dense fog had set in over Lower Manhattan by the time Zapata arrived at Union Square. He was too dejected to go down to Broome Street to confront his wife with more bitterly bad news after being expelled from City College. He thus limped around the square in a haze. His arms were folded tense and pressed tight to his aching chest. He was desperate to ignore the myriad rabble rousers, anxious to bide time, put his thoughts in proper order, and devise a way of explaining the calamity of losing his job and being expelled from school in the same day to Maria without further diminishing her trust and affection. He feared she might finally be fed up enough to leave him.

The keen-eyed International Brigade recruiter with the thick French accent – a diminutive and middle-aged man with a thick and coarse moustache and droopy blue bags under his gray eyes – spotted Zapata leaning disconsolately against a lamppost on the corner of Broadway and Sixteenth Street. Zapata was easy to pick out of the crowd considering his forehead was swollen and his cheek was stained with dry blood. The recruiter honed in on Zapata, tracking him like a wolf after a wounded wildebeest. "You look lost, lad," the recruiter said in a thick and empathetic French accent as he placed his hand gently on Zapata's sore shoulder.

"I'm not lost," Zapata hesitantly replied while glancing suspiciously at the man's mangled arthritic hand nestled on his shoulder. "I've lived in the city my whole life."

"No, I mean 'lost,' like in need a new and profound sense of purpose and direction in life," the recruiter qualified.

"Let me guess," Zapata said snidely while slightly rolling his eyes, "you're just the man I need to give me the direction I'm so fucking desperate to find?"

"Not me," the man said graciously while slightly chuckling. "I'm just a humble servant who can help introduce you to your destiny."

"Look buddy," Zapata said flatly while brushing the man's hand from his shoulder," whatever you're selling, I'm not buying,"

"Do I look like a salesman?" the recruiter rebutted as his steely eyes scanned down at his stained brown trousers to his torn and tattered work boots. "I'm simply the man offering you the opportunity for freedom, power, and a chance to make history."

Zapata scoffed, smiled wryly, and then limped painfully down a few steps towards the subway tunnel under Sixteenth Street. The persistent recruiter was undaunted by the slight. "I can tell you are a working man!" the grizzled Frenchman called out to Zapata as he followed him towards the steps descending into the dark tunnel. "I'd be willing to wager that your family has been exploited by the capitalist system for most of if not all your life. I imagine you are trapped in an economic death roll that you see no way of escaping. Tell me I'm wrong and I'll leave you be forever more!"

"You're not entirely wrong," Zapata said despairingly while rummaging through his pockets for a subway token. He reluctantly turned towards the eager recruiter. The recruiter's face lit up. He revealed a shiny new subway token from his pocket and held it in front of Zapata, who begrudgingly accepted it with the pained reluctance of a starving atheist taking communion from a high priest.

"I offer a glimmer of hope," the Frenchman said as Zapata shoved the token into his trouser pocket. "I'm offering you a slingshot and rock with which to strike a blow at the Greatest Goliath the world has ever known— capitalism. The war in Spain is a glorious stage in a worldwide revolution pitting the forces of fascism and capitalism versus those who are on the side of enlightened democracy and economic equality. Spain is the next glorious chapter in a story that dates back to the American, French, Haitian, and Russian Revolutions. All of those epochs, like the war in Spain, centered on defeating the landed aristocracy, redistribution of land and wealth, and equal political rights to 'the people,' all people! Defense of the democratically elected government in Spain against those fascist Nationalists should be the cause of every working man and woman and everyone who believes in political and economic equality. The International Brigades represent all the things Americans should stand for: a little less power to The Church, a little less land for aristocrats, more power and equality for 'the people,' and universal education."

"I don't disagree with you, sir," Zapata hollered as a train down the stairs screeched to a halt. "But I have a wife and child. I can't leave them to go to Spain. Besides, it's illegal for Americans to even travel to Spain now that the U.S. has imposed the embargo. Besides, I'm not exactly a Communist."

"Let me ask you, son. Do your wife and child have enough food to eat? Do they have enough warm clothes in winter?" he asked as his beady and bloodshot eyes peered deep into Zapata's weary and tattered soul.

"No, of course not," Zapata grumbled despondently. Hardly anybody has enough of anything now-and-days. Times are tough for nearly everyone. But this Depression can't last forever."

"Times are not so tough for those goddamned Wall Street bankers downtown, or those aristocrats eating caviar and drinking schnapps in their townhouses on Park Avenue, are they?"

"No," Zapata reluctantly agreed. "I don't suppose so."

"Those money-grubbing whores are the reason Roosevelt and his so called 'Brain Trust' cowed to the so-called neutrals such as ITT and Texaco, who are in bed with Franco. What does it do to your manhood to not be able to provide for your family like they need you to?" the recruiter prodded.

"What manhood?" Zapata said sullenly. "My sense of manhood is dependent on the whims and needs of management. They keep my balls locked away in a mason jar in my supervisor's desk."

"Exactly!" the recruiter said, wild eyed and grinning as he draped his arm around Zapata's shoulders and led him down the stairs and into the station. "You have the opportunity to reclaim your manhood in Spain. Show your wife the man you can be by striking a blow at those Wall Street bankers, Hitler, Mussolini, and Franco. Join the International Brigades and we will provide you with food, shelter, and we'll honor your sacrifice to the cause by paying you $225 a month to send home to your family, all while striking a death blow at economic and political injustice here and throughout the world. Look, I know it's hard to leave family. I have a wife and three children of my own in Lyon. But think of the hero you'll be to them when you come back from Spain after making history!"

Zapata hesitantly dropped the token into the turnstile, pushed through the barricade, and began to make his way towards the L-train downstairs. "I greatly admire what you and the International Brigades are doing," he explained. "But Spain is not my fight." He then descended another flight of steps down into the darkness below.

"You've never been more wrong in all your life, my boy!" the recruiter hollered into the abyss as Zapata faded from sight. The sullen Frenchman shook his head disappointedly, turned around, hurried up the stairs leading out of the station, and scanned the sea of humanity milling around Union Square. He spotted a disheveled hobo hunkered down at the base of the War Memorial statue in the middle of the square. The hobo was shivering violently and desperately trying to get warm next to a modest fire deep inside a metal trashcan. The recruiter rubbed his icy hands together and breathed warm breath on his fingers as he honed in on the hobo.

Fear of losing one's family and wishful thinking can both make a person believe things that just are not so. That helps explain why Zapata, his head still swollen and stained with dry blood, arrived at the Domino Sugar factory at dusk. The nightshift had only just begun when he limped onto the factory floor. The hope of keeping his job and not losing his family deceived him into thinking that all might be forgotten and forgiven since he had almost always been a model employee in the months prior to the walkout and subsequent fight at daybreak. He was proud of the fact that his work ethic and character demanded that he almost always arrived at the factory a few minutes early and stayed a few minutes late. "That must count for something," he thought as he slid his punch card into the time clock on the wall outside the break room.

He dutifully worked the entire shift, careful to keep his head down and to ignore the quizzical looks and whispers of the AFL-affiliated workers. At dawn, as the buzzer to end the nightshift sounded and the bleary-eyed, sweaty and exhausted workers began to file out onto cold and windy Kent Avenue like automatons seeking sleep, the foreman finally summoned Zapata into his office.

"I'm awfully sorry about yesterday," Zapata blurted nervously as he plopped down in the vinyl seat across the small desk from Rogers. "I'm a member of the IWW, so if one of the men walks out, we all walk out. I hope that you, since you used to also be a laborer like us men, understand my predicament."

"I do understand the difficulties of being unskilled labor, especially in the midst of an economic depression," the foreman said graciously. "I was unskilled in the 1890s down at Carnegie's Homestead Plant. There were walkouts and fights with Pinkertons at least once a fiscal year. See this?" he pointed to a small scar under his right eye. "I got this from the butt of a Pinkerton's pistol."

"I'm glad you understand," Zapata said quietly as his weary and swollen eyes scanned the dust on the floor between his scuffed and battered work boots. "I really do appreciate you letting me stay on board. Who knows, maybe someday I can work my way up to being skilled labor, and maybe, if I'm lucky, a foreman like you."

"I hope so too," the foreman forced an awkward and toothless grin, "I really do. But I can't keep you on board here. Management has a strict policy of not retaining any worker who commits an act of violence against our security force. Had you just walked out, maybe we could have forgotten the whole thing. But I can't let you stay after committing violence against our boys."

"Please sir," Zapata pleaded. "We were provoked by those Goons. It was fight or else flight. Those Goons were hired to beat the hell out of us! What choice did we have? I couldn't let them strip me of my dignity – my manhood!"

"Son, you've got it all backwards," Rogers coldly retorted. "A man's dignity depends on him having a job, of being a breadwinner for his family. You should have just kept working and minded your business when that nigger broke a bag of crystals open. If you kept working and didn't get involved with business between me and that clumsy nigger you'd not be in this predicament. You had a really good thing going here, but you couldn't let well enough alone. Had you had the good sense to support me, the foreman, rather than that nigger you'd still be able to put food on your family's table. Hell, I may have even recommended you for a skilled labor position somewhere down the line. As is, you, that nigger, and the rest of those goddamn commie Wobblies are all out on your asses and ain't nothing in this world going to change that."

"Please sir," Zapata pleaded. "I have a wife and child. I need this job. I've always been a good worker. I helped make Domino lots of money."

"Sorry, son," the foreman said emotionlessly. "I think you're an alright fella deep down, and my heart does go out to your family, especially since it is Christmastime. But my hands are tied. You and those godforsaken

Wobblies caused us to lose thousands of dollars' worth of production time last night. If it was up to me, I might consider keeping you and a couple of the other fellas on board. You're a hard worker and a decent enough fella. You're almost always on time and I can't ever recall you being drunk on the job, which is a hell of a lot more than I can say for half of these bastards. But, at the end of the day, we all got to live and die with the decisions we make. I'm sorry. But my hands are tied by company policy. I've got no choice but to let you go." He stood and ushered Zapata to the door. "You'll find a new job soon. I'll keep you in my prayers," he patted Zapata on the shoulder. "You'll see; this will end up being for the best. The Lord works in mysterious ways."

"Please sir, I'm begging," Zapata's meek voice quivered softly. "I have a wife and child. Have some compassion, please. I swear, it won't happen again; on my honor."

"I'm sorry, son," Rogers said as his beady gray eyes darted towards the cold concrete floor beneath Zapata's boots. Your old position has been already been promised to an Irish fella fresh off the boat. These micks save the company money—they work for less than nothing and they are Catholic, so usually not interested in joining unions. It's nothing personal, son. It's just business. Someday, if you're ever lucky enough to land a supervisory position, you'll understand my position... my hands are tied." He held his wrists together, as though an invisible wire bound them together, and momentarily held them aloft. "No hard feelings, I hope," he said as he forced an oafish smile and patted Zapata on the back, ushered him out of the door with a gentle nudge, and then swung the door shut behind him.

Zapata shook his head disconsolately and staggered nauseously down the iron staircase leading down towards the factory floor. He felt as though the world were caving in on him. Bulbous and terrified tears welled in his tired brown eyes as he exited the factory into the cold and biting wind whipping up Kent Avenue from the East River. He winced slightly as a frigid wind ripped into the wounds on his face, which were soaked with burning salt from his tears. He was, however, too emotionally devastated and afraid of what fate might befall his family to be altogether conscious of the salty stinging of his facial wounds.

Maria was busy quickly bundling Versailles in a purple winter onesie when Zapata glumly entered their tiny apartment on Broome Street. "Where the hell were you?" she asked. "I thought I was going to have to smuggle Versailles into work with me."

"I worked the nightshift at the factory," he said.

"You did?" her surprised and optimistic eyes grew wide. "Domino let you keep your job?"

"No," he said in a flat and dejected tone. "The bastards let me work all night before telling me I was officially canned. Rogers probably figured I owed the company a day due to money lost as a result of the work stoppage yesterday."

Maria's heavy and aching heart sank even further. She stopped bundling her baby and handed Versailles to Zapata. Though scared, angry and depressed, Maria gently rubbed the remnants of a blood-crusted tear from his swollen black-and-blue cheek. "Well," Maria said warmly, "you'll find a new job soon. Maybe you can find a work-study position at City College. The good news is that you can stay home and watch the baby until you find a new job. At least we won't have to pay for daycare for a while." She gave him a soft peck on his battered cheek.

"I'm going to Spain with the International Brigades," he blurted.

"The International Brigades?" She glared at him, wondering if he had lost all sense. "The hell you are. Look, I know you are angry and upset, but you can't leave school; not after all the time, energy and sacrifice you've put into it. You'll find a new job soon, even if it's just temp work. We'll find a way to make it work, no matter what. Nobody said graduating college and getting a farm on Long Island was going to be easy. If it was, everyone would do it."

"I was expelled from school this afternoon," his weary eyes scanned the hardwood floor a moment before settling on the bloodstain that resulted from his father's death the previous year.

Maria looked deep into her husband's depressed and pale face, hoping he was telling some sadistic and incredibly unfunny joke. "What the hell do you do you mean, 'expelled'?"

"I socked a Silver Shirt and broke his nose. The guy might press charges."

"Silver Shirt?" She was befuddled. "What the hell are you talking about? I think you might need to see a doctor. You must have a severe brain injury!"

"The class went to see some fascist give a lecture," he rambled. "A Silver Shirt said Jews were meant to be slaves," Zapata stammered as he struggled to explain his motive. "One of my classmates, Bethany, hit the guy with an egg and he charged at her like he aimed to punch her, so I decked him. A fight broke out. It's a long story… all you need to know is, I was expelled. I can't go back to City College."

"Please, Zapata, tell me you're kidding," she said while buttoning up the top button of her crushed-cherry colored pea coat. "You've got to be kidding. Please, you can't be serious!"

He slowly shook his head, trying to shake cobwebs loose. His weary eyes then soaked into the stained hardwood floor next to the window of their Broome Street apartment as if he was lost in another dimension.

"What were you thinking?" Maria seethed while tightening her scarlet scarf around her neck.

"I guess didn't think things through," his voice was sullen and filled with regret. "I just reacted. I'm just angry all the time since mom and dad died. I'm just sick and tired of being pushed around all the time. I want to join the fight.

I need to go to Spain." He began to sob disconsolately, which slightly disarmed Maria.

"My love," she said as she softly caressed his bruised cheek, "don't cry, you'll find another job."

"I don't want just another goddamned job," he whimpered. "I'm tired of being as 'replaceable as toilet paper.' I want to make a real difference in this godforsaken world. I don't just want to figure out a way to get by; I want to get over. I want to feel like a man who can stand on his own two feet, who can control his own destiny."

"But what about your father?" she asked while wiping a bulbous tear from his bruised and battered cheek. "You saw what happened to him when he embedded in France. If you join the International Brigades, you might come back in a similar condition, if you are lucky to come back at all."

"Things are different now than they were in 1918," he explained. "War is more modern and civilized now than it was back then. Besides, with Soviet support, it's just a matter of time before Franco counts his losses and goes back to Morocco. The fascists are fighting on the wrong side of history, so they can't possibly win. There's also a good chance that the U.S. will end the embargo if enough of us Americans have the courage to join the Republic in its fight. The government might even provide the Republic with weapons and fuel if enough of us go over there to influence policy. If the U.S. gets on the right side of history, maybe France and England will too. Then we might see some real positive change throughout the world.

Maybe I can help turn the tide of oppression throughout the world by going to Spain. Besides, the International Brigades provide food, shelter, and $225 a month to send home."

"$225 a month?" her sympathetic eyes instantaneously morphed into optimism. "Well," she said reluctantly, "if you need to go, you need to go. But just make sure you come back to me in one piece, especially with a sound mind and spirit. I don't want you to leave as the man I love and come back a shattered shell of yourself. I don't want to have to go through what your mother did with your father." Feeling especially pressed for time, Maria swung the door open to depart for work as Zapata sat plopped down at the tiny dining table with Versailles in his lap. Maria gave her Versailles and Zapata a quick though warm and supportive hug and kiss, wiped a bit blood and tears from his face with her tattered brown mitten, and then hurried out of the apartment and down the stairs towards Broome Street. Though physically and emotionally exhausted, Zapata had a renewed and profound sense of optimistic purpose as he bobbed Versailles up and down on his knee. "Don't worry, my love," he softly whispered. "Daddy will make things right. You won't ever want for anything again."

CHAPTER FIVE

Downtown Manhattan, January 1937

Nearly forty percent of the eighteen hundred American volunteers for the International Brigades that went to Spain between 1937 and 1938 were Jewish. That forty percent seemed particularly cognizant of the fact that they were fighting a brand of fascism designed, in part, to annihilate their race. More than ninety of the eighteen hundred volunteers were African Americans. Many of the black volunteers' political consciousness had been shaped in part by the threat of Ku Klux Klan fascism and lynch terrorism. Many African-American volunteers were also black nationalists who felt particularly compelled to fight fascism in part due to Italy's invasion of Ethiopia in 1935. Stono was greatly inspired by Paul Robeson – the thespian and baritone singer who popularized the classic "Moon River" – who, like Henry Fonda, was an ardent advocate of Spanish democracy. The Spanish Civil War, not inconsequently, was the first time in American history that black soldiers were fully integrated with white soldiers as full and equal partners. Some of the more well-read black nationalists, including Stono, had read Marcus Garvey's *Message to the People,* Karl Marx's *Capital*, W.E.B. Du Bois's *The Souls of Black Folks,* and C.L.R. James's *Black Jacobins.* Stono and many of the better-read volunteers thus saw the oppression of peasants in Spain, the exploitation of working-class people throughout the world, and the extermination of Africans in Ethiopia as a many headed hydra. Many of the volunteers, including Zapata and Stono, saw defense of the democratically elected government in Spain as the next inevitable chapter in a series of interconnected revolutions stretching back to the American, French, Haitian, and Russian Revolutions, all of which had toppled ancient monarchial regimes and subsequently implemented at least limited forms of democracy. Many American volunteers were also members of Popular Front affiliated organizations and were guided to Spain by a sense of idealism, most particularly a belief in liberty, fraternity, and equality, which many felt was especially threatened by fascism. But just as many volunteers, Zapata included, were lured to Spain by financial desperation to and need to provide a living as much, if not more than, by quixotic idealism.

Forty-two new American recruits, including Zapata, arrived at the Ukrainian Hall on East Third Street at 9 a.m., New Year's Day, 1937. Stono was reunited with Zapata, who was somewhat surprised to see that Professor Benjamin, who spoke so passionately about the importance of non-violence on a number of occasions, had also enlisted with the International Brigades. Benjamin, like Zapata and Stono, was as desperate to earn a living as he was guided by a sense of idealism.

The ragtag collection of forty-two enlistees drilled for an hour with broomsticks, since no guns had been provided by the Communist Party of the USA—the group tasked with organizing the brigade and getting them to Spain. After clumsily drilling for a while, the men were led a few blocks in a single-file line to the Yiddish Theater on Second Avenue where they were provided with a kosher meal, given some razors, packs of instant coffee, a few bars of soap, a couple cartons of Lucky Strike cigarettes, and a flimsy black cardboard suitcase with a yellow carry strap. Anyone sans passport also had their picture taken so that the CRUSA could furnish them a fake passport they could use to travel to France, then to Spain.

After their modest meal, many of the men eagerly ripped open their Lucky Strikes and enjoyed a cigarette or two. The recruiter with the thick French accent and bushy moustache, who had recruited Zapata on Union Square days earlier, thanked the men for "their courage and sacrifice to the cause of liberty and equality." He also reiterated that the volunteers would be "making history, striking a blow at Goliath," and all that bombast. For the first time, however, the little Frenchman also betrayed a sense of dire trepidation as he warned of the perils of traveling to a foreign country to fight in a war, especially when the United State Government was officially neutral and had imposed a strict travel embargo.

The volunteers were ordered to not to let anyone know they were traveling together, which seemed exceedingly difficult, since they were all given the same black cardboard suitcase with a yellow strap. Under no circumstances were the volunteers permitted to tell anyone that they were affiliated with the International Brigades or CPUSA, lest they risked "losing the war for the Republic and landing themselves in prison." The men were told to create believable alibis to tell anyone who might prod them for information. After arriving in France, the men were informed, they'd be smuggled into Spain via boat or train known as the "Red Express," which would escort the volunteers as far as the foothills of the Pyrenees Mountains on the French side of the border. If caught attempting to sneak into Spain, the men risked having their passports taken and their citizenship revoked. That was the best-case scenario as far as traversing the Pyrenees was concerned. The worst-case scenario was they'd all be killed by the fascist forces embedded in the forested foothills along the bordered between Spain and France. Extreme secrecy, in short, was imperative.

The North Atlantic, January 1937

January 5, 1937—Zapata's twenty-fourth birthday—the American volunteers for the International Brigades began their long, winding and treacherous odyssey to the Spanish Civil War. Maria had to work and to take Versailles to daycare, so she was unable to see her husband off as he disembarked at the Port of New York. At the dock, the volunteers' passports, many of which had been forged a few days prior by the CPUSA, were stamped with "NOT VALID FOR TRAVEL IN SPAIN" in bold red lettering before boarding *The SS Paris*, a ship bound for Perpignan, a small town on the Mediterranean Sea. But just getting to France, never mind Spain, was by no means no facile. The journey was marked with peril from the moment *The Paris* lost sight of land beyond the western horizon. A violent thunderstorm tossed ship back and forth.

Stono, Zapata, and Benjamin shared a tiny, windowless, third class cabin in the deepest bowels of the 744-foot-long ship. Stono, who had never been on a boat before, was especially susceptible to nausea once the ship was in the open waters of the icy North Atlantic Ocean. He was vomiting profusely into an aluminum mop bucket provided by a crewman when a loud THUMP THUMP THUMP sounded on the heavy metal door.

The hollow banging sound reverberating through the cramped cabin jarred Benjamin from his slumber. Zapata, however, who had great difficulty sleeping on anything moving, was wide-awake. He leapt from his musty cot and cautiously opened the thick aluminum door ever so slightly until the opening between the hall and cabin was but a few inches wide. A suspicious and disgruntled man, standing taller than six-feet and four inches and donning a spotless gray flannel suit and freshly polished black wingtip shoes, looked past Zapata into the cabin at Benjamin, who was gently rubbing his sleepy eyes, and Stono, who was puking into the bucket. "What are you three up to?" the intruder gruffly demanded in a thick South Carolinian accent.

"Who the hell wants to know?" Benjamin, wearing nothing but boxer shorts and a white cotton t-shirt, said as he stood fast from his cot and approached the door.

The South Carolinian in the gray flannel suit flashed a chrome FBI badge. "Agent Calhoun is who the hell wants to know. I'm on this boat in the interest of preventing Americans from illegally entering Spain. Let me see your passports?"

"Of course," Benjamin said tersely while trying to conceal his angst, "but I'm afraid you're wasting your time and ours, sir." Benjamin's passport was genuine, but he was especially nervous because he knew Stono's and

Zapata's passports were forgeries that could very easily lead to felony convictions for his cabin mates. Zapata and Stono, who had pending court dates due to their brawl outside the Domino Sugar factory and were technically fugitives from the law, were especially concerned as they handed their passports to Benjamin. Stono was particularly concerned that he might also have a warrant out for the deaths of the deputy and cabbies in Miami the previous year.

Calhoun snatched the passports from Benjamin's hand and quickly flipped them open one by one, then scrawled the trio's names in his tattered notepad. "What's the nature of your business?" Calhoun demanded as he glared deep into Benjamin's weary and bloodshot eyes.

"I'm a history professor at City College in Harlem," Benjamin said as he glanced back over his shoulder at Zapata and Stono. "These men are graduate students I am working with while they research their dissertations. We're on our way to Paris to research Negro Jazz musicians who fought in "The Great War" and helped establish the Parisian Jazz scene in the 1920s."

"You kikes and niggers from New York sure do love jazz, don't you?" Calhoun snickered a bit while exhaling deeply through his nose, hoping to incite a reaction. Benjamin was shrewd enough to know that the agent was shamelessly attempting to goad the trio into losing their cool, thereby providing the provocateur ammunition to revoke their passports.

"Jazz is one of the few things of true cultural value the United States has actually given to the rest of the world," Benjamin said while smirking, "so of course we love it. We're all incredibly proud to be American."

"Sure, you are," Calhoun chortled somewhat sarcastically while comparing the picture of Stono in his passport to Stono, sweating profusely, hunkered over the soiled mop bucket. "Well, enjoy your stay in France," the detective sighed disappointedly as he handed Benjamin back the passports. "If you do end up in Spain, make sure you die there because you won't much like what Uncle Sam has waiting for you back in the states." Benjamin kept his cool and calmly shut the door. He then gave Zapata a 'whew, that was close,' raise of his eyebrows with eyes wide open. He then crawled under the musty wool blanket atop his cot and pulled the covers over his head. Zapata sat down next to Stono and gently patted him on the back. "Hang in there," he whispered and handed his friend a canteen half-full with water as rolling thunder rumbled through the swaying cabin. "The storm will pass soon."

CHAPTER SIX

Perpignan, France, January 1937

Calhoun's interrogation was the only time crossing the Atlantic when Stono, Zapata, or Benjamin felt completely uneasy about being detected and sent back to the states. After all, none had actually violated federal law, not until they actually stepped foot on Spanish soil. There was an odd, somewhat naïve, optimism on board *The Paris* as the ship carved through the North Atlantic and down the western coast of Europe, especially considering the American volunteers were all determined to scoff federal law to fight in a war in which so many men on both sides of the battle lines had already perished. The pervasive demarcation of the social classes aboard *The Paris*, however, seemed to justify in many of the volunteers' minds the necessity of sojourning into the heart of darkness of the Spanish Civil War. Most of the American volunteers were quartered in the third-class bowels of the ship and spent the majority of the two-and-a-half trip journey from North America to Europe plotting the downfall of the first-class passengers. The camaraderie resulting from the prevalent sense of 'us versus them' amongst the volunteers in contrast to the first-class passengers was a psychological necessity for most of the men because regaling in the divisiveness helped keep an otherwise overwhelming sense of fear, doubt, and regret at bay. Not one of the volunteers decided to dodge their mission of getting to Spain to fight for the Republic.

Things, however, grew far more tenuous soon after disembarking in Perpignan, a small port town not too far from the French-Spanish border. All forty-two volunteers on board *The Paris*, including their matching black-cardboard-with-yellow-strap suitcases, were herded down a narrow boardwalk and then into a cramped customs office where they were all but confronted by a morose and suspicious official baring a strange resemblance to Charlie Chaplin, but with a black pencil moustache. He donned a scarlet and yellow cap made of linen pulled low over his forehead, resting just above his bushy and unkempt eyebrows.

"How do you men know each other?" the suspicious customs official garbled the words through a mangled French accent.

"Why do you assume we all know each other?" The volunteers elected Benjamin, who was the most erudite in the group, to be their spokesman.

"Assumption?" the official snidely chuckled. "You mean to say that it is but a strange coincidence that all forty-two of you just happen to have bought such ridiculous Soviet-made cardboard suitcases?"

"They are ridiculous," Benjamin sheepishly admitted as he slightly chuckled. "But they are not necessarily evidence of us being communist operatives, I assure you sir. I'm a history professor at City College in New York. This is my class. We are touring South France's ancient ruins. These are the cheapest suitcases we could find and we wanted to be sure to be able to find each other if one wandered off; the suitcases make it easier to identify each other."

"In the middle of winter? That is when you are taking a tour of the ruins?" the official suspiciously asked as he pushed his wire-frame spectacles up the bridge of his nose.

"Yes, you see, winter is when it is least expensive to travel," Benjamin explained. "Plus, the sites are not nearly as crowded during the wintertime as they are during the other more temperate seasons. Viewing the ruins during winter makes it somewhat easier for the students to conduct research."

"Both of these men are your students?" the incredulous official said pointing his finger first at Stono, who was one of the youngest in the group, then pointing at, Morris, an especially grizzled and bedraggled "The Great War" vet turned coal miner who was aged forty-four years old, but looked nearly sixty.

"Yes, uh," Benjamin nervously cleared his throat, "you see, uh, City College is a commuter school, so many of the students live in the city, work during the day, and attend night classes. We have people of all ages, most of whom are hoping to use education as a means of finding a job that might lift them out of the working class."

"Ah, I see," the official said while smugly smirking. "And is City College co-educational, or no?"

"Uh... the College has both men and women attending," Benjamin said as he glanced over his shoulder at the cadre of men assembled behind him. "But most of the students tend to be men. It would have been nice to have a lady or two along on the trip. But it's probably best for any women with good sense to steer clear of this pack of savages." He smiled charmingly.

"Alright, alright, enough of the charade," the weaselly official grinned and rolled his eyes. He had finally grown tired of his intelligence being insulted. "Your passport, s'il vous plait," he held out his hand and wiggled his fingers invitingly. Benjamin nervously handed his passport over. He was afraid he'd not get it back. To Benjamin's delighted surprise, the official stamped it merrily, winked, smiled wryly, handed the passport back, and whispered, "Viva La Republique." Benjamin grinned slightly and very briefly and surreptitiously flashed a closed fist, which was a sign of solidarity amongst those who supported the Republic of Spain's fight against Franco's fascist forces.

"No pasarán" Benjamin whispered the phrase written all over Madrid after the Nationalists had failed to take the city during the coup.

All forty-two volunteers were elated to have avoided apprehension by federal authorities on the high seas, dodged German U-boats patrolling the Strait of Gibraltar and the Mediterranean Sea between France and Spain, and then successfully navigated French customs. Arriving in Spain seemed all but inevitable, as if it were meant to be.

The cadre, though exhausted and anxious from the fortnight odyssey, quickly settled into their musty motel rooms, which overlooked the Gulf of Leon. The men washed up and met in the lobby at dusk. They quickly convened and ultimately decided to explore Perpignan a bit, and to have a nice final supper and a few drinks to alleviate the stress of having to traverse the treacherous Pyrenees Mountains into Spain the very next day. Prior to disembarking from the Port of New York, the volunteers were warned against interacting with each other on the boat ride across the Atlantic any more than absolutely necessary for fear of stoking suspicions of other passengers. Being blessed with the chance to chat over dinner and drinks was thus a fine bonding experience for most of them, the vast majority of whom were working-class Jews from the New York City area, and thus had many of the same philosophical, political, and financial concerns. Stono, the only southerner and African-American amongst the first batch of American volunteers to make his way across the Atlantic Ocean to Spain, especially enjoyed being integrated into the group. For the first time in his life, he felt as though he were not actively ostracized because of his race. He thus experienced a sense of belonging, camaraderie, and pride in being American like he had never known before.

Most of the men were visibly drunk by the time they left the little Italian restaurant where they had dined. Some staggered and stumbled and generally had a hard time navigating the quant cobblestone steps of the tiny Mediterranean town. Many of the fellas took small casks of wine with them from the restaurant and took heavy stress-induced swigs as they wandered around the festive pastel-painted structures near the church and bell tower in the heart of the village, all of which were built hundreds of years earlier.

Morris, the coal miner who looked decades older than he actually was, was three sheets to the wind by the time the group had wandered onto the town square. He began to belt out the *Star-Spangled Banner*. Many other volunteers, especially the more inebriated and/or patriotic, joined him until the chorus grew so boisterous that a spattering of lights in the buildings lining the square began to flash on one by one. Stono, Zapata, and Benjamin, the three of whom were splitting a bottle of chardonnay at towards the back end of what seemed to be quickly evolving into a drunken mob, ran fast to catch up the men assembled by the grand fountain in the middle of the square. By the time the concerned trio had caught up to the rest of the group, a concerned citizen who happened to be the mayor of the village had come to the window looking terribly tired, disheveled and somewhat worried. Benjamin raced to the front of the group, where Morris and a dozen others were boisterously bellowing the song between gurgled burps.

"Shut the hell up!" Benjamin demanded in a tone halfway between a whisper and yell. "You want us to get arrested before we even get there?" He shoved Morris, who drunkenly stumbled on the cobblestone under foot. The shove angered and slightly sobered Morris. He took a hard step at Benjamin. But their compatriots quickly separated both men.

A pudgy constable soon stumbled around the quarter and reluctantly entered the square at the north end, not far from the mayor's townhouse. The sudden appearance and the very presence of law enforcement sent the American volunteers scurrying across the square in all directions like a pack of wild rabbits fleeing starving wolves in full stride. The constable, who was also quite drunk off brandy by the time he was alerted of a disturbance on the square, did not bother to chase after anyone. The mayor, however, hurried to his desk and telephoned the proper authorities. He alerted them that Americans were most assuredly on their way to Spain.

The morning after the incident on Perpignan's town square, the forty-two volunteers, most of whom were at least slightly hung-over, met with a dozen volunteers from Montreal outside the Americans' motel. The men loaded onto two buses en route to the train depot, but were soon stopped at a roadblock that had been set up by a non-intervention patrol tasked with preventing foreigners from illegally entering Spain from France.

One of the non-intervention agents seemed particularly disheveled. He demonstratively flailed his hands about while speaking to both bus drivers. The buses were surrounded and then escorted to the station by law enforcement. The American and Canadian volunteers were soon booked and crammed into two holding cells for several days before a French attorney, who was funded by the Comintern, arrived to inform the men of their rights and what next to expect in the process.

The volunteers were ultimately promised a speedy hearing and informed they'd be back in the New York before February, where they'd eventually be handed over to American authorities to be tried and prosecuted. "But first," the attorney explained, "You will have to face French justice." The volunteers were, however, somewhat lucky because the attorney paid for by the Comintern had gone to law school together before the 'Great War' with the presiding judge and shared a cordial relationship. The volunteer's lawyer knew the judge had volunteered for service during "The Great War" and was hopeful he'd be sympathetic to his clients. The attorney shrewdly cajoled Morris, the most senior of the American volunteers who was also "The Great War" vet, to speak on behalf of his clients.

"Your honor," Morris' baritone voice was contoured by a grizzled West Virginian accent, "I am appalled by this false accusation levied against us. We came to France, me in particular, because we have a great love for your country. I came here as a young man during the 'Great War' to defend this beautiful land from the Kaiser and his malicious Hun invaders. I've never regretted it, not until last week, when my comrades and I were falsely accused of being in this beautiful land in order to go fight in the Spanish Civil War."

"Well then," the judge asked suspiciously, "why exactly have you come to Perpignan, this tiny village on the Mediterranean, in the dead of winter?"

"We are students at City College in New York City," Morris explained. "We have come to visit the ancient Roman ruins here and relax a bit while doing research. I myself have especially longed to come back here since I left in 1918 in the hopes of enjoying this land in which I lost so many friends defending French liberty, fraternity, and equality."

Benjamin slightly rolled his eyes, fearful that Morris was being too syrupy and romantic and that he'd ultimately insult the judge's intelligence and help incarcerate every one of the American and Canadian volunteers.

The skeptical and somewhat impatient judge ran his long and skinny fingers through his thinning white hair. "I'm afraid I do not entirely believe you," he said matter-of-factly. Morris swallowed hard and nervously clutched his cap between his calloused hands. "I do, however," the judge continued, "very much appreciate your sacrifice to France during its most dire time of need. I myself am a proud and unapologetic veteran of the 'Great War.' As a small gesture of my appreciation for your service and the memory of your fallen comrades on French soil, I will release you and the others on your own recognizance so long as you give me your word of honor, from one soldier to another, that you will not go to Spain and that you will leave France on the next boat back to the United States."

"On my honor, from one soldier to another," Morris nodded emphatically. "My classmates and I will not go to Spain until their great and terrible war ends, if ever." He glanced back at the other volunteers packed into the gantry behind him. He smiled slightly and surreptitiously flashed his mates a closed fist, the nonverbal salute that expressed support for the Popular Front.

The Pyrenees, January 1937

Within a few hours of being released from jail, the American and Canadian volunteers were loaded onto two diesel-powered buses in the dead of night and taken to a nondescript train depot forty miles from the coast. The volunteers nervously hurried onto a railcar nicknamed the "Red Express," which carried the men within a few miles of the French-Spanish border at the foothills of the Pyrenees Mountains, just a dozen or so miles from Andorra La Vella, Spain, and – it was believed – the relative safety of Republican lines.

For the most part, the men were in a reservedly jovial mood. Although all of them felt trepidation about defying federal law to risk their lives fighting a war, there was also a palpable lightheartedness evident amongst the men aboard the "Red Express," as if the non-intervention patrol had caught the volunteers with their hands in the proverbial cookie jar, but they got to eat the cookie anyway.

Aboard the "Red Express," the volunteers boisterously sang folk songs written by Woodie and Arlo Guthrie at the top of their lungs over and over and louder and louder the faster the train propelled them towards the Pyrenees and Spain. The singing was a means of alleviating stress and tension swelling deep inside each volunteer anxious hearts and minds. After an hour of belting out tunes, the men tired of singing, so they took turns reading

"*¡No pasarán!*" – an impassioned speech made by the firebrand of the Republic's struggle, Dolores Ibárruri – as a means of stoking courage and keeping their emerging fear at bay. The tattered and wrinkled copy of the famous speech was finally handed to Stono, who mimicked Paul Robeson's deep baritone as recited "*¡No pasarán!*" with great pride and panache.

"Workers! Farmers! Anti-fascists! Spanish Patriots! Confronted with the fascist military uprising, all must rise to their feet, to defend the Republic, to defend the people's freedoms as well as their achievements towards democracy! Through the statements by the government and the Popular Front, the people understand the graveness of the moment. In Morocco, as well as in the Canary Islands, the workers are battling, united with the forces still loyal to the Republic, against the uprising militants and fascists. Under the battle cry 'fascism shall not pass; the hangmen of October shall not pass!' Workers and farmers from all Spanish provinces are joining in the struggle against the enemies of the Republic that have arisen in arms. Communists, Socialists, Anarchists, and Republican Democrats, soldiers, and other forces remaining loyal to the Republic combined have inflicted the first defeats upon the fascist foe, who drag through the mud the very same honorable military tradition that they have boasted to possess so many times. The whole country cringes in indignation at these heartless barbarians who would hurl our democratic Spain back down into an abyss of terror and death. However, THEY SHALL NOT PASS! For all of Spain presents itself for battle. In Madrid, the people are out in the streets in support of the Government and

encouraging its decision and fighting spirit so that it shall reach its conclusion in the smashing of the militant and fascist insurrection.

Young men, prepare for combat! Women, heroic women of the people! Recall the heroism of the women of Asturias of 1934 and struggle alongside the men in order to defend the lives and freedom of your sons, overshadowed by the fascist menace! Soldiers, sons of the nation! Stay true to the Republican State and fight side by side with the workers, with the forces of the Popular Front, with your parents, your siblings, and comrades! Fight for the Spain of February the 16th; fight for the Republic and help them to victory! Workers of all stripes! The government supplies us with arms that we may save Spain and its people from the horror and shame that a victory for the bloody hangmen of October would mean. Let no one hesitate! All stand ready for action. All workers, all antifascists must now look upon each other as brothers in arms. Peoples of Catalonia, Basque Country, and Galicia! All Spaniards! Defend our democratic Republic and consolidate the victory achieved by our people on the 16th of February.

We especially call upon you, workers, farmers, and intellectuals to assume your positions in the fight to finally smash the enemies of the Republic and of the popular liberties. Long live the Popular Front! Long live the union of all anti-fascists! Long live the Republic of the people! The fascists shall not pass! THEY SHALL NOT PASS!"

"Man," Stono grinned as he handed the copy of the speech to Benjamin," I can't wait to slay me some fascists." The level of excitement and merriment had reached a fevered pitch by the time the sun had slinked beyond the ridgeline Pyrenees Mountains. But just as darkness subsumed the valley, an earth-shaking explosion derailed the "Red Express." Men, luggage and cargo hurtled violently forward; the train screeched to a halt and folded like an accordion.

Stono, who had a deep gash above his right eye, struggled to wrench the exit open as Nationalists, who'd been hiding in the woods awaiting to ambush, bombarded the derailed and toppled cars with heavy waves of machinegun fire and sporadic shelling. Fifty-caliber bullets mowed down a few of the volunteers the moment they exited the train. The unfortunate fallen, however, served as modest cover for Stono, Zapata, Benjamin and a half-dozen other men who fled as their snow-covered Keds could carry them until they made it somewhat unscathed to the woods at the foothills of the mountains just as the full moon was beginning to creep above the horizon.

The Nationalists, who were very heavily armed, cautiously chased the aghast and disheveled American volunteers, who were armed only with Stono's trusty switchblade, into the dense and dark forest at the bottom of the mountain range. The volunteers hiked as fast as they could all through the night, up into the snow-covered Pyrenees peaks. None of them had ever experienced such a prolonged combination of extreme cold, lack of oxygen, and blinding terror. But the terror was, quite ironically, likely what kept them one step ahead of the Nationalists tasked with keeping them from arriving in Spain alive. The adrenalin caused by sure death was the only thing that kept the volunteers alive through the night. They finally navigated the summit as the full moon was directly overhead. They were not, however, able to make it down into the valley until the sun was just beginning to peak over the eastern horizon.

Once the volunteers were relatively sure they were on the Spanish side of the border, necessity forced the exhausted, famished, and frightened collection of men to rest a while at the edge of the forest leading into a vast, open, and sun-soaked valley. But soon after setting up a camp sourced with the most modest of provisions, the dozen or so men who survived the Nationalists' attack stood stock still and frozen by fear at the sound of footsteps slowly approaching.

Zapata had wandered off a while in the hopes of relieving bowel pain he'd been struggling with since eating the jailhouse gruel provided while awaiting their hearing in Perpignan. He was squatting like catcher Bill Dickey behind home plate at Yankee Stadium over a hole he had dug into the snow with his nearly frost-bitten hands when a snarling wolf that was bigger than a Volkswagen, methodically crept towards its prey. The hungry behemoth of a beast was especially excited at the prospect of a hearty meal, particularly since meat was so scarce all through the winter in the Pyrenees. The monster ferociously lunged at Zapata, who fell prone on his back like a mantis. The wolf's ice pick-like canines ripped into Zapata's forearm.

Stono, who was alerted by the hollow sound of paws crunching in stiff snow, hurried from a thicket and jumped on the beast's back, slashing deep into its ribs with the blade he had inherited from his slain father. The wolf squealed, flinched and winced as Zapata punched it in the snout and choked it around its massive mane. Stono thrust the knife into the wolf's plexus, causing it to give up the fight. It dragged its mangled body back into a dense thicket of woods, leaving a crimson trail of blood in the pristine snow.

Though Zapata's injuries from the battle with the Domino Goons and Red Squad had yet to mend completely, the pure burst of palpable adrenaline provided by surviving a vicious attack from a wild wolf permitted him to lug himself the last three miles of their arduous and exhausting hike across the valley to Andorra—the last safe haven he'd have the great honor of knowing before confronting the unspeakable hell on earth known as the Spanish Civil War.

Surviving such a horrendous ordeal and officially and relatively safely crossing the border into Spain felt, at that moment, as if it were sure to be the first of many monumental victories the volunteers would surely enjoy. They slowly traversed the wide and verdant valley to a dilapidated farmhouse – the safe house where they would wash up and have a warm meal before being transported to their training grounds. The bucolic valley and charming farmhouse looked like an inviting postcard, replete with deer paths and dried-up creeks that would be overflowing with water when spring came.

The sudden droning sound of a distant airplane engine on the French side of the range, however, frightened the men. They, though terribly exhausted, ran as fast as their weary feet would take them as they raced towards the farmhouse. Morris, who was wild eyed, exhausted, malnourished, and beginning to lose his grip on sanity, manically shouted as he made his way deeper into the valley. "You bloody fascist bastards, Franco, Mussolini and Hitler!" his trembling voice echoed through the valley. "We've come a long way and waited a long time for this opportunity to join thousands of other anti-fascists from all over the world to form the International Brigades. By God, we're finally here on a battleground that may one day help to decide the fate of the human race. We may not be the most skilled warriors in this world, but one thing's for sure: we're going to make you pay for every indignity you committed. We intend to give a good account of ourselves. From here on, you're going to know we're here."

CHAPTER SEVEN

Belchite, Spain, March 1937

The American volunteers had been drilling hard as they could and living a hand-to-mouth existence for seven weeks at an abandoned monastery at Villanueva de la Jara on the outskirts of Belchite, just east of Madrid, before Soviet Central Command, who was responsible for training the International Brigades, considered them to be even remotely war ready. The walls of the monastery where the Americans were encamped had been severely battered by time, neglect, and periodic shelling. The inside walls of the barracks were adorned with Propaganda posters and graffiti donning slogans such as "Viva la Republique," "¡No pasarán!" and "Down With Fascism." The posters and graffiti were strategically placed by a French Brigade who had earlier trained at the monastery prior to their deployment to Madrid and prior to the Americans' arrival in Spain. The propaganda plastered to the walls was intended as much to serve as a kind of wall paper that very modestly insulated the cold and drafty interior of the monastery as much, if not more, as they were meant to inspire a sense of duty and courage amongst the ill equipped and poorly trained volunteers.

Upon arrival at the monastery, each man was outfitted with one mud colored International Brigade uniform that included: one helmet, one hat, one pair of brown trousers, one brown shirt, one brown undershirt, a jacket, and hand-me-down trench coats worn by Russian soldiers in "The Great War", some of which had bullet holes and blood stains in them. The men were not provided combat boots. While training, many volunteers wore the same shoes – whether Keds, Converse, Oxfords, work boots, or wingtips – they wore whilst they hiked through mud, ice, and snow over the Pyrenees seven weeks prior. Many men, whose shoes were all but in tatters, wore used up newspapers and paper bags wrapped around their frigid and frostbitten feet with rubber bands. The battalion, in short, hardly looked like a cohesive fighting force able to save the world from fascism. Even after seven weeks of dedicated and intense training, the Americans were not even remotely adequately prepared to win any battles, never mind a war, against the vastly more experienced and equipped fascist fighters.

Zapata, who was already a bit malnourished and underweight by the time he left Maria and Versailles in New York, looked especially pale, gaunt and depressed. Heavy blackish blue bags hung under his sleep-deprived eyes, which had sunk into his head a quarter inch. He had never experienced the level of bitter cold, aching starvation, deafening loneliness and despair he was forced to confront his first seven weeks in Spain. Not an hour passed that he did not wrestle with thoughts of deserting the battalion.

Morale was abysmally low since the men were so woefully undersupplied, on the verge of starvation, and had not been paid a dime since disembarking from the Port of New York in early January, and none had yet to receive correspondence from loved ones back home. Zapata, who was especially desperate to receive warmth words from his wife, was particularly suspicious that central command was not letting letters reach their intended destination. His suspicions seemed unfortunately justified by the fact that none of the volunteers had received letters since arriving in Spain. Zapata grew increasingly paranoid each day that passed that Maria might be angry that he had actually left for Spain. He never doubted, however, that even if she was furious, she'd still have the decency to send him a quick line or two about his daughter every now and again.

The glaring paradox that first seven weeks in Spain for the American volunteers was being incredibly excited to confront the enemy in battle, but knowing they had not been properly trained or prepared to confront such finely equipped and experienced killers as the Italians, Germans, Franco's Nationalists, Moors, and Falangist forces. The only slight bright spot and reason for celebration since arriving at the monastery in early January was Professor Benjamin being unanimously elected to serve as squad leader and liaison between the American volunteers and Soviet Central Command. He won special acclaim amongst the men by reluctantly accepting the accommodation by declaring: "the last capitalist we hang will be the man who sells us the rope!"

The optimistic enthusiasm that marked that solitary and fleeting moment in the first week in Spain was, however, short lived. Hunger, homesickness, and constant second guessing of the quixotic logic of traveling to Spain to fight a war against a much more experienced and superiorly equipped fighting force significantly diminished morale, which contributed to the Americans quibbling over just about everything, including what to name the XVth International Battalion of the International Brigades. One volunteer from Chicago, for example, argued that the battalion should be called the Leon Trotsky Battalion, since Leon Trotsky was, like him, an artist who advocated global revolution. Most of the men, those who believed they were indeed taking part in a working-class revolution with global implications, warmed to the idea of being part of a fighting force named after Trotsky. But the company commissar, a bitterly angry, paranoid and megalomaniac Bolshevik Ukrainian named Alexander Zubov who had fought with Lenin and Stalin against the Imperialist Whites in 1919 suggested the Chicagoan be shot by firing squad and "left to die like a bloated swine in the snow" for even mentioning Trotsky's name. What none of the Americans were privy to was that Trotsky had run afoul of Stalin and had been forced to flee Russia for Mexico, lest he be sent to a Siberian Gulag or, perhaps worse yet, face the hangman Trotsky, like Karl Marx, vociferously believed that the revolution must be a worldwide conflict between the working class and capitalists. But Stalin was not concerned with a global economic revolution; he was simply concerned about maintaining his authoritarian power in Russia; the legitimacy of which was increasingly challenged by revolutionaries such as Trotsky during the economic hard times of the Great Depression.

The XVth eventually settled on the Abraham Lincoln Battalion as its moniker. But even that moniker incited vitriolic debate amongst the volunteers since, as a few argued, Lincoln was partly responsible for opening the western half of North America to railroads, the lifeblood of nineteenth century capitalism, the Gilded Age, and the subsequent genocide of Native Americans west of the

Mississippi River. Stono, however, was the deciding vote and settled on the Lincoln Battalion since he was the President who, albeit reluctantly, confronted the sin of slavery in the United States, which ultimately, as Stono ominously reminded the men, "cost the president his life."

Benjamin, however, insisted that the infantry company in the Lincoln Battalion, which included he, Zapata, Morris, and Stono be named after John Brown, the infamous abolitionist who was hanged after leading his sons from Kansas to Harpers Ferry, Virginia, in the hopes of starting a slave uprising in 1859. Stono, who was one of the few members of the battalion who knew of and admired John Brown, recited in a deep and powerful tone evoking Paul Robeson, the last words Brown said on the scaffold before being hung from the neck until his death: "If it is deemed necessary that I should forfeit my life for the furtherance of the ends of justice, and mingle my blood further with the blood of my children and with the blood of millions in this slave country whose rights are disregarded by wicked, cruel, and unjust enactments, I submit; so let it be done!" The entire battalion, including Daley, the fair-haired medic from Holland, cheered and applauded.

Dusk had descended over the monastery. Zapata, a longtime insomniac, tossed and turned in his cramped second-hand knapsack atop the icy and uneven stone slab beneath his tattered, ragged and musty pillow in the corner of the nave turned makeshift barracks. He finally abandoned hope of getting any sleep at all and was somewhat frustrated as he lit a little candle. He softly blew the match out. A swirl of white smoke wafted towards the pigeon nest in the rafters above. Zapata wedged the stump of worn-down pencil with bite marks between his nearly frostbitten fingers. 'My love,' his trembling, dehydrated and calloused hands scribbled on a yellow notepad, 'I don't know if you have received any of my letters, or if anything is wrong and you simply don't care to respond. I know you didn't love the idea of me coming to Spain. Truth be told, often times I also very much regret coming to Spain. Morale amongst the men is at an all-time low. Starvation, relentless cold, lice, depression, and desperation to hear from home are all we know of Spain. Central Command has only allowed us to fire five rounds of live ammo into a hillside as preparation for battle, which gives us all a great lack of optimism when considering how well fed, trained, and equipped the fascists are. Plus, many of us, me included, came to Spain because we needed the money as much as we needed to restore a sense of our manhood and self-worth. But none of the volunteers have been paid a cent since leaving New York. I feel more than a bit duped because had I stayed in the states at least I could see, smell, touch, taste, and feel you; I could have taken care of Versailles while you worked. I'm of no use to anyone stuck here in this godforsaken place. My life has less value and meaning here than it did in New York.'

A sudden clattering in the darkness distracted Zapata from the letter. His eyes darted from the candle-lit page and peered into the dark corners of the quarters. Some men were quietly playing cards by candlelight, others were trying to sleep. Zubov, the commissar, flicked the light switch on, filling to nave turned barracks with artificial light. A disgruntled murmur amongst the men did not dismay Zubov, who stumbled into barracks like a lost toddler. He wore a long mud-brown trench coat and commissar hat with a little red five-pointed star on it. He'd never entered the men's quarters before. Everyone thus froze momentarily, and then reluctantly stood at dismayed attention. "Lieutenant Benjamin?" Zubov hollered in a thick Russian accent while squinting into the dimness. "Yes sir," Benjamin said as he hustled double-time to his company commander. "Your men are being sent to Jarama at 0:500." A collective gasp mixed with terror, optimism, and awe filled the room.

Benjamin quickly scanned Zapata and Stono's gob-struck faces. "But sir," Benjamin stammered, "do you really think we're ready to be sent to the front?" His weary eyes darted around the room at his terrified comrades. "The men are starving," he continued. "They've not been able to send one lousy dime home to their families. Besides that, we've not been adequately trained to fire our weapons, never mind confront fascist bullets."

"You insolent and spoiled American brats," Zubov grunted as he slapped Benjamin across the face with a pair of black leather gloves. The slap was more emasculating, insulting, and surprising than painful. Benjamin's ability to maintain humility and control was nothing short of miraculous. "What in the bloody hell gave you the notion that you could question my authority?" Zubov slurred. "To win a war, there must be a rigid chain of command. Don't you ever dare question my authority again, especially in front of the men!"

"I'm by no means trying to be insolent, sir," Benjamin graciously said while gently caressing his stinging cheek. "I'm simply trying to reason with you. Our weapons are antiques from the 1860s. Many of the rifles don't even fire. They're nothing but props! I'm simply trying to convey that I and some of the others are afraid we are being sent to the trenches as lambs are to slaughter."

Benjamin glanced over and slightly nodded at Stono and Zapata. Their nervous eyes darted towards the cold stone floor below. Zubov's fist collided with Benjamin's nose. The former professor dropped to his knees. Blood gushed from his face. "You will do as I say without question or face a firing squad," Zubov grunted.

Benjamin was slightly concussed and somewhat nauseous. He also felt terribly emasculated as Zubov stormed out of the room. Stono and Zapata helped Benjamin up to his feet. He wavered a bit and nearly fell back over before finally steadying himself. "You heard him, men," Benjamin said. His quivering voice quaked as he put all his energy into not crying for fear of being further humiliated. "Let's try and get some sleep," he pulled his mothball smelling wool blanket over his blood-covered face. "Tomorrow we'll show those fascist bastards what hell is."

CHAPTER EIGHT

The Jarama Valley, March 1937

The restless anxiety the Lincoln Battalion experienced their last night at the monastery before being sent to Jarama was a sweet dream compared to the actual terror of trench warfare in the dead of winter on the side of a frozen mountain. The ill equipped, undersupplied, and barely prepared American volunteers were pinned down by machinegun fire and artillery shelling for days in trenches filled with icy slushy mud and blood up to their knees, and rats feasting on mangled and bloated corpses.

Zubov, who was safely fortified inside a secure bunker high upon a ridge nearly a mile from the frontlines, was visibly frustrated as he glared through a pair of binoculars pushed against his round and pink face. He finally radioed Benjamin, who was knee-deep in bloody mud. "Why are your men not leaving the trench?" Zubov screamed into the phone.

"We're pinned down!" Benjamin's muffled voice could hardly be heard over the sound of machinegun fire, exploding shells, and a chorus of screams as maniacal as though produced by madmen doused with mustard gas. "It's an impenetrable wall of bullets! Anyone who tried to get out of the trench has been killed or wounded. Where the hell is our air support?"

"Air support has been delayed," Zubov grunted after throwing back a warm shot of cognac. "Our comrades are in a dogfight with the Germans. They will arrive as soon as they can! But if your men don't get out of the trenches soon, air support will be a moot point! The fascists will have invaded your lines and most of you will be dead anyway. Get your men out of those goddamn trenches or I will see to it personally that you all face a firing squad for cowardice. Is that clear?" Benjamin, who was flabbergasted, stammered but was ultimately to overwhelmed to respond. "Is that order clear, Lieutenant?" Zubov demanded.

"Crystal," Benjamin sighed and then hung up the radio receiver. His sorrowful and fearful brown eyes gazed listlessly at Stono and Zapata, both of whom were wild eyed and full of dread.

"What did he say?" Zapata's hollowed voice was barely audible over the sound of exploding shells, machinegun fire, and frantic screaming.

"He said either the fascists kill us or he will," Benjamin yelled.

"It's a suicide mission to leave the trenches now!" Stono said exacerbated. "Where the hell is air support?"

"God knows if we'll ever actually get air support," Benjamin lamented. "We can't trust anything these Russian bastards say. But I'd rather take my chances with the fascists than Zubov, that drunken fucking madman." Neither Stono or Zapata questioned the logic.

Italian and Moorish troops sprayed round after round of machinegun fire as they inched ever closer to the Lincolns' lines.

Benjamin blew into his little wooden whistle as loud as he could, which alerted the couple dozen or so men in the trench that were still alive. "Alright men," Benjamin screamed at the top of his lungs. "We'll soon be surrounded by fascists! We're sitting ducks in this trench! We've got to get a move on!" He blew all the air left in his lungs into his whistle then climbed quickly up the rickety wooden latter towards the top of the trench. He tried to fire his mud-scuffed rifle, but the gun jammed. A German-made bullet smashed into his metal helmet, shattering it into pieces; shrapnel ripped into his cheek. He fell ten feet back down the latter, landing on top of Stono and Zapata. All three were dunked under the bloody rat-infested mud by the force of Benjamin's fall from the top of the trench.

Benjamin winced as Daley, the fair-haired Dutch medic embedded with the Lincolns, sloshed through the knee-high bloody mud towards him. Daley's mud- and blood-stained hands quickly stitched the wound Benjamin's lacerated cheek. A renewed and palpable sense of blinding despair set in the moment the radio buzzed. "The goddamned fascists are almost to your line!" Zubov screamed into the radio. while glaring into his binoculars at the Lincolns' trench. "Why the bloody hell haven't you and your men left that godforsaken hole in the earth?"

"We tried sir," Benjamin pleaded, "but my weapon wouldn't fire, I was shot, for Christ's sake!"

"You insolent coward," Zubov slurred, "I told you to keep your weapon clean for that very reason!"

"It's impossible to keep anything clean in this fucking trench," Benjamin said defiantly as his manic eyes quickly scanned the mud-filled trench.

"Get your men ready to fight!" Zubov seethed. "Air support is just a few miles away. They'll be there any moment. If you can't repel the fascists you will all be killed, or worse yet, prisoners of war. Now, get out of that fucking trench and prove you're a man!" Zubov slammed the radio receiver down, slurped another shot of warm cognac, and peered attentively into his binoculars down the hill at the Lincolns as they prepared to exit the trench, which was under especially heavy fire.

The high-pitched sound of fighter planes approaching the valley was so deafening that it even muffled the sound of machinegun fire, artillery shells, and dying men screaming for their mothers. A few Russian fighter planes strafed the Moors and Italians' lines, which enabled Benjamin, Stono, Zapata, Morris, and a few other members of the John Brown battalion to scurry out of the trench with a fifty-caliber machine gun. Though the fascist barrage of bullets was briefly put on hiatus by Russian air support overhead, the Italians and Moors had made great progress towards the Lincolns' trenches, making air support only the most modest relief for the Americans. The two combatants were so proximate that strafing from above imperiled the Lincolns as much as the Italians and Moors.

The Lincolns' only option was to fight to certain death, or flee and live to fight another day. Instinct dictated they flee. The men lucky enough to be alive ran as hard and fast as they could towards the heavily fortified hill where

Zubov was embedded. The enemy shot a few of the Lincolns in the back as they struggled to ascend the icy and rocky ridge. The retreat permitted the fascists to advance all the way to the Lincolns' trenches. The victorious Italians cheered wildly as they captured the red tri-point International Brigade standard.

The forest between Jarama and Belchite, March 1937

Zubov was so disgusted with the Lincolns "cowardice in the face of fascist aggression" in the Jarama Valley that he denied them transport back to the monastery in Belchite. The battalion was, as such, forced to risk capture or bombardment as they trekked thirteen grueling miles through the treacherous forest, which was an especially trying task considering so many of the men were already suffering from frostbite, trench foot, nervous exhaustion, shell shock, and influenza.

"It's a death march," Benjamin quietly confided in Stono and Zapata. "The Russians don't care whether we live or die. We're nothing but fodder in Stalin's geopolitical pissing match with Franco, Hitler, and Mussolini."

"Maybe we should make a run for it," Stono whispered. "I hear there are anarchists up in Catalonia at war with both Franco and Stalin. Maybe we could find dome of them."

"You guys crazy?" Zapata, who was ever cognizant of his wife and daughter's wellbeing, asked as he glanced nervously over his shoulder, fearful that their

146

commiseration might be considered treasonous. "Maybe this isn't what we hoped for or signed up for. But we did sign up. As men, we need to honor our commitment, to the glorious or bitter end."

"We signed our fuckin' death warrant," Stono lamented, then took a long and hard swig from his mud-covered canteen. His eyes grew wide as he screwed the lid back on his canteen.

"Is it ours or theirs?" Benjamin asked as his weary and frightened eyes scanned the gray dusk sky above the tree line. A plane was near, but none of the Lincoln's could detect it to identify whether the plane was friend or foe. The Lincoln's hunkered down until after dark, then humped a half mile east to the Ebro River.

"It might make us an easier target to follow the river back to Belchite," Benjamin explained to the men," but it might get us back to the monastery quicker since the ground will be more even and level." The men, all of whom were so exhausted they were certain death was all but inevitable anyway, unanimously voted to risk following the river. The Lincolns finally had a slight bit of good fortune; the river posed no incident on the way to Belchite.

As forlorn as the vast majority of volunteers were to have lost so many courageous comrades that were killed during the fascist onslaught in the Jarama Valley, many of the survivors of the ordeal were equally elated that they had looked certain death square in the face and somehow lived, if only for a little while longer. As miserable as the men were on the horrendous hike back to Belchite, there was also an odd sense of relief and elation the last half-mile of the march. Stono concocted a song, which helped the men keep some semblance of a cadence the last grueling leg of the journey.

"There's a valley in Spain called Jarama, it's a place that we all know so well.

It was there that we gave our manhood and so many of our comrades fell.

We are proud of the Lincoln Battalion and the fight for the Republic it made.

In Jarama we fought like true sons of the people as part of the Fifteenth Brigade.

Now we're far from that valley of sorrow.

But its memory we'll never will forget.

So before we conclude this reunion let us lament our glorious dead."

Stono sung the song over and over on the march back to base as a means of maintaining some semblance of sanity as much as cadence. Some of the other men, including Zapata and Benjamin, hummed the tune the last quarter mile of the trek. They arrived back at the monastery just as the sun was rising. Zapata, who achingly missed his young family and was desperate to find meaning and some kind of silver lining in the hideous ordeal he'd managed to survive, hoped the sunrise over the monastery might be a sign of glorious new beginnings.

Belchite, March 1937

Most of the Lincolns lucky to have survived the Jarama Valley hoped the war would somehow cease before they could be sacrificed to another battle. By the end of the march through the forest from Jarama back to the monastery in Belchite most of the formerly optimistic and gung-ho survivors, including Stono and Morris, had grown so fretfully pessimistic that many of the men no longer cared who won or lost the war because, as Stono lamented in confidence to Zapata somewhere on the trek from Jarama, "violence leads to more and more violence... you can't fight evil with evil."

It was near midnight by the time Zubov's surly and indignant assistant, a very short man with a bushy moustache named Molotov who hailed from Minsk that spoke almost no English, beckoned Benjamin to the commander's quarters. Benjamin, half expecting to be shot by Zubov, reluctantly complied with the order. Zubov was nearly drooling drunk and completely unreasonable by the time Benjamin inched into his comfortable and dimly lit office. "I am so fucking ashamed to be the commander of such spoiled and cowardly children as you Americans are," Zubov slurred as his dark and heavy eyes stayed glued to Benjamin. "You know, I have a good mind to have all you swine slaughtered by a firing squad."

"You wouldn't dare do that," Benjamin snickered as he sneered. His insolence seemed to revive Zubov, alerting the commander with a renewed sense of justified rage.

"Oh no?" Zubov chuckled and burped as he placed his hand limply on the handle of his holstered revolver.

"No," Benjamin continued determinedly and unafraid, "you need us Americans to die so that you and the Spaniards have a chance of surviving a while longer in this unwinnable farce."

"Farce?" Zubov seethed. "We could win this war if you and the rest of those faggots were not such cowardly Nancys."

"You're the fucking coward," Benjamin seethed. "Worse yet, you have less value for our lives than the capitalists you think you're so anachronistic to. You Soviets promised the volunteers willing to risk our lives in this godforsaken meat grinder of a war three meals a day and money to send back to our loved ones back home. But we've received not one dime of what we earned, of what you agreed in a contract to pay us for services rendered. Half the battalion is already buried in the Spanish earth. Not one was paid a dime. They died so you could drink cognac."

"You are a soldier," Zubov grunted. "Your job is to fight. If you die, you die. That's war. War is hell. Your job is to follow orders and understand that there are things beyond your comprehension. We'll never defeat fascism and overthrow the capitalist system if you and the others are quibbling over fractions."

"You forced us from our trenches against better supplied and trained soldiers to face all but certain death,"

Benjamin almost started to cry, but the thought of Zubov having the satisfaction of breaking him down fortified his nerves. "You're so much worse than any capitalist I've ever met. I'm ashamed to be associated with you, Stalin, and the Comintern. You are as evil as Hitler, Mussolini, and Franco. You're all cut from the same cloth. We can't defeat the fascists because fascists also lead us. It's a paradox."

Zubov fumbled his revolver a bit as he freed it from its holster. He cocked the hammer and aimed the gun squarely at Benjamin's unflinching face.

"You don't have the balls," Benjamin smirked. "You're not man enough."

"Oh no?" Zubov said as his index finger slid onto the trigger.

Benjamin exhaled a deep and tense breath as he stepped calmly towards the egress of Zubov's office.

"Come back here!" Zubov demanded. "I didn't excuse you!"

Benjamin ignored the order and trudged out of the room and across the courtyard of the monastery to the volunteers' dim and drafty quarters in the nave. Stono's slight case of trench foot was being treated by the overworked by Daley, the Dutch medic embedded with the Lincolns. Zapata, fearful he'd soon be dead, scribbled a farewell letter to Maria and Versailles as he sniffled and coughed due to the terribly debilitating case of the flu that he had caught on the frigid march back to base the previous night.

Zubov staggered into the Lincolns' quarters with a fistful of American hard currency in one hand and his cocked revolver in the other. He marched determinedly towards Benjamin, who was sitting atop his sleeping bag untying his cold wet boots. Zubov threw the wad of cash in Benjamin's face. The stunned silent volunteers watched eagerly as billfolds fluttered in what seemed to be slow motion to the cold and dirty floor. "Here's your fucking money, coward!" Zubov slurred condescendingly. "That's all any of you fucking Americans pigs care about anyway. Fuck liberty, fraternity, equality, and victory. Money! Money! Money! 'Give me more money!' That's all Americans value. Divide your fucking money amongst yourselves, you disgusting, greedy, unprincipled, spoiled American children. Oh, and do be sure to enjoy your evening. For many of you, it'll be your last night alive. Tomorrow you are being sent to Brunete." Zubov stumbled out of the door into an icy wind ripping across the courtyard outside the nave turned barracks. "Brunete?" Stono whispered frightfully under his breath. He and Benjamin shared a long and ominous glance as Zapata hurried to scrape the cash scattered on the floor into a tidy pile as the other men clamored around him, eager to get their cash.

CHAPTER NINE

Brunete, April 1937

The Lincolns had been so decimated during the defense of the Jarama Valley that Soviet Central Command merged them with Washingtons, a battalion comprised mostly of volunteers who hailed from west of the Mississippi River, with the Lincoln Battalion. The Washingtons had been in Spain six weeks fewer than the Lincolns, but they likewise suffered heavy casualties and captures during the debacle in Jarama. Like the Lincolns and many other International Brigade battalions, had a growing mistrust of Soviet Central Command, which had likewise taken dangerously unnecessary chances with their lives.

Soon after the merger, both American battalions were ordered to take Brunete, which was a heavily fortified village citadel that had been emptied of citizens and repopulated by Moorish troops from Spanish occupied Morocco. They were some of the best equipped, best trained, and most feared enemy fighters. Many of the Moors were Muslim mercenaries whose relatives had, like the Jews, been forced out of Spain during the Inquisition, which began in 1480 and was sponsored by Catholic Monarchs Ferdinand II of Aragon and Isabella I of Castile, the same family Franco traced his roots to. The irony of the fact that the Americans, many of whom were Jewish, were fighting the ancestors of the very same Muslims who had been forced out of Aragon on behalf of ancestors of Ferdinand and Isabella was not lost on Benjamin, whose

PhD dissertation focused on the evolution of feudal lords into fascist regimes during the industrialization of Europe.

The Moors had been embedded in the village for more than a month. They thus knew almost every nook and cranny of Brunete, a tiny village on the outskirts of the Aragon Forest. The Moors had all the strategic advantage enemy combatants could possibly desire against a terribly supplied shock force of invaders entering a city they had never heard of, let alone been to, before. The Moors had all the best sniper nests, particularly the bell tower of St. Francis Church, which they dastardly used to their great advantage once the Lincoln-Washington Battalion commenced the siege the city.

The one advantage the Americans arguably had during the siege of Brunete is that most men, Zapata included, had reconciled themselves to the fact that they would almost certainly be buried in the Spanish earth and were thus far less fearful than they had been in Jarama. They thus fought with the courage of Lakota Warriors facing General Custard in what they believed to be bulletproof shirts. Unfortunately, the Americans had about as much success repelling the Moors as the Lakota had repelling the Union Army. The Americans suffered especially heavy casualties at the start of the invasion of Brunete. Soviet Central Command dictated that wave after wave of Americans approach the town square in the heart of the village, which was directly below the sniper nest in the bell tower. Morris, the "The Great War" veteran and coal miner, was felled by a sniper in the first quarter hour of the siege. Daley, the Dutch medic embedded with the

Americans, tried to provide Morris aid, but was unable to save him.

The Americans lucky enough to survive the sniper fire during the invasion of the village fought house to house. Troivoika, The Washingtons' commissar, had taught them the art of manufacturing glycerin bottle-bombs, which they used to great effect in Brunete. Since the village was made up mostly of narrow alleys and walkways undulating from around the town square, the snipers in the bell tower at St. Francis were increasingly ineffective as the Americans made their way into the nooks and crannies of the ancient hillside village.

The Americans fought with a reckless and ruthless abandon and were actually beginning to develop into a fierce fighting force to be reckoned with. Plus, the fact that the Moors were deeply embedded inside buildings actually worked in the Americans' favor because they could simply batter front doors open, toss a grenade or glycerin bomb inside. The carnage got so bad so quick that the mercenary Moors, who were fighting not for national pride or political ideology but simply for money paid by colonial overlords, quickly cut their losses and fled into the Aragon forest, which was just beyond the village ramparts.

By dusk, the Americans had, to Soviet Central Command's surprised bewilderment, taken control of the village, including the bell tower. The fleeting taste of victory in battle was very sweet indeed, but quickly soured by the dozens of mangled Americans the survivors were tasked with burying in the Spanish earth all through the night.

155

Dawn finally broke over the eastern horizon beyond the Aragon Forest. Benjamin, Zapata, and Stono were all covered in blood and dirt as they placed the final and most cumbersome and heavy sandstone over Morris's makeshift grave.

"How many of us are left?" Zapata asked while wiping a tear from his cheek.

"Less than half," Benjamin said dejectedly.

"What did Zubov say about our victory?" Stono asked. "How long are we going to have to stay here? The fascists aren't going to let us keep it without a fight."

"I've not been able to get a hold of him," Benjamin shrugged. "He stayed at the monastery in Belchite and hasn't answer the radio since we were deployed."

"He's probably passed out, piss drunk," Stono sneered. "Either that, or his conscious is weighing down on him for sending us on this fuckin' suicide mission."

"Zubov has no conscious," Benjamin said matter-of-factly. His downtrodden eyes stayed cast on Morris' grave. "He sent us here to die, simple as that. But we showed that bastard, didn't we? Well, some of us any way." Zapata and Stono nodded slightly in unison as their eyes stayed trained on Morris's tomb.

"I say to hell with this war," Zapata said as his eyes rested on Benjamin's dejected countenance. "All I care about at this point is making it home to my family alive. Fuck everything else."

A tense silence hung in the air a moment.

"No," Benjamin said as he stared at the pile of rocks atop Morris's mangled corpse, "we can't quit now. We've got too much invested to quit before we finished the job we came to do."

Another tense silence dragged on for a moment.

"I guess you're right," Zapata's weary voice quivered. "How the hell would we get out of here anyway?"

Tense silence hung between the trio as they gazed as the pile of rocks meant to protect Morris from wild scavengers.

"I can hotwire a car," Stono said as he slightly shrugged his shoulders and nodded his head. "If we can figure out a way to make it to Catalonia, we can make it to France. If we can make it to France, we can make it home."

"No," Benjamin said begrudgingly as he sighed." I hate to pull rank, but we have to win this war. If we don't win here, there won't be anything left for us back home. I agree with the notion that we were sent to this village to die. But against all odds, we're still here; we're still standing, still alive. We took this godforsaken village, which nobody, especially Zubov, believed was possible. I understand that right now surviving, never mind winning, this war seems impossible. But we'll find a way to win it and make it home alive. We simply have to. The only other option to winning this war is dying; dying is simply not an option. We have to stay and win this war. We owe it to our family and friends." Benjamin slowly knelt down next to Morris' makeshift grave and lovingly repositioned a stone ever so slightly.

The trio started to lumber and lug themselves back towards the town square and bell tower. A fleet of Fiats, Messerschmitt Junkers, and Savoia Manchettis however arrived from beyond the mountains lacing the horizon in what seemed like an instant.

TWOOT TWOOT TWOOT TWOOT. The hollow and deafening sound of machineguns mounted to the Fiats overhead caused the men to duck and cover. The planes strafed the trio as they rushed frantically for the relative safety of the burned-out buildings inside the village.

A half hour after the planes strafed the town square, a fleet of tanks and nearly ten thousand Italian infantries began their siege. Heavy and deadly artillery shells were scattered all over the village, causing incredible carnage. The world literally seemed to be crashing around the Americans huddled inside the crumbling citadel. Doom seemed not merely inevitable, but imminent. One by one, then five by five, and then ten by ten, the Americans began fleeing the village, making their way towards the Ebro River, which had a particularly fast moving current and heavy undertow.

The earth seemed to rattle as the planes circled back. They strafed the Americans as many fled towards the river, which bisected the Aragon Forest. More than a few men were mowed down in the open field between the village and the river bed. Once in the icy river, it was like shooting fish in the barrel for the gleeful and wide-eyed fighter pilots. The water in the river soon turned blood red at the bend by the forest.

Zapata nearly drowned. He was, however, dragged from the water by Stono into the relative sanctuary provided by the thick elm canopies of the Aragon Forest. Stono and Zapata shivered violently as they waited a while in the hopes of reuniting with Benjamin, who stayed behind in the bell tower with many men who were too petrified to flee the village. Stono and Zapata watched body after lifeless body float by until nightfall. They, however, never found Benjamin either dead or alive.

CHAPTER TEN

Belchite, April 1937

Both Stono and Zapata were hypothermic and nearing death as the sun finally began to rise in the east. They had walked and crawled along the river through the forest seven miles back to Belchite in the dead of night on a cloudy, moonless, and starless night.

Benjamin and a few dozen other survivors had been swept downstream by the river current and nearly drowned. But he had quite miraculously found his way back to the monastery just after noon.

Zapata, who was overcome by a cocktail of intense emotions, sobbed when he first saw that Benjamin arrive alive to the monastery. The professor turned reluctant soldier and his former pupil shared a long, warm, and tearful embrace.

"I thought I'd never see you again," Zapata wailed and exhaustedly then dropped to his knees as he neared a nervous breakdown. "I'll never see Maria or Versailles again, will I?" he repeatedly incessantly and disconsolately. Benjamin assured him he would soon enough.

"We're going to find a way to win this goddamned war," Benjamin promised. "You'll return to your family a hero."

All told, less than twenty of the original forty-two American volunteers on the Paris in January of 1977 had survived Brunete. More than ten of them were significantly wounded physically, All of them would be deeply scarred, if not completely shattered, by emotional and psychological scars for the remainder of their days on earth. Some of their days on earth were numbered, including Benjamin's.

Many of the volunteers terribly regretted coming back to the monastery at all, especially after Zubov forced them to hand over their weapons to Central Command. Even those desperate to desert the battalion after the debacles at Jarama and Brunete were paralyzed by the fear of getting lost and captured by the fascists, who had set up concentration camps that – due to non-intervention policies established by France, England, and the United States – blatantly violated the Geneva Accords and thereby violated basic human rights of captives.

After impounding the men's weapons, Zubov ordered the survivors to attend an assembly in the dimly lit chapel. The chapel was especially drafty due to the broken and shard stained-glass windows, which once depicted Christ's crucifixion. The tired survivors endured a horrendous and nonsensical haranguing delivered by Zubov, who was already three sheets to the wind. "Your cowardice has significantly hampered our ability to win the war," Zubov slurred. "The Republic's lines have been broken in half and it is highly likely that, barring some unimaginable miracle, a mere matter of time before the Nationalists take Madrid, and then take Barcelona, and then all of Spain. Your spinelessness in both battles means that all of the sacrifices the International Brigade and Comintern have made, all the lives and treasure that have been lost, will most likely be for not. I, unfortunately," he seethed, "am as much to blame as you men. I have failed to extirpate the cowardice from you! I have failed to properly motivate you. I will not fail you anymore!" He vehemently shook his closed fist and banged it with all his might on the podium. "To that end, Lieutenant Benjamin will choose five men who will serve as an example."

"Example?" Benjamin was equal parts confused and offended." What the hell for?"

"The firing squad," Zubov explained. "I am going to remove the cowardice from this company like cancer from a dying man. Pick five of your men to die."

"I will do no such thing," Benjamin said defiantly.

"You will follow my orders at once or you will be shot too!" Zubov seethed and pounded his fist on his podium.

"It is an immoral order," Benjamin's voice quaked. "I am bound by common decency to ignore the order."

"You signed the contract," Zubov's voice bellowed. "You will do as I say or face direst consequences!"

"You will have to kill me," Benjamin said flatly as he shrugged his shoulders.

"So be it," Zubov said as he gestured for four of his most loyal henchmen to block the egresses to the pew where Benjamin was flanked by Zapata and Stono. Benjamin was manhandled after a short and half-hearted scuffle, and then dragged outside the chapel by the henchmen and tied to the wooden post of a clothesline outside the volunteers' barracks.

Zubov was followed tentatively out of the chapel by what remained of the bedraggled, exhausted, mortified, and decimated American volunteers out into the glare of the late-afternoon sun, which was high in a cloudless early spring sky. "Victory has a thousand fathers," Zubov said sneeringly through Vodka-soaked breath, "failure is but an orphan." Benjamin betrayed no fear. He simply refused to give Zubov the satisfaction of fear. He stared resolutely and unflinchingly into Zapata's tired, frightened, tear-filled eyes. Zubov's massive hands struggled to remove the revolver from the holster on his hip. He finally fired a solitary shot into Benjamin's cerebellum, killing him instantly. His body remained tied to the post, but sunk listlessly. Crimson blood stained the brown earth below, which created a black puddle around the post. Pink brain matter and tissue oozed slowly down Benjamin's cheek and forehead. A splattering of hot blood was splattered on one of the henchmen's faces. He smudged it, but was not able to wipe it completely clean, with his snot-crusted handkerchief. Benjamin's lifeless eyes stayed wide open, staring at Zapata. The bedraggled and mortified survivors were stunned silent. Stono momentarily fantasized of attacking Zubov, but was restrained by Zapata and a few other volunteers.

"The rest of you flunkies pick a new lieutenant," Zubov demanded while holstering his revolver. "You lot will be joined by the British battalion in Brunete first thing in the morning. Your objective will be to take the village back from the fascists and to restore allied lines; that or die trying." He, followed closely by his weaselly henchmen, stormed into the building bound for his private quarters. Stono and Zapata hurried over to the clothesline post where Benjamin's corpse was slumped over. "I'll dig the hole," Stono said dejectedly as he used his father's blade to cut the chords from Benjamin's hands. Zapata, who was sobbing disconsolately, wrapped his trembling arms around the corpse so that it would not collapse into the puddle of blood below. Benjamin's brains and blood soon soaked Zapata, who was as nauseated as he was heartbroken. But he refused to let his friend go.

Stono was, to his great dismay, elected as the battalion's new lieutenant to replace Benjamin. He was the first African-American to be put in charge of white American combat troops in the history of the United States. As remarkable as the commendation was, he especially dreaded the notion that he might be the next man assassinated by Zubov for 'cowardice' if what was left of the Lincoln-Washington Battalion failed to take the village back from Nationalist forces. It seemed like an insidious catch-22 that caused him even greater dismay than he was already suffering.

"I'm getting out of here, tonight," he confided to Zapata.

After lights out, as most of the volunteers squinted as they scribbled letters by candlelight that would likely never be read again or stared at the shadows on the ceiling.

Stono and Zapata, meanwhile, plotted their escape from the monastery. "It's now or never," they both concurred.

What neither knew, however, was that hundreds of soldiers had deserted the International Brigades in the previous months. Zubov thus enlisted spies to embed amongst the enlistees. Stono did, however notice Daley, the Dutch medic, eavesdropping from a nearby bunk, and then quickly exiting from the barracks. Stono momentarily wondered to himself if Daley might be a snitch. But the medic had never given Stono a reason to mistrust him, so he quickly dismissed the thought as exhaustion- and fear induced paranoia. 'Daley's good people,' he thought, 'he's one of us.'

But Just as Stono and Zapata were fast shoving their most prized garments and keepsakes into their knapsacks in preparation to desert the battalion, Daley rushed into the room with two of Zubov's henchmen, both of which were toting rifles that were presumably loaded. Daley surreptitiously pointed out Zapata and Stono to the henchmen before hurrying back to his bunk. The henchmen kept their rifle trained on Zapata and Stono as they spirited the two frightened Americans out of the nave-turned-barracks to Zubov's quarters.

A half-moon was directly overhead as Stono and Zapata were being led across the square towards Zubov's office. The surly commissar was drunk and swaying a bit back and forth on the balls of his feet with the palms of his hands planted firmly atop his desk, engrossed by the fluttering of a moth about the table lamp.

Stono slashed the henchmen's throat open with the switchblade he had concealed under the cuff of his jacket sleeve the moment he was shoved into the office by his captor. Stono then cut the strap of the henchman's machinegun, and pointed it at Zubov, who drunkenly fumbled to retrieve the revolver from the top drawer of his desk. Zubov wildly fired a round. The shot, however, whizzed past Stono, and hit the second and somewhat stunned henchmen square in the head, killing him instantly. Stono blasted a round of ammunition into Zubov's chest. The force of the blast shoved the drunken Ukrainian into the cushy and hand sewn leather chair adjacent the desk. "Grab his gun," Stono excitedly urged his comrade as he motioned towards Zubov's desk. "See if he has keys, quick!"

Rigor mortis caused Zubov's hand to cling to the revolver with viselike grip. Zapata thus had a great deal of difficulty prying it loose. He finally separated the revolver from Zubov and then tucked the gun into the waistband of his trousers.

Zapata hurriedly rummaged through the desk drawers and cabinets. He was grief-stricken to find hundreds of letters, most notably his letters to Maria and letters from his wife to him, bundled in a pile and stuffed into the cabinet. He quickly and dejectedly flipped through them. "He kept all my letters," Zapata said dejectedly. "The bastard kept our letters. Maria doesn't even know if I'm alive or not!"

"Come on, man," Stono pleaded while glancing back at the egress to the office. "We gotta go. Somebody had to have heard those shots!!" Zapata ignored his friend's order and continued to frantically rummage through the bottom drawers of the desk. His eyes grew wide assure moons when he found a massive key ring with dozens of keys next to a manila envelope stuffed to the brim with hundred-dollar bills. Zapata shoved the keys into the folder full of cash and held it tight under his arm like a football. He took a handful of the letters penned by Maria as Stono finally pried him from the desk and pulled him towards the office exit. "Maria and Versailles don't even know if I'm dead or alive," Zapata muttered disconsolately.

"Forget about that!" Stono urged his friend as they raced down narrow hallway. "The sooner we get out of here, the sooner you see them!"

They cautiously inched out of the monastery and crept toward a transport truck parked just steps from where Benjamin's listless tied to the clothesline post body was left. The vultures feasting on his corpse ignored Stono and Zapata as they inched by towards the truck.

Two henchmen loyal to Zubov had been awakened and alerted by the percussion of gunfire. They, both of whom were donning pajamas and bathrobes and toting machineguns, moved into position for an ambush as Stono and Zapata climbed into the truck. Stono fired a round at them, so they were forced to scramble for cover inside the building, which bought the aspiring deserters a few moments of time. The henchman with the machinegun sprayed bullets at the truck. Bullets ripped into the driver side door. Zapata ducked and covered in the hope of avoiding being doused by broken class. He, however, could not avoid injury. Metal and plastic shrapnel as well as tiny shards of glass lodged in his leg and arm.

Zapata was terrified. His trembling hands fumbled with the keys.

Stono, who had learned great deal about car mechanics as a result of being a cabbie, finally ripped open the panel under the steering wheel. He cut three wires with his switch blade, then twisted two strands of copper together. The cab of the truck shook slightly as the grumbling diesel engine sparked on, which provided a shot of optimism and adrenalin to the escapees. Zapata placed the car into drive and pressed the gas pedal with all the strength he could muster in his malnourished, sleep deprived, and grieving body, mind and soul. The two henchmen wearing bathrobes chased after the truck frantically firing bullets at it.

The front bumper of the truck smashed through the fortified gate on the dirt road at the bottom of the hill from the monastery. The collision was so violent that it tore the front bumper clean off the truck. Stono leaned cautiously out of the passenger side window and fired a few haphazard rounds of ammunition from the machinegun he had confiscated from the henchmen lying dead in Zubov's office.

The two Soviets donning sleepwear chased after the truck, but were slowed by the fact that they had difficulty running in slippers. Both Soviets fired several rounds of ammo as their bathrobes flapped in the wind, but only a few bullets hit their target, lodging harmlessly in the back bed of the truck. Despite the fear associated with trying to defy death or capture, Zapata and Stono felt freer than they had since boarding *The Paris* four months earlier. But the danger of driving a troop transport truck with the three-pointed star Republican insignia painted on the side of it so soon after the Popular Front's lines had been broken in half quickly set in heavily on the deserters as they raced along a narrow and winding dirt road leading towards the only highway linking Madrid to Barcelona.

CHAPTER ELEVEN

Daycare, Lower East Side of Manhattan, April 1937

Versailles was bundled tightly in her royal blue winter onesie. A red scarf was wrapped snugly around her neck. Her concerned and doughy brown eyes gazed up at her mother's pale and gaunt face, which was sallow from deep grief and exhaustion. Maria's mind seemed scattered and distant as she bobbed the toddler gently on her knee. The mix of not receiving a single letter, wire, phone call, or cent since her husband left for Spain four months earlier had exacted a tremendous emotional, psychological, spiritual, and physical toll on Maria, who looked as though she had aged a week for every night that she suffered without receiving word from her husband. Her shoulders slunk forward and her face expressed perpetual dread. All the light and twinkle in her formerly brilliant, sensitive, and expressive eyes had flickered dim. Though she'd been working double shifts at the cabana wear factory, she could hardly make ends meet, especially since the cost of childcare, rent, food, and utilities had spiked concomitant to wages being depressed in the months since Zapata left his family behind in New York to fight a seemingly winless war in Spain. Not being afforded the simple luxury of spending quality time with the father of her child was difficult enough. But not being able to see her own child grow and develop due to hour after hour in a factory polluted with the sound industrial machinery and carcinogenic fibers perpetually wafting through the air was especially soul crushing to Versailles mother, who was beyond burnt out and suffering from a terribly painful stomach ulcer. What little time during the evening Maria was fortunate enough to spend with her daughter was by no means quality time because the shifts at the factory were just too damn exhausting, and thus left her no time and even less energy to play with her daughter, to talk to her, hug her, love on her, or assure her that she was adored. Though doing her very best she possibly could with the scant time and resources available to her, Maria suffered especial dread at the fact that her very best effort never ever seemed even remotely close to enough to adequately providing all the emotional, spiritual, and financial support that her fast developing daughter needed. Maria thus grew to resent, and, in her darkest and most quiet moments, detest her husband for leaving his family high and dry to fend for themselves so he could jeopardize his life and theirs in order to retrieve some godforsaken sense of masculinity lost in a war an ocean away.

"Please," Maria's voice quivered as she pleaded with an ancient woman on the other side of a coffee stained mahogany desk. "I can't take her to work anymore. I've been warned and threatened with termination. The fibers in the air and racket of the machines make her too fussy. The spectacle of her crying upsets my manager."

"I'm quite sorry, ma'am," an elderly lady with thinning white hair said in a thick Irish accent while pressing the center of her Coke-bottle-thick glasses up from the bridge of her nose, "truly, I am m'dear. But times are tough for us all, you know. I can't afford to care for your lass any more than you can afford to take her to work with you."

"Please, I'm begging you for just a bit of time," Maria's upper lip quivered and her eyes grew moist as she struggled to maintain her composure. "The heating bill was especially high this month due to the blizzard last month. My husband will send money any day, I just know it. When he does, I swear to everything holy that I will pay you five dollars extra for your trouble and ten dollars extra for your graciousness."

"That's precisely what you said last week, ma'am." the elderly woman replied. "Your bill is already more than two months past due. I am sympathetic to your plight, believe me I am. But I simply cannot afford to tend to your child sans compensation any longer than I already have, ma'am. Times are tough for us all. This Great Depression affects us all, don't you know?"

"Please," Maria pleaded a solitary bulb of tear slid down her porcelain cheek, "I'm begging you a bit of compassion. My husband is fighting fascists in Spain. I've not heard from him in months and don't even know if he's alive." Another bulbous tear streamed down her flushed white cheek and dripped on her daughter's tiny and pudgy hand. Versailles's gaping and concerned brown eyes beamed up at her grief-stricken mother.

"I'm awfully sorry ma'am, truly I am," the woman replied, struggling to conceal her angst and frustration. "But, you see, you've been promising to pay the balance of your bill for far more than a month now, saying your husband would send along some money any day now. Now you're singing a different tune, saying you don't even know whether he's dead or alive. In other words, you don't even really know if you'll ever be able to pay me at all, now do ya?" The decrepit woman winced achingly as she struggled from her chair, stood, and held her veiny and wrinkled hand towards the exit of the dilapidated Victorian townhouse. "If you'll excuse me, ma'am," the woman said as she swung the door open, "I have pressing matters to tend to."

Maria sighed deeply and stood slowly as if carrying the weight of the world on her weary shoulders, wiped the streak of tear from her cheek, held Versailles tight to her bosom, and walked stoically out of the Victorian, and down the steps to Houston Street where she stood stock-still a moment as a bitingly frigid wind ripped into her.

Cabana wear Factory, Lower East Side of Manhattan

Maria sat as dutifully at her machine tending to a spool of thread in the cabana wear factory while bobbing her daughter up and down in her lap. Versailles was, however, very fussy. Maria pleaded with her to "shoosh" and "please, be quiet." But the stench of textile fibers, fumes, dyes, and solutions, together with the grating banging and clanging sound emanating from row after row of sewing machines and weavers, all operating in unison, discomfited Versailles. She was far more fussy than usual.

Maria's supervisor, Mr. Angelo Pisano, was a perfidious letch. He originally hailed from Rome. He, however, harbored no sense of being her countryman or fellow traveler. No. He was management. She was labor. He was also paid well enough to not complicate the arrangement too far beyond that binary, unless, perhaps, the complication was of a sexual nature.

173

"Miss Abrahams," he hollered from the threshold of the doorway leading into his office, which was just adjacent to the factory floor. Maria, whose attention was centered on her fidgeting and fussy daughter, did not immediately hear or notice Pisano calling her. She finally heard him calling her name in a muffled tone above the din of the machines. He beckoned her towards his office with a quick flick of his index finger. "A word in my office, please." Maria sighed anxiously as she nodded, then reluctantly scooped Versailles into her arms, and trudged past dozens of machines, begrudgingly following the man into his office.

Maria, fortunately, had never been summoned into the Pisano's office before. It was largely reserved for his private time in which he needed a respite from the noise and stench of the factory floor, and for his not too uncommon trysts with a few of the girls. Maria had long believed him to be a single man due to the frequency of factory girls he had shared liaisons with coupled with the fact that she'd never noticed him wearing a ring. She was thus a bit dismayed when he turned the photo atop his desk around to show her a portrait of his stay-at-home wife and their two young boys posing for a picture in front of a shiny new Buick and four-bedroom house on a little plot of land in suburban New Jersey. He had also hung a portrait on the wall behind his cushy leather chair of Mussolini smugly scowling for the camera. Maria was already a bit nervous and shaky. The portrait, however, clenched Maria's stomach into a painful volleyball-size knot. She cautiously sat in a stiff and creaky second-hand chair across from Pisano's quaint Cuban mahogany desk and plopped Versailles in her lap.

Pisano swung the door shut behind him, then lowered the blinds a bit, lit the cigarette he retrieved from the small silver case in his top desk drawer, and sat attentively at his desk on the edge of his seat. He looked hard at Maria and Versailles for a long and awkward moment as he enjoyed his cigarette. He finally launched into a chastising lecture in which he flailed his hands about as though conducting a symphony. "I hate to," he said gruffly and animatedly, "but you leave me no option but to scold you about your lack of productivity the past few months. Now, you bringing your child back to the factory again, after I've already told you already not to is the final straw on the camel's back! This place is far too dangerous for a baby. It needlessly exposes the company to all kinds of liability, which puts my job and family in jeopardy."

"I'm sorry, sir," Maria said softly. "I don't have any choice; My husband has been gone since January. I'm barely able to raise her on my own. I can't afford daycare. I had no choice but to bring my child to work." Anguished tears began to well in her exhausted and lifeless eyes.

"And where is your husband?" Pisano asked curiously with a slight predatory glint in his beady black eyes. The edge of his tongue eased onto his upper lip ever so slightly.

"To be honest," Maria seemed embarrassed, "I'm not quite sure where he is just now." Her bloodshot eyes darted surreptitiously at the portrait of Mussolini scowling down at her, before glancing nervously towards the dusty floor beneath her dilapidated boots.

"Are you saying you and your husband are getting a divorce?" he asked bluntly as he rolled his eyes and sighed.

Maria, not wanting to discuss her personal life with her employer, slightly shrugged.

"I know how you Italian girls can become Americanized and blame your husbands' for all your problems and want to get divorces at the first sign of the fairy tale ending. I imagine you expected to find the America of the movies and may have been disappointed that the reality is nothing like Hollywood backdrop of New York we see in the movies. But you shouldn't blame the man for that!"

"No sir, I am not getting a divorced," Maria resented being forced to explain. "He left months ago. I don't quite know where he is. I have not heard from him."

"That's a relief," Pisano blurted through a toothless half grin as he sauntered suavely from behind the desk. He knelt close next to Maria and placed his slender hand gently onto her shoulder. "Look at me, Mrs. Abrahams," he demanded. She reluctantly made momentary eye contact before her eyes darted back towards the floor. "There is nothing more obscenely sinful than a divorce," he said as his hand crept from her shoulder and down onto her neck and upper back between her shoulder blades. "Look Maria," he said in a soothing tone as he tenderly placed a raven curl behind her ear with his thumb, "I like you. I think you are a pretty and sweet young thing. I hate the idea of having to fire you, but the fact is, your work has been subpar for months now. If it was up to me, it'd be no big deal. But it's not up to me. Your lack of productivity costs the company money. That, I'm afraid, jeopardizes my position with upper management. Lucky for you, I decided I will keep you around a while longer so you can prove yourself under two simple conditions."

"What conditions?" she glared suspiciously. He gently caressed the nape of her neck with the back of his index finger. "One, you never bring your child to the factory again."

"And the second?" she demanded.

"The second condition isn't even really a condition," he grinned and gently nibbled his bottom lip with his top incisors. "It'll be fun for us both. Every now and again I'd like to summon you in here for some quality time."

Maria stood abruptly from her chair and tucked Versailles tight under her arm. "I'm a married woman, sir," she said tersely and offended. "I'm not the kind of woman to engage in a tryst with an employer, especially a man with the self-control of a child molester."

His lusty grin instantly transformed into a jaded sneer. He grabbed a fistful of hair on the back of her head. Her eyes stayed locked on the portrait of Mussolini. She tried to pry herself free. But his grip was as powerful as an alligator chomp. The sudden fear and pain of the assault nearly caused Maria to fumble Versailles to the cold hard floor below. But she was barely able to keep her child from plummeting by holding her tight around Versailles' little wrist.

"You had better watch your tongue and tone, you naïve little peasant girl," he said in a tone voice laced with venom. He finally let loose of her hair and composed himself by taking a deep breath while straightening out his navy blue and pinstripe waistcoat and tie. "I am a married man, too. But I am still a man, if you catch my drift. You are being so childish and naïve. You are a modern working girl living in the big city now. You don't have any idea where your deadbeat husband is. He could be shacked up with some other girl, for all you know. This isn't the old country, little girl. God does not, of course, forgive divorce any more than he does abortion. The almighty man in the sky is, however, gracious enough to forgive a scorned wife whose husband is unfaithful for engaging in carnal pleasures of the flesh with men besides her husband. All you have to do is ask your father during confessional for forgiveness and God's grace will wash you clean." His sneer instantly transformed back into a lustful grin. "Live a little."

"My father is dead," Maria said flatly. "He was disappeared by Il Duce." Maria was both disgusted and flabbergasted. Versailles, who was especially fussy, scowled at her mother's tormenter. "I have a good mind to find your wife and tell her just the kind of man you are!" Maria threatened.

"Go ahead," he laughed haughtily. "Who do you think she will believe – a peasant girl whose father was dumb enough to find himself on the wrong side of Il Duce, or me – the father of her sons who puts food on her table and a roof over her head? Don't be so daft as to think you can threaten me, little girl. I could dump you in the East River and nobody, not even your husband or daughter, would give a damn."

Maria caught herself losing her cool like Zapata had at Domino in December. She took a deep breath in an attempt to rectify the situation. She was disgusted with herself for having to swallow her pride in a humiliating attempt to calm the situation enough to keep her job. "I'm sorry, sir," she forced the words from her mouth, "I didn't mean to lose my temper with you. It's just that I love my husband very much and would never dishonor him in any way, not even if it meant keeping my job. I'm sure you would not want your own wife to dishonor you. Please, Mr. Pisano, forgive me. I need this job. My daughter needs me to have this job. I will work harder than ever. But I could never dishonor my husband."

"My wife wouldn't dare dishonor me with another man," he said snidely as he wiped a bead of sweat from his pasty forehead. "She knows I'd kill her if I ever found out."

"If you'll please excuse me, sir," Maria said timidly, "I need to get back to work. I'd hate to waste the company money. I will try to find an arrangement for my child before Monday, you have my word." She took a quick step towards the door leading out of the office to the factory floor.

"That won't be necessary," he said callously. "Your days with this company have concluded. I do, however, wish you the very best with your marriage and finding new employment opportunities, though it'll be tough in this job market."

He hurried to the exit of the office. He swung the door open and ushered her towards the egress. Nearly every woman on the factory floor ceased tending their machines and watched wide-eyed and curious as Maria, who was obviously disheveled and downtrodden, exited the office. Pisano swung the door shut and locked it. Maria squeezed the knob and tried to jar the door open. But it would not budge. She pounded on the door with her fist. "Please," she pleaded, "you can't do this!" Versailles began to bawl disconsolately. Maria quickly realized that creating a spectacle with Pisano would never win her job back. She, an uneducated immigrant woman raising a child on her own, likewise began to bawl the moment the weight of her situation began to swallow her.

She walked stoically across the factory floor as the other seemingly unsympathetic girls began to reluctantly tend to their machines. An icy and biting wind ripped into her as she stepped out of the factory onto Bowery Street. Cold pellets of rain fell from the bleak gray sky above. Versailles, sensing her mother's angst, anger, desperation, fear, and despair sobbed uncontrollably at the top of her lungs. Maria's fragile veneer of stoicism finally crumbled under the weight of her stress, anxiety, and need to know where her husband was and how he was doing. Her sobbing became hyperventilation. For a moment, she feared she might have a heart attack. But she finally composed herself with a few deep breaths and by tapping into Maria the character he had developed as a result of facing the adversity associated with the abduction and disappearance of her parents and her subsequent exodus to New York by herself. She finally composed herself enough to stop crying, which caused Versailles to calm as well. "Don't worry, my love," Maria whispered into her daughter's tiny and cold ear. "Everything will be all right."

Broome Street, April 1937

The calamity went from horrendous to worse when Maria, with Versailles held tight to her bosom, rounded the corner onto Broom Street. Though the rain had subsided a bit, she was stunned and dismayed to find most of the belongings that were previously in her apartment had been scattered on the sidewalk outside the building. Two inebriated hobos heaved her couch around the corner. "Stop! Thief!" she demanded as she chased them. "That's my property!" The spooked hobos simply scurried faster as they fled the scene of the crime, causing one of them to drop his end of the couch. The hobos abandoned the couch and hurried to flee Maria. She shuffled back towards the steps leading into the apartment building.

A cadre of middle-aged immigrant women wearing house dresses wrapped in school bus yellow raincoats who lived in the tenement across the street from Maria's apartment building frantically rummaged through Maria's clothes and cutlery. "Most of this is rubbish," the eldest of the woman grumbled in a deep Yiddish accent. Maria was dumbfounded at the sight of her possessions pushed onto the sidewalk in the rain being picked through and evaluated. "Stop! Thief!" she blurted as she sobbed, which caused Versailles to wail even more egregiously than she was in the cabana wear factory earlier. The rain-soaked cadre of elders quickly bundled their misbegotten wears under their slick raincoats and hurried into the dark and dank tenement building across the street.

Maria, with her daughter in tow, raced up the steps of her dilapidated Brownstone apartment building and into the dimly lit foyer. She walked cautiously down the hall towards her apartment and struggled due to the darkness and Versailles' fussing to locate the key to the front door. Her key would not budge the lock. What Maria did not understand was that the super, as ordered by the landlord, had changed the lock a few hours earlier, soon after Maria left for work.

Maria rushed down to the basement level of the building, where the super resided. She pounded her fist into his door until her hand throbbed. Versailles cried disconsolately. The super, a surly little man with a shiny bald head who originally hailed from the Dominican Republic, reluctantly opened the door ever so slightly. His beady and bloodshot eyes glared into the dimly lit hall. "What the hell do you want?" he said in a broken English accent. His breath reeked of coconut rum and cheap cigar smoke.

"My key, it won't work," Maria fumed. "I can't get into my apartment! All of my belongings have been thrown outside in the street!"

"Your rent has been past due for more than a month," he said cautiously. "I warned you that if you didn't pay all money owed management by the first of April that I'd have no choice but to evict you."

"I did pay you last week!" she yelled.

"I have no recollection of any payment," he explained.

"The hell you don't!" she seethed. "I slipped the cashier's check under the door myself, just as you said to."

"I'm afraid you are mistaken," he sneered. "If there is one thing I remember, it is the rare luxury of being paid by tenets. Besides, I already found a new tenant who will pay twenty-five dollars more a month for the apartment."

She was stunned stock still for a long moment as she tried to reconcile the absurdity of the calamity her life was becoming. "You are as crooked as a dog's hind leg, you miserable old bastard," her anguished and angry voice quivered. "You are pure evil."

"Pure evil?" the landlord glared disagreeably as he subconsciously clutched the gold crucifix around his neck between forefinger and thumb, both of which were stained by tobacco resin. "I was very gracious to let your husband stay in apartment after that nasty episode between his father and the FBI. I'm actually very lucky I could find anyone else willing to rent the apartment with that blood stain in the floor. I also let you stay in the apartment for more than two months even though your rent was past due. You have some real nerve calling me evil after how generous I have been with you fucking communists!"

"We're not communists! She grunted. "But if we were, we'd have far more decency than you, you fucking slumlord! If you had any soul left at all, you will learn to regret the day you did this. My husband is going to properly sort you out when he gets back from Spain, so help me God."

"Your husband?" the super chuckled antagonistically. "You silly little dego. Your husband will never come back from Spain alive. All of those idiots fooled into going to Spain by Stalin will be lucky if they come back in pine boxes. If the Nationalists don't kill them, Stalin will send them all to labor camps in Siberia for losing the war. Your husband is a dead man and I suggest you place your child up for adoption, lest you ruin her life completely too." He slammed the door shut.

Maria was stunned and dejected for a long moment as the weight of the super's vicious words soaked into her tattered soul. She finally pounded on the door, demanding fairness, sympathy, and satisfaction. Versailles wailed louder and louder.

"Shut that damn baby up!" One of Maria's former neighbors hollered from the stairwell. "Go to hell!" Maria yelled as she hurried up the stairs and toward the exit of the building. She nearly slipped and fell down the icy salted steps leading down to Broome Street. For the first time since meeting Zapata, Maria contemplated suicide. It seemed the only logical way to proceed. She imagined herself leaving Versailles on the steps of the orphanage on Houston Street, then walking to the top of the Williamsburg Bridge and hurling her cold, hungry, exhausted and dispirited body into the icy East River below. The idea of suicide equated to a finality of her seemingly endless heartache and travail, which soothed her mind and soul for a fleeting moment. As grief-stricken and filled with angst, anxiety, desperation and depression as Maria was, the notion of her daughter not having known either of her parents helped fortify her resolve just enough to overcome the nefarious ideas of suicide for a while longer.

Chinatown, April 1937

Maria wandered around in a dense fog that had set in over Chinatown between Delancey Street and the Williamsburg Bridge. Versailles, who had exhausted herself, had finally stopped crying and had fallen asleep. Her head nestled gently on her mother's rain-soaked shoulder. Maria, however, could not stop herself from whimpering restlessly, nearing a nervous breakdown. She walked in a haze through the fog for more than a half hour and was somewhat surprised to find herself standing at the spot she and Zapata had met the year earlier on the footpath atop the Williamsburg Bridge. Her tired eyes gazed at the wake of a pleasure cruiser gliding through the East River below.

She was focused and had a kind of tunnel vision as she began to climb over the chest-high fence railing from the footpath to the ledge over the river. A tall, slender, elegantly dressed, young Chinese woman about the same age as Stono gently put her hand on Maria's shoulder and asked, "Is anything the matter?" Maria flinched as though suddenly waking from a dream. She fell to her knees and sobbed.

185

The young Chinese beauty tenderly caressed a tear from Maria's cheek. "Please," she tried soothing Maria, "you can tell me what's wrong. Maybe I can help."

Maria was crying so hard she had great difficulty explaining her horrid predicament on the walk back down the bridge towards Delancey Street: not knowing if her husband was dead or alive, not being able to afford daycare for her child, being fired, and then evicted. The Chinese girl, who had fled grinding poverty, deprivation, and oppression in China soon after the Wall Street crash of 1929, was especially sympathetic to Maria's plight.

"Have you ever thought of working at a parlor?" the young woman asked somewhat coyly through a thick Mandarin accent once the three had made their way to the Lower East Side.

"A Parlor?"

"A massage parlor," the young woman explained while pointing to a nondescript doorway on the corner of Ludlow Street. "Chinatown has many parlors."

"I don't know the first thing about giving massages," Maria said somewhat queasily. "Besides, I don't like touching or being touched by anyone but my husband."

"It can a bit uncomfortable and take some getting used to at first," the young woman said shyly, afraid she'd offended Maria. "But after a while, you get used to it. It's just a job, like any other. It's certainly better than plucking dead chickens, which is what I used to do. And the money can be very good. Most of the clients work on Wall Street. They suffer from lots of stress. The better the massage, the better they tip."

"How good is the money?" Maria asked as she glanced down at Versailles, who was beginning to stir.

"It depends. But a nice, young, clean pretty European girl like you could make up to $50 dollars a day, maybe more. And you can choose whatever hours you want. You can even bring your baby to the parlor with you, if you like. Lots of girls do. We all look after each other. We're sort of like a little family."

"Fifty dollars a day?" Maria's amazed eyes grew wide as windows. "I didn't make thirty dollars in a whole month at the factory!"

"I work just two days a week and spend the rest of the week doing whatever I want," the girl said as she wrapped her scarlet lips around a freshly lit cigarette. "I can introduce you to my boss right now, if you like. She's always looking for new girls, especially Europeans. Wall Street men love good clean girls from the old country."

"Well," Maria said hesitantly while bobbing Versailles gently up and down in her arms, "I don't suppose there's any harm in meeting your boss." She squeezed Versailles just a bit tighter yet more tenderly as she followed closely behind the young, tall, slender, and elegant Chinese woman leading her towards the nondescript parlor on the corner of Ludlow Street.

CHAPTER TWELVE

Barcelona, April 1937

The buzzing of the fire alarm caused by bombs dropping outside the piñata factory in the Sant Andreu district of Barcelona where Azure worked shook dust from the machines and cobwebs from the corners of walls where they intersected the ceiling. Azure hated the mind-numbing repetitiveness of factory work and terribly missed the land she'd known all her life. But she did not dare think of leaving the city for fear of being apprehended by the authorities and charged with murder.

"The Nationalists are getting terribly close," the frightened and disheveled little old lady hunched over the machine next to Azure on the assembly line shrieked. "It's just a matter of time before it's all over now!"

Azure, however, did not notice the woman's trepidation. She barely noticed the buzzing sound emanating from the fire alarm or the sounds of bombs shattering concrete outside the confines of the factory. She was intently focused on stuffing candy and plastic trinkets inside a piñata bound for Guadalajara, Mexico. She had long grown accustomed to shattering sounds of shelling, the rat-ta-tat of gunfire, and the drone of plane engines overhead. She thus hardly noticed when emergency lights began to flash and think black smoke began to fill the factory. Her terrified co-workers, including the little old lady at the machine next to hers, scurried towards the double doors leading from the factory floor out to the street. But Azure did not pay much mind to the panic or bustle.

"Come on, Azure!" her co-worker pleaded. "Get out of here. or you're dead." The elderly woman's tiny and arthritic hands clutched at Azure's sweat soaked sleeve. Azure finally and reluctantly let loose of the piñata and calmly followed her coworkers towards the egress of the smoldering factory.

Outside the factory, a fleet of two-ton trucks was parked on every street corner as far as the eye could see. Men, woman, and children were hurriedly handing out rifles to anyone who might be willing and able to defend the besieged city from the Nationalist onslaught. The somewhat centrist and tepid Popular Front government had previously been reluctant to arm the anarchist revolutionaries in Barcelona for fear that paramilitary leftist groups such as Confederación Nacional del Trabajo (CNT) or The Workers Party of Marxist Unification (POUM), which acclaimed British author George Orwell was embedded with, would turn on the centrist government and thereby threaten Soviet support for the Republic in its war against Franco's fascists. By the time the Nationalists had surrounded Catalonia, however, it was glaringly apparent to any thinking person that the Soviets had left both the leftists and centrists to largely fend for themselves. The Republican government thus finally decided to count their losses, rather than hedge their bets, by arming the city's civilians.

Azure, who had been recruited by POUM not long after finding work at the piñata factory, was especially eager to fight. She had fallen into a deep despair after the death of her parents and separation from the land she had known her whole life and was thus, like many of the International Brigade volunteers, especially eager to exact a bit of retribution from Nationalists, even if it meant death, which she had no fear of since witnessing the murder of her parents.

The Road to Barcelona, April 1937

A few miles from Villanueva de la Jara, on a narrow dirt road leading towards the only paved road linking Madrid to Barcelona, Zapata and Stono were ordered to stop at an International Brigade checkpoint. The checkpoint was not entirely formidable, consisting of just two half-drunk flunkies, a rundown Indian Chief motorcycle with sidecar, a waist-high wooden barricade weighing no more than fifty-five pounds, and a two-way radio depot inside a small booth collecting dust at the side of the road. The checkpoint had been built in the opening stages of the war so that Zubov, who suffered from booze-induced paranoia, would be provided ample warning of any potential invasion of the monastery via the dirt road. The checkpoint would have done nothing to stop the fascists from taking the base, but it might have provided Zubov just enough time to escape in a small fishing boat via the Ebro River.

Stono, who had just one clip for the machinegun he took form Zubov's dead henchman, and was especially wary about running out of ammo, thought it best to try and talk their way through the potential ordeal at the checkpoint. "We need to save some bullets if we want to make it to Barcelona," Stono said loudly over the rumbling and hum of the diesel engine, "so be cool; let's try to sweet talk our way through this."

"What the hell are we supposed to say?" Zapata asked worriedly as his right food began to ease down on the brake pedal.

"I'm not saying a damn thing," Stono said while pushing the machinegun under his seat. "You do the talking. Tell them we are going to Madrid for supplies – food, munitions… whatever. Just be cool," his voice quaked nervously. "No matter what, be cool."

The two guards, both of whom hailed from Minsk, cautiously exited the booth and waived the grumbling truck to a squeaking stop in front of the barricade. Both spoke English about as poorly as Stono and Zapata spoke Russian, which inhibited the Americans' potential of charming their way out of the tension filled situation.

The smaller and cleaner shaven of the two guards begrudgingly trudged out of the tiny roadside depot connected to the barricade and fluttered his hand to indicate 'pull the truck here, out of the road.' The young guard had seen very many transport trucks enter and leave the checkpoint in the preceding months. He, however, had never seen a truck with its front bumper missing, 42-caliber bullet holes in the side, and a shattered driver-side window. All coupled, the guards were especially suspicious when Zapata smiled and waved his hand as though nothing was at all out of the ordinary. Stono, meanwhile, stared straight ahead in a futile attempt to appear nonchalant. 'What the

191

fuck is this?' the younger and cleaner shaven of the two guards wondered silently.

"Where you go?" the bigger, bearded, and elder of the two guards asked in a mangled English accent.

"Commissar Zubov commanded us to resupply in Madrid," Zapata said timidly while clearing his throat. "Our supply of food, munitions, and other provisions is critically minimal."

"Zubov is sending you for more food?" the younger of the two guards, knowing how stingy and coldhearted Zubov was, asked suspiciously.

"That's right," Zapata said softly as he wiped a newly formed bead of sweat from his upper lip.

"What the hell happen to truck?" the bearded guard grumbled.

"It was attacked on the way back from Belchite," Zapata said. The two guards glanced at each other quizzically a quick moment.

"I thought Zubov made Americans find way back from Belchite without transport?" the smaller guard said while smirking and squinting his suspicious beady blue eyes.

"Oh, that's right," Zapata nervously stammered a bit as Stono slightly shook his head. "I meant to say on the way *to* Belchite. In fact, I think I did actually say *to* the first time. Maybe there was something lost in translation."

Zapata forced an awkward and nervous grin. "Zubov wants us back before noon, so if you don't mind." He began to ease his foot off the break. The two-way radio in the barricade-booth suddenly crackled. A muffled voce said something frantic in Russian. A long and tense pause in conversation lingered for what seemed like a week. A bead of sweat raced from Zapata's forehead down to his chin. His heart pounded harder and harder; so hard he thought the booth attendants might hear it.

The bigger of the two guards rushed inside the booth to answer the radio. He nervously stroked his beard a bit while listening intently. He glanced surreptitiously at Zapata and Stono, and then spoke suspiciously frantic in Russian to the person on the other end of the line. He took a conspicuously deep breath in an attempt to compose himself. He tried to act nonchalant and hung up the phone cool as could be – way too calm for Zapata's liking. The bigger and elder guard mumbled something in Russian to the smaller guard, who glanced nervously back over his shoulder at Zapata. The two guards began to approach the truck. Zapata meanwhile took his foot off the break and mashed the gas pedal with all his might. Stono snatched the machinegun from under the seat and sprayed the motorcycle that was adjacent the checkpoint full of holes. The cycle's tires exploded and fumes spewed from the engine.

A thick cloud of brown dust and wavy grey diesel fumes filled the air as the transport truck went from zero to sixty in what, for Stono and Zapata, felt like a decade. The bigger of the two guards hurried out of the booth haphazardly firing his antique Enfield rifle. A few 32-caliber rounds ripped into the back of the truck, but not enough to disable the behemoth of a machine. Stono and Zapata had successfully managed to navigate the first hurdle on what they expected to be a veritable Homeric odyssey on the way to Barcelona through Nationalist occupied territory.

Neither Stono nor Zapata spoke for nearly 300 miles. Stono, who was utterly exhausted from the battles in the Jarama Valley and Brunete, nearly drowning, the arduous and frigid trek back to base along the river bank, and suffering Benjamin's assassination, was able to calm down just enough to catch a few winks of sleep. Zapata was equally exhausted. The only thing that kept him conscience was the fear-induced adrenalin of being caught by Nationalists coupled with the glorious fantasy of surviving and soon being reunited with his family.

The sun was just beginning to rise in the east as Stono and Zapata approached Barcelona's suburbs from the southwest. They were surprised to not have experienced resistance on the 313-mile highway leading from the monastery in Belchite to Barcelona. Though Nationalist troops had been transported in big trucks in both directions, nobody seemed to pay Stono and Zapata much mind. That's likely because the Nationalists were well aware that victory was nigh. The troops en route to the eastern and western front and the last and most crucial conflicts of the war had also seen lots of deserters along the highway, way too many to stop, question, and incarcerate them all. The troops in transport to the frontlines were also surely well aware of the heavily fortified checkpoints set up at the main avenues leading into and out of Barcelona.

"Wake up, man," Zapata said brusquely as the truck exited the highway leading into the city. Stono shook violently awake, as if coming out of a terrible dream into an even worse one. "It's like fucking Fort Knox," Zapata said dejectedly. Bright spotlights illuminated row after row of tanks, trucks, and motorcycles, all of which were guarded by dozens of determined men with machineguns slung over their shoulders. The stolen transport truck fast approached a heavily fortified concrete barricade that made Zubov's checkpoint seem like a dollhouse. "Just drive man!" Stono frantically demanded. "If we stop, we're dead!"

The moment the Nationalist guards assembled at the checkpoint realized the truck was accelerating, rather than slowing, and thus had no intention of stopping, troops started firing machineguns indiscriminately at the truck. Stono, who was especially wary about wasting ammo, reluctantly fired a few rounds at the barricade booths leading in and out of the city, which sent Nationalists running for cover. Stono and Zapata slumped low in their seats, even lower when a 40-caliber machinegun shell blew out the back window. The truck barreled over the waist-high concrete barricade, incurring significant structural damage, but miraculously kept on going, albeit at significantly diminished speed. Stono fired a few more rounds out the shattered back window, hitting a Nationalist just as he was mounting a motorcycle, which caused other cycles to topple over like dominoes. The concrete barricade was disabled by the collision with the truck, which kept the Nationalists' motorcycles and trucks from being able to chase Zapata and Stono. A tank was deployed. It had no trouble rolling over the damaged concrete barricade left in the stolen trucks wake, but it was too slow to keep pace. The tank thus lobbed a massive bomb at Stono and Zapata, missing the battered truck by less than ten feet. Concrete and metal shrapnel caused the truck to fishtail a bit. It took all the strength in Zapata's weary body to wrestle the steering wheel straight and to keep the truck from careening into the ditch adjacent to the highway.

A minute or two passed. It seemed like a lifetime. For a fleeting moment, Zapata and Stono had the temerity to think they might actually make it to Barcelona alive, which, although under siege by the Nationalists, was still, for the time being, considered a Popular Front stronghold. Zapata and Stono's primary goal at that particular moment in time was to make it to the port and find a ship – any floating vessel really – that could get them to France safe and sound.

The moment of optimism was, however, fleeting. "Ah shit," Stono said dejectedly as a humming sound overhead caused him to cautiously poke his head out of what was formerly the back window of the truck. A Messerschmitt with two forty-four-caliber machineguns swooped low within thirty feet of the truck and opened fire. The first battery of rounds missed the truck by a matter of inches. Concrete shrapnel from the street, however, ripped into the driver-side door. The plane raised its elevation slightly and swooped back around. Again, it fired. Rattatat-tat! Pop! A large bullet ripped into a back tire, causing the truck to careen and fishtail wildly. Zapata almost lost his grip on the steering wheel, but was able to hold the truck as steady as could be hoped for under the circumstance.

The truck was just about to enter Les Corts, a section of the city with a number of businesses and residences that the Americans hoped they might be able to hide in. The plane swooped low once more and fired a direct hit into the engine block of the truck. Diesel fuel, fumes, and fire began spewing from the engine and hood. Zapata lost power steering. The disabled and fiery truck coasted for another hundred yards before slamming into the front entrance of a bombed out and abandoned post office.

The fire quickly spread from the engine to the cabin of the truck, forcing Stono and Zapata to flee from the post office as fast as their exhausted and sore feet could carry them. The truck exploded, but both men avoided being burned by the blast. They raced into a nearby neighborhood and cowered for what seemed like hours under an abandoned pushcart tied to a dead and decomposing donkey carcass, a feast for maggots. The gut-wrenching stench reeked so badly that Stono vomited several times. But neither he nor Zapata dared to crawl out from under the pushcart until long after the humming sound of the plane's engine vanished beyond the mid-afternoon horizon.

Stono and Zapata were terrified of the plane returning. Both were also terribly nauseous from the death smell of sun baked donkey flesh rotting just a few feet from their hiding place. The stench grew so odious that both eventually agreed to flee. They cautiously made their way on foot through backyards and alleys towards the Ciutat Vella section of the city, which they hoped would get them closer to the port and ultimately to France. To their great dismay, they happened upon the front steps of the University of Barcelona library.

Their sudden appearance on campus rekindled a bitter firefight between Nationalist invaders and POUM defenders that had been on hiatus since the morning. Stono and Zapata found themselves caught in crossfire between POUM and Falangist fighters. Stono fired his last few rounds at the Nationalists hunkered behind two dead and rotting horses turned barricade outside the library, which allowed the Americans just enough cover and time to safely enter the building. POUM, many of whom were devout Trotskyites and thus in part responsible for the inter-war leftist revolution in Catalonia, hated Stalin with a snarling disgust. They thus did not quite know whether Stono and Zapata, who were both donning their mud colored International Brigade uniforms, were friend or foe as they ran frantically into the foyer of the library.

Albion Algernon, a young Englishman covering the war for Oxford University's student newspaper, was hunkered down behind a giant stack of Encyclopedia Britannica, white-knuckling a machinegun. He assumed Stono and Zapata must have, like so many International Brigade volunteers before them, deserted and found their way to Barcelona in the hopes of getting to France, and eventually matriculating back home. The young Englishman, who was by now a grizzled veteran of guerilla warfare, was keen to have company, especially if the potential ally had a machinegun. He, as such, called out to them as they ran past.

"You there!" Albion hollered. "Bring that bloody hardware over here, old boy!" Stono and Zapata were running frantic, so hopped up on fear-induced adrenaline that they did not even notice the young Englishman hunkered down behind the barricade of books. They doubled back just as the blast from an artillery shell tore open the front doors of the library. Nationalist troops, most of whom were Moors followed by a battalion of Italians, crept towards the cavity at the library entrance. They fired round after round of blazing hot metal through the crater and into the building towards the barricade of books Albion, Stono, and Zapata had found refuge behind. Stono, who had already expended all his ammunition, hunched behind Zapata, who hunkered down behind Albion. Edward soon ran out of ammo too. It was but a matter of time before the Nationalists, who seemingly had an endless supply of men, munitions, ordinance, and weapons, entered the library.

The outgunned and overwhelmed trio fled on foot out the back of the library by the humanities section – which had caught fire – and then raced across campus, followed closely by many other men and woman associated with POUM and CNT, all of whom had ran out of ammo. They ran full speed for what seemed like an hour through the Sant Pere neighborhood, which was adjacent the university, where myriad factory workers lived clustered together in tiny apartments and bungalows. Zapata and the other combatants fleeing the carnage at the university finally came upon a non-descript blue-collar cottage at the dead end of a cul-de-sac a few miles from the port. The cul-de-sac had been heavily bombarded and battered during recent air raids. The residence, however, was largely undamaged structurally. It was a kind of anarchist safe house/headquarters replete with a modest cache of arms; the walls were adorned with red, white, and black propaganda posters hailing the plight of the world's workers versus fascism.

Even though Albion, who had been embedded with POUM since a month after his arrival in Spain two years earlier, was very much trusted, liked, and respected by many members of the anarchist labor union, Stono and Zapata invited widespread suspicion and a bit of scorn, even after they had explained that they had killed their commissar, Zubov, after he had murdered their friend, Professor Benjamin. The Americans in the anarchists' mist also explained that they had confronted peril and the threat of death to in order to desert the International Brigades in the hopes of making it safely to France and ultimately back to the United States. The fact that they had murdered their commissar seemed to ease tension a bit, especially considering POUM was well aware that many volunteers had deserted the International Brigades and made their way to Barcelona in the preceding months. The anarchists were well aware of the fact many International Brigade deserters had ended up being quite inspired and capable combatants against Stalinists as well as Nationalists. Stono nor Zapata also earned a degree of trust because neither spoke the same lamebrain, obtuse, simplistic, and automaton-like jargon and slogans common to devout Stalinists. But still, the Americans were going to have to prove their worth in battle before the anarchists would even consider feeding and providing shelter, never mind helping the deserters escape Catalonia.

After a few hours of tense interrogation, Stono and Zapata were invited by Albion to stay with the group, provided they were willing to join the cause of repelling both the Nationalists and Stalinists, and were willing to fight and die for the workers' revolution in Catalonia. Of course, they were willing fight and potentially die for the cause. What choice did they have? POUM represented their only and thus best chance of surviving the final stages of the war and ultimately navigating their way to France, and then back home to America.

"Successfully complete three missions," Albion promised, "and we'll figure out a way to get you back home."

Stono did not need any extra incentive. He, unlike Zapata, was not desperate to get back to America, where nothing worthwhile awaited him anyway. He was also extra invested in fighting amongst the anarchists after being introduced to Azure his first night at the safe house. Azure had, along with some other combatants, claimed a corner of the cottage as her own not long after fleeing Martinez's land.

Even Zapata, who wanted nothing more than to make it back home to New York alive as soon as possible by the time the siege of Barcelona began, agreed to fight with POUM. Albion promised the young husband and father that he could help him mail a letter to his wife and child and could possibly eventually arrange safe passage to France on a fishing boat if and/or when the Nationalists were finally repelled from the city. Despite Albion's promises and assertions, Barcelona was under heavy fire all through the summer and early fall of 1937, which prohibited most mail from getting in and out of Catalonia. Albion was completely unaware of the fact that none of his correspondence to his mother or article's penned for *Cherwell* had made it out of Spain in months.

Stono – who had developed a crush on Azure – and Zapata, who was more homesick each day, fought on behalf of POUM all through the summer of 1937 as the Nationalists invaded the city. The anarchists treated Zapata and Stono with an appreciation, dignity, and respect that they had never known with the International Brigades or at home in the states. Zapata also intuitively knew that his chances of fleeing to France and eventually making his way home to his wife and child in New York were significantly diminished if Franco and the fascists regained power. He thus never questioned the logic or wisdom of orders. He fought tooth and nail beside Azure, Albion, Stono, and the rest of POUM. Plus, many ships entering and leaving the port during the summer and fall of 1937 were torpedoed and sunk by German U-boats patrolling the Mediterranean. The frequency with which ships plying the sea between France and Spain were sunk created a catch-22 for Zapata;

he had the option of staying in Spain to do his part in defeating the fascists, or take his chances drowning at sea. Though he achingly longed to be reunited with his wife and child, he was determined to finish the three missions he vowed to complete before attempting to flee Spain. Besides, Stono and Zapata came to Spain to win the war. Keeping Barcelona from falling into fascist hands was the only chance the Republic had of surviving. Though he was desperate to get home, Zapata was determined to regain a sense of manhood lost by staying in Spain to fight until he could proudly return home a hero who had created a better world, future, and life for his wife and child to enjoy.

CHAPTER THIRTEEN

Gracia, Spain, summer 1937

Spring dragged on and on for Stono and Zapata. That was especially so for Zapata, who achingly missed his wife and child. For him, each day of winter and spring of 1937 seemed like a lifetime. The pace, however, quickened a bit during the death-defying summer embedded with POUM.

The Americans' first operation with POUM was relatively successful. A combatant who had been captured but had managed to escape an abandoned jailhouse turned short-term detention center in Gracia, a suburb of Barcelona, convinced POUM of the importance of an operation at that specific location. The detention center served as a staging ground with which to collect and process captured enemy combatants, then ship them to internment camps. Being sent to one of Franco's internment camps was tantamount to death for anarchists. Actually, a quick death in battle was a much better alternative to the systemic humiliation and torture that transpired for interned captives.

Azure's father taught her to shoot rabbits when she was just as tall as a rifle is long. She was raised shooting incredibly agile rodents in the dim early morning light from more than a hundred meters. Shooting fully grown fascists moving at a slow and predictable rate of speed was thus easy compared to picking off squirrels. Her prowess as a crack shot helped her to fast establish herself as one of POUM's most potent and dependable weapons. She was vital to Stono and Zapata's survival during the series of missions during the summer of 1937. She had established a carefully concealed sniper's nest in a dense forest on the side of a hill, a couple hundred yards from the jail.

Albion, Stono, Zapata, and a half-dozen POUM regulars donned camouflage fatigues and painted their faces with black shoe polish. They hunkered down at the perimeter of the forest adjacent to the jailhouse. Guards patrolled back and forth all through the night. At one point, a keen German Sheppard seemed to smell and hone in on Stono, Zapata, Albion and the others, which likely would have cost them their lives and led to an aborted mission. The impatient guard, however, convinced the dog to continue on without inspecting whatever had piqued its interest.

At daybreak, thirteen combatants were led from inside to outside the internment camp at gunpoint. The captured combatants, whose hands were securely tied with twine behind their backs, were forced to climb aboard an open-bed transport truck similar in model and make to the one Stono had hotwired at the monastery a month earlier. "That's Xavier," Albion whispered to Stono, "he saved my life last fall." Albion instinctively started towards his friend, but Stono grabbed him by the arm, which seemed to center the determined Brit a bit. "Wait for Azure," Stono reminded Albion. Albion nodded apologetically while coming back to his senses.

The bedraggled captives were made to stand in the back bed of the truck shoulder to shoulder, like cattle being shipped to a slaughterhouse. Two nationalists, a driver and a passenger toting a Madsen machinegun, were tasked with transporting the captives to a prison camp somewhere far and securely behind Nationalist lines. Once the captives were taken behind enemy lines, saving them was nearly impossible – a suicide mission. Foreign nationals such as Albion, Stono, and Zapata stood a chance of surviving captivity because they could conceivably be used as bargaining chips in global politics; Spanish captives were treated as traitors and they were thus shown no mercy by their virulent captors. Tens of thousands of captives simply disappeared and were never heard from or seen again.

Azure perhaps understood best of all how vital it was to save her comrades before they were taken from the jail turned staging area in Gracia. It was literally a matter of life and death for captives. Just as the engine of the truck began to rumble and started to roll down the hill towards the front and heavily fortified exit of the compound, Azure composed and focused herself with a soothing deep breath in through her nose and out through her mouth, then fired her rifle. A forty-caliber bullet shattered the front windshield and lodged in the driver's cerebral cortex. His lifeless yet intense eyes stared straight ahead. The passenger watched helplessly as the two-and-a-half-ton truck continued to roll down the hill before it finally smashed into a dense concrete barricade at the bottom of the hill. The powerful collision sent the captives who were standing shoulder to shoulder in the back bed of the truck flying violently forward. A few of them were badly lacerated.

Albion, Stono, Zapata, and the other POUM combatants, all of who were toting submachine guns hurried from the forest.

Stono clipped the razor wire atop of a ten-foot fence at the perimeter of the jail compound with his switchblade. He, followed quickly by his comrades, climbed over the fence and sprinted headlong towards to idling truck wedged against the concrete barricade at the bottom of the hill. They haphazardly sprayed bullets back towards the detention center, which bought a bit of time for the captives to escape from the truck bed. Albion and Stono kept gunmen inside the detention center pinned down by machinegun fire as Zapata and the others helped the captives flee into the relative safety of the nearby forest. One of the captives, who was concussed and thus staggering as a result of the truck's collision with the concrete barricade, and one of the POUM regulars who was trying to guide him into the forest, were shot and killed by the machinegun wielding Nationalist in the passenger seat of the truck. A precisely aimed bullet from Azure's rifle ended his life.

The escapees ran as fast and deep into the forest adjacent to the detention center as their weary legs could carry them. After ten minutes in a dead sprint the men finally located Azure. She was sitting in the driver's seat of the Rolls Royce she had taken from Martinez after he had killed her mother. "Hurry!" she demanded while firing up the diesel engine. "Come on!"

The escapees and their saviors piled into the sedan like it were a clown car or a phone booth in some fraternity's lark. Two of them were desperate enough to crawl into the truck, which was actually quite spacious compared to other popular cars on the market. Four others were able to hang onto the side of the car by standing on the foot rail of the sedan, as if they were secret service agents. Azure's boot mashed the gas pedal. She drove as fast as she could, which was actually quite slow, considering the terrain – a rocky and narrow mule trail leading from the forest into the San Marti section of the city. San Marti was, relatively speaking, a safe haven for leftists at that late stage of the war. The cadre of fugitives and their saviors dispersed soon after arriving in San Marti. By nightfall, all of them had assembled at the safe house in Sant Pere, eager for a glass of wine to calm their jangled nerves and the details of their next mission.

Montjuic, Spain, summer 1937

POUM strategists spent about a month plotting the Americans' next mission. In the meantime, Barcelona was enduring incredibly heavy bombing by German and Italian fighter planes. Franco's Nationalists gained more ground each day. The Republic's collapse seemed imminent. POUM thus grew increasingly impatient, desperate and vicious.

The Americans were told to borrow nice clothes from Albion and then attend a matinee screening of *Pépé le Moko*. They thus did without asking questions. The theater was less than half full. Zapata and Stono nonchalantly slunk into seats in the back corner of the theater a quarter hour after the opening credits rolled.

The audience seemed enthralled by the plot during the first and second act, But Stono and Zapata were too on edge to enjoy the merriment, especially considering the theater was deep in the heart of the Montjuic section of the city, which had recently become a Nationalist stronghold. They were apprised that one of the movie's attendees was a local police captain who had been working hand-in-glove with the Nationalists to undermine the Republic's effort to win the war by systemically arresting and incarcerating leftists, especially members of both POUM and CNT. The captain was the target. Stono and Zapata, however, had no idea which of the movie watchers was their target. Both thus spent the entire time they were in the theater predicting which man was their enemy. The Americans' mission was simply to yell "fire!" sometime soon after the start of the third act, which would cause a mass and frantic exodus from the theater. Stono and Zapata were then supposed to wait three minutes before exiting the theater. Azure and Albion, Stono and Zapata were informed, would handle the rest.

Shortly after the gangster who ran the Kasbah and the young Parisian girl sent to tempt his fate first kissed in the final act of *Pépé le Moko*, Zapata frantically screamed "Fuego! Fuego! Fuego!" Panic, as predicted, ensued. The theater was all but empty within thirty seconds of Zapata's frantic declaration. A middle-aged man and his young son, who was no older than ten, lingered in their seats a spell before cautiously making their way towards the back of the theater. The alert father clutched onto his son's trembling hand. The surly father glared daggers at Zapata and Stono as they slunk suspiciously low in their seats.

"You don't see too many Africans or Americans around here, huh?" the man grunted as he slightly pulled back the hem of his smoking jacket in order to reveal the firearm holstered to his hip.

Stono stammered, trying desperately to think of a way to explain his peculiar presence in Spain without stoking further suspicion. The sudden sound of machinegun fire outside the theater, however, made responding moot. The suddenly frantic man gripped his son's wrist tight as a vice and dragged the boy back towards the screen, which was adjacent to the emergency exit at the front of the theater. Night had descended on the city. The worried father very cautiously crept the emergency exit open and poked his head out into a narrow and dark alley, which led out to the main thoroughfare, which was bustling with cars and foot traffic. He plucked his son up into his arms, and held the boy tight to his chest. He glanced back once more at Zapata and Stono – both of whom remained hunkered down in the back corner of the theater – and then nervously crept into the dark alleyway leading out to the busy avenue.

"Is three minutes up?" Stono asked Zapata.

"I don't know," Zapata shrugged, "close enough, I guess."

The pair cautiously but quickly walked towards the screen and crept open the emergency exit door next to it.

Stono peeked into the alley. The father and his son had just arrived at the main thoroughfare. The father, however, was cowering behind a dumpster, frightened to leave the relative cover and safety provided by the dark alley. He, however, glanced back at Stono and Zapata and surmised that they had been sent to assassinate him. He thus, still clutching his son tight to his chest, finally stepped onto the well-lit sidewalk next to the congested avenue. Mangled and bloody bodies ripped to shred by machinegun fire, including a few children, littered the sidewalk outside the theater's box office. The father instinctively rushed in the opposite direction. Stono and Zapata followed him. The absconding father glanced back and saw Stono and Zapata pursuing him. He began to run as fast as he could, which was not very fast due to the weight of his son. He did not make it one hundred yards from the theater's box office before a solitary and deafening CRACK sound reverberated through the neighborhood. A merlot colored mist exploded in front of the father's face. A brunt force knocked the father forward, squarely atop his son, who was covered in blood, which oozed from the boy's head. The father was on all four haunches. His frantic eyes stared down at his lifeless and blood-soaked son. Zapata and Stono stood stock-still and shocked twenty feet from the father and the son's bloody corpse. The surprised horror in the father's face was quickly replaced by a look of determined anger and vengeance. He snatched the pistol from his hip and aimed it squarely at Stono's petrified face. Both Americans crept back a few inches and held their hands aloft. The bitter and heartbroken father cocked back the hammer of his pistol. Another solitary shot reverberated through the thoroughfare and echoed as if in a canyon, followed in rapid secession by another less hollow shot. A bullet lodged in the father's eye at the very same moment a bullet lodged in Stono's arm.

Azure, who had established a sniper's nest a few windows up from where Albion and his machinegun had established a position, shot the police captain and his son. A stray bullet from the captain's pistol lodged in Stono's arm. It was the worst physical pain he had ever known. Zapata helped his friend up onto to his feet. Both trudged clumsily past the dead police captain and his boy, and hurried away from the theater as fast as they could. Zapata snatched the captain's pistol from sidewalk as the sound of heavy boots fast smacking the pavement behind him and Stono. He turned around ready to fire a round, but was relieved to see Albion, who was clutching tight to his machinegun, hurrying after them.

"Follow me!" Albion demanded.

He led the Americans back into the dark alleyway back towards the theater. Zapata shot the outside lock off the emergency exit and they rushed back into the theater. The credits were rolling. The room was empty of all but one young usher who was cowering behind a row of seats close to front of theater. Albion then led his comrades down a long hallway and into a screening of *La Grande Illusion*, which was in the middle of the second act. There was a panicked murmur in the theater as a result of the recent machinegun fire outside. Most of the people in the theater had ducked and covered in front of their seats. They were especially terrified to see Albion, Stono, and Zapata hurrying down the aisle towards the emergency exit adjacent to the screen. Albion cautiously peered into the dark and narrow alleyway that led to a less congested thoroughfare than the one littered with dead bodies out front of the box office. Albion, Zapata, and Stono – whose arm was now covered in blood – cautiously crept out of the theater and into the alley. Azure skidded the Rolls Royce to a stop in the gutter next to the rain slicked sidewalk. The trio jumped into the car as it sped from the scene. Stono winced and curled into a ball and rocked back and forth, afraid he might he might die. Albion unbuttoned his shirt, took it off, ripped it in two, and fashioned a tunicate, which he tied tight around Stono's arm. He then cradled his friend in his arms and assured him he would "be alright."

Azure, Albion, Zapata, and Stono all managed to survive to movie theater mission; their target did not. On the surface, the mission thus seemed a success. But this mission, for Azure especially, felt different than the others. There was no great sense of jubilation that the operation had helped to bend the will of the fascists. Killing the cop and his kid was pure revenge that would ultimately do nothing to turn the tide of the war in favor of labor unions. If anything, killing children gave the fascists a kind of moral high ground to claim, and would only inspire further reprisal. Nobody in the Rolls Royce said a word until long after they arrived back at the safe house in Mont Pere.

Albion and Stono cracked open a bottle of Johnnie Walker Blue the Englishman had brought with him from London and had been saving for a very special occasion.

Albion had always envisioned drinking it with a few comrades after the fascists had finally been defeated. He, however, decided to split it with Stono before attempting to pry the bullet embedded in his friend's arm out with the tweezers in his shaving kit. Zapata sat close by and watched Stono biting into a towel with all his might, scowling, and making a terrible sound snarling that he imagined might be similar to the noise a cow might make while giving birth to a giraffe.

He could also hear the muffled sound of Azure speaking very fast and determinedly to a few of the POUM regulars in the back room of the cottage. "What the hell have you made us do?" she demanded. "I never agreed to kill any children. Now we've been reduced to what we hate most. We are no better than Franco!"

Zapata could hear male voices retort in a murmur, but could not quite make out what they said. He assumed they were trying to explain their methodology and simultaneously calm Azure, who was full of rage.

"No!" she retorted. "I'm no murderer! If we had a chance of winning the war, I would consider it. But at this point, all we are doing is risking our lives to exact revenge on people who may or may not even deserve it. I'm done!"

Zapata could hear the men explaining something to Azure, but could not quite decipher any details. One of the POUM regulars had plopped the afternoon edition into Azure's lap. She had taken some reading classes since arriving in Barcelona after her parent's died. But her comprehension was still not great. She, however, recognized the face of a startlingly familiar looking man wearing a crisp white tuxedo and standing next to a glorious marbled Olympic sized swimming pool. She could also phonetically sound out the headline, which read: 'Falangist Playboy Opens Five Star Resort in Tarragona.'

Her hands began to tremble and she suddenly felt a terrible pain in her sternum caused from intense nausea. A tidal wave of repressed anger, anxiety, and despair crashed into her. Her mind momentarily raced back to the farm and fields she had known her entire life, and specifically to the fateful day her parents were killed by Martinez – the playboy on the front-page of the paper donning the tuxedo.

"But how?" she muttered. "I thought he was dead..." Her memory flashed back to seeing him bleeding profusely from the chest in the middle of the cotton field next to the barn and cottage. The agonizing memory transformed in her mind into a hypothesis: Father Ramon, who, along with the constable, had been peppered by buckshot did not die. The sound of Azure igniting the engine of the stolen sedan stirred Father Ramon, who regained consciousness. He, after shaking the dizziness from his head, laboriously dragged himself to his feet and stumbled out of the dark barn, where, thanks to a glorious new moon shining overhead, was able to find Martinez, who was at the threshold of death. Father Ramon, who knew Azure's shortcut to the village through the forest, was able to find a telephone with which to call for help. The local doctor arrived with his black kitbag just in time to ensure Martinez' survival, and ultimately, after a great deal of rehabilitation, his full recovery. That was Azure's hypothesis, anyway.

She was assured that assassinating Martinez could be her last mission if she wished to leave the organization. She had their blessing to leave POUM, if she believed that was in her best interest. She was also guaranteed that her friends, Stono and Zapata, would be provided safe passage to France upon successful completion of the mission. The thought of letting Stono down terrified her. She thus very reluctantly agreed to a final mission, so long as she was able to plan as well as execute it.

Azure had grown up on the outskirts of Tarragona. Martinez had built his palatial resort atop the lands that had sustained her family for generations, which added a bit of extra incentive to kill the real estate baron. She took more than a week to formulate a plan of attack, which provided Stono the opportunity to mend a bit before being thrown back into battle.

The night before the mission, Azure and Albion broke into a formalwear boutique in Sant Andreu. His task was the find three tuxedos. She was determined the find a ball gown. It was a quick smash-and-grab that took less than two minutes total.

The next evening, Zapata, Stono, and Albion bathed and shaved in the Besòs River while Azure used the bathroom back at the cottage to prepare. She had never worn a gown or makeup before. Albion, who had known her for more than a year, did not immediately recognize her dressed to the nines. Stono, who had been romantically involved with her since soon after arriving in Barcelona, immediately grew even more smitten with her due to how awkward and uncomfortable she seemed to be covered in such finery. Albion looked especially smart and dapper in his midnight blue tuxedo, which fit like a glove. But Stono and Zapata's tuxedos were designed for men much better fed than they were. They thus looked foolish, as though they might drown in black fabric and bowties.

The drive from Barcelona to Tarragona was relatively quick and somber, just ninety minutes with the Rolls Royce running top speed on the newly paved asphalt highway. Nobody in the car spoke much at all, except for Azure, who rehashed the details of the plan. They also crafted a somewhat solid cover story in case they were stopped at a checkpoint. The road to Tarragona was, however, conspicuously wide open. Madrid was days from falling into the Fascists' hands and Franco therefore concentrated the bulk of his manpower and firepower in the capital city, which was the biggest domino. Once Madrid fell, the rest of Spain would too in a matter of weeks, if not days.

Azure's excitement and nervous energy on the highway from Tarragona to Barcelona transformed into fierce determination as night fell, and especially with each mile closer the car darted towards her ancestral homeland – the fields that provided her and her family life for generations.

Stono, who was driving the sedan, eased the break-pedal to the floorboard as the car approached a security gate built to resemble a Romanesque victory arch, which was down the hill from Martinez' resort. Albion, meanwhile, furtively shoved his machinegun under the passenger side seat. "Let me do the talking," Azure, who was in the seat directly behind Stono, said softly while rolling down her window.

Two handsome gentlemen with slicked back black hair and donning crisp white tuxedos exited the gaudy victory arch as soon as the sedan rolled to a stop. The taller of the two exuded suspicion, especially because Stono, a black man, was driving.

"How can I help you," the guard smiled cheerfully, trying to mask his uneasiness.

"Hello there," Azure, who was sitting in the seat directly behind Stono, confidentially retorted, "we have a reservation for four suites."

"Of course! What name is the reservation under?" the guard asked in a syrupy tone.

"Garcia," Azure replied politely.

The suspicious guard hurried into the victory arch and checked his registry. His finger finally settled on a line that read: 'Garcia: four suites.'

The two guards whispered nervously amongst one another, which stoked worry inside the sedan. "Is there some kind of problem?" Azure prodded.

"I do indeed see your reservation here in the registry," the taller guard said, "but…"

"But what?" Azure demanded.

"Well, you see," the guard's face turned fire engine red from embarrassment.

"What seems the problem?" Azure was trying hard to not lose her cool.

"Well," the guard stammered, "you see, we've never had a guest of African ancestry visit the resort before. I'm not quite sure what our policy is."

"Do you have even the slightest idea who this man is?" Azure chuckled condescendingly, which underscored the guard's boorish ignorance. "This man – 'of African ancestry' – as you put it, is a prominent real estate tycoon from Miami, in America. All of these gentlemen were considering investing in this property. Your ignorance could, unfortunately, cost your employer a great deal of money."

"I'm terribly sorry, senorita," the guard blanched. "Please, just permit me one short moment to call and clarify what exactly our policy is. I won't be a minute."

A frustrated and tense sigh escaped Azure as she rolled her eyes. The daunted guard rushed into the victory arch. He dialed the rotary phone, which made it feel as though an hour had passed before the call was placed. Martinez, who was already completely sauced, answered a gold-plated telephone next to the Jacuzzi in the palatial bathroom his penthouse suite. He listened as intently as a drunk man could as the guard explained the imbroglio with the foursome in a luxury sedan at the front gate of the resort.

"I don't care if the nigger is a goddamn Martian," Martinez slurred. "If he has a Rolls Royce and wants to help me get richer, he's welcomed to stay as long as he has cash to burn." He had a bit of difficulty placing the receiver in the gold-plated cradle, but finally managed it, then poured himself another tall class of Dos Lunas Grand Reserve, and turned the RCA on. Duke Ellington's "Take the A Train" blared. He shimmied over to the window, down the hill at the Rolls Royce idling at the victory arch at the bottom of the hill.

The tall and dapper guard at the front gate seemed relieved as he pushed a button inside the victory arch. The wooden barricade in front of the Rolls Royce's chrome bumper went skyward. The guard smiled as he waved the foursome in the sedan by. The car roared up the hill towards the resort, which, to Zapata and Albion, seemed to be an impenetrable fortress and a suicide mission. Both, however, kept their misgivings mum.

A raucous and hedonistic soirée that reminded Albion of a scene from F. Scott Fitzgerald's novel, *The Great Gatsby* was spilling out of the bar adjacent to the lobby of the hotel. Azure, Stono, Albion, and Zapata left the car with the valet at the front entrance to the hotel, but they did not permit the bellhop to touch their luggage.

Azure checked in at the front desk, and then met her comrades with their respective room keys on the third floor of the resort, where their suites were. A submachine gun was stuffed in Stono's suitcase. Zapata and Albion's cases were each full of four one-gallon canisters, each filled to the brim with petroleum. Albion left his submachinegun under the front passenger seat. Azure brought nothing but a pearl-colored pocketbook with a tiny plastic packet stuffed full of scopolamine, a powerful sedative, crushed into a fine white powder.

The band down in the bar played a Dixieland classic so loud that the bass reverberated in the suites on the third floor. Azure sat fretfully at the foot of the queen-sized bed and took a deep breath to compose herself. She, however, shivered more violently, the more she concentrated on calming herself. Instinct compelled her to the terrace. She basked in a warm late-summer breeze and humidity as she leaned over the railing. Her eyes sopped up the horizon she had known all her life. She could faintly see the crucifix above the tree line of the church her mother made her attend each Sunday morning.

She wiped a bulbous tear from her cheek as Zapata, Albion, and Stono each conspicuously carried their suitcases across the front lawn towards the Rolls Royce parked in the lot. She took a long and deep breath in an attempt to center herself, snatched her pocketbook from the edge of the bed, gave herself a long and determined look in the vanity mirror, and then casually exited the room and made her way down a long and lush hall towards the gold and marble elevator.

Her nerves got the best of her a bit and she vomited on the elevator ride down. The elevator operator was kind enough to pretend he did not notice her get sick. On ground level, she pushed her way through a crowd of drunken revelers wedged between the bar and dance floor. She perched at the edge of a stool at the end of the bar and ordered a glass of pinot noir, which she had seen someone do in a movie.

Outside the hotel, Stono was fast approaching thick brush, the woods that used to separate Azure's farm from the village, with his suitcase stuffed with a submachinegun. Nobody seemed to notice him. Zapata and Albion were far more conspicuous. They shoved the suitcases back into the trunk of the Rolls Royce, then proceeded to remove the canisters of petrol from said suitcases.

Back inside the raucous bar, Martinez, who was a bit out of breath, had just left the dance floor and made his way to the bar in search of refreshment. He noticed a young woman all by her lonesome sitting conspicuously at the edge of her stool at the end of the bar. He straitened his bowtie and hair and then approached.

"Can I get you another?" he grinned suavely.

Her breath shortened and she trembled slightly the moment she heard his voice cut through the loud music. Her eyes darted nervously from his smiling face to the bottom of her glass of wine.

"Okay," she forced a gentle grin. "Please, sit."

"You look very familiar," he said while motioning for the bartender to bring her another drink. "Have we met?"

"I don't think so," her voice quivered as she brushed her bangs down over her forehead a bit.

"Have you been here before?"

"No, this is my first time here."

"This is my property," he was proud. "I'm as rich as I am handsome." He grinned haughtily. She smiled and nodded, feigning like she was impressed. "What brings you to my resort?"

"Oh, I don't know," she shrugged her shoulders slightly. "Adventure, I guess."

"Who are you here with?"

"Nobody," she replied, and then gulped down the glass of wine provided by the bartender.

"It's so loud in here," Martinez said as he glanced over his shoulder at the boisterous band playing a raucous tune and frenzied partiers flailing on the dance floor. "Would you like to perhaps chat and have a drink in my penthouse upstairs?"

"I guess so," her eyebrows raised slightly, "why not?"

Martinez' face beamed a half-surprised and half-pragmatic grin. He dug deep into the pocket of his trousers and placed a copper key in the palm of Azure's dainty yet calloused hand.   "I'm in suite 400, on the fourth floor," He said. "I've got to say goodnight to a few friends. Why don't you go upstairs and fix us a drink? I'll be up in two shakes of a lamb's tail." She forced a faux seductive smile and made her way from the bar, to the lobby, and back onto the elevator, where a disgruntled bellhop was cleaning the vomit that she had deposited on the way downstairs.

Back outside the hotel, Stono was hunkered down in a ditch, lying flat on his belly behind the submachine gun, which he had trained on the double doors leading from the lobby. He gazed through the magnifying scope attached to his weapon at the front entrance of the hotel, which was obscured by the valet retrieving the keys from a Mercedes owner who was anxious to engage in the revelry spilling from the bar into the lobby. Stono's eyes then scanned the perimeter of the hotel. His heart sank as he noticed the taller of the two guards Azure had interacted with at the front gate bisecting the grand lawn in hot pursuit of Albion, who was dousing the outside of the east wing's foundation in petroleum. Zapata, who had already emptied both of his canisters on the foundation of the north wing was having trouble lighting matches due to a stiff breeze.

Back inside the hotel, Azure had just fixed Martinez a tall class of small batch tequila and dumped the entire packet of scopolamine into the drink. Martinez was already loosening his bowtie by the time he exited the elevator and made his way into the penthouse. Azure was uneasy as she gazed out the sliding-glass door leading out to the terrace, which overlooked the grand lawn, as the guard was fast approaching Albion below.

"I apologize for the delay," Martinez said suavely as he stepped off the elevator and into the suite. "Please permit me a just another quick moment while I slip into something less constricting than this monkey suit."

"Of course, no problem," Azure said softly, "here's your drink. I hope tequila is okay."

"Tequila is wonderful!" he exclaimed as he took it from her and hurried into the master bedroom and shut the door behind him. She hurried back over to the terrace door, slid it open, and leaned over the railing to get a better look at the potential disaster unfolding below on the lawn. The guard, who had confronted Albion, was gesticulating frantically. Azure feared the confrontation between Albion and the security guard could doom their mission before it was accomplished. Her heart raced.

Albion and the guard were both agitated as they strode towards the front of the hotel. Albion suddenly dropped the canister of petrol in his hand, pulled a two-shot derringer from the breast pocket of his tuxedo jacket and blasted the guard square in the head twice. The valet parking the Mercedes heard the shots and saw the white-hot gun blast, then watched horrified as his coworker dropped face first onto the dew-covered grass like a sack of wet towels. Rather than parking the car, he drove fast to front gate in order to apprise the other guard of the tragedy he had witnessed transpire.

Zapata, meanwhile, had finally lit a match, which set a hedgerow lining the north wing on fire. He crouched down behind another nearby hedgerow and tried to catch his breath as he watched the fire spread until it finally started to devour the north wing of the hotel. He then tried to compose himself by breathing in through his nose and out through his mouth as he hurried back towards the Rolls Royce in the parking lot.

The fire alarm began to blare, which caused the band to cease playing and caused a general panic to ensue. The revelers rushed frantically from the bar, then into the lobby, and finally outside of the hotel where they lingered. The blaze spread rapidly. Albion lost his cool and sprinted conspicuously across the lawn towards the parking lot. He and Zapata arrived at the Rolls Royce at the same time. Both waited anxiously in the backseat of the sedan, gazing helplessly at the blaze engulf the hotel as if spectators watching at a movie through the windshield. "What if Azure gets trapped inside?" Albion uttered. Zapata nodded ominously but did not verbally respond. They watched helplessly as the guard hurried after the valet, who was running full speed, from the gatehouse up to the hotel.

Martinez exited the master bedroom fully naked. His penis was half-erect. Azure's eyes honed in on the glass of tequila wedged between his thumb and forefinger. It was half-full. He was already three-sheets-to-the-wind. But now, he was staggering as though one would in a heroin stupor. "What's happening?" he slurred.

"The hotel…" she said matter-of-factly, "it's on fire,"

226

"Fire?" He slunk towards the terrace and witnessed the gathering commotion below on the lawn. "Stay here," he demanded," I'll be right back." He clumsily pulled a scarlet silk robe around his torso and hurried out of the suite and onto the elevator. Azure's determined eyes fixated on a gold envelope opener atop his oaken desk. She took a deep and composed breath while waiting for the elevator to return from the ground floor. She steadied her nerves on the elevator ride from the penthouse to the ground floor. The lobby was filled with black smoke. She had difficulty breathing and seeing, but finally managed to make her way out of the hotel lobby and onto the lawn. Bewildered and suddenly sobered patrons packed the front lawn and drive. Azure's eyes were burning and filled with smoky tears. But she finally located Martinez, who was being fast approached by the valet and guard. She slipped the heels from her feet and ran as fast as her tight and heavily sequenced evening gown would permit.

"This is for my mother and father," she fearlessly declared as she plunged the envelope opener into Martinez' neck. He fell to his knees. She stabbed him again and again until he fell face first on the dew-covered lawn. Blood gushed from his throat. The guard removed the concealed pistol from the holster wrapped around his waist, and cocked back the hammer. Stono, who was still hunkered down at the perimeter of the property behind his submachinegun, mowed the guard and valet down with a hail of bullets just before the guard could shoot at Azure. She left the gold envelope holder stuck into Martinez' jugular and ran as fast as she could towards the Rolls Royce in the parking lot. Stono abandoned the gun and likewise ran as fast as he could towards the parking lot. He jumped into the driver's seat of the sedan, leaned over, and popped the passenger side open. Azure slid inside. The car barreled down the hill and smashed through wooden barricade attached to the victory arch. Stono glanced in the rearview mirror, relieved that nobody seemed to be pursuing them. Azure gazed hard and silent at the conflagrated resort for a long moment, and then broke into a maniacal laughter, unburdened of a lifetime of trauma that she had not even been conscious of lugging. The laughter was infectious. Albion, then Stono, and finally Zapata laughed hysterically most of the ride back to Barcelona.

CHAPTER FOURTEEN

Barcelona, September 1937

In September 1937, Juan Negrín y López, the Spanish Premier who had been in exile in Switzerland since shortly after the coup began in July 1936 spoke earnestly to the League of Nations about the dire situation the Republic was in. He feared the democratically elected Popular Front government could not hold out much longer. He lamented to the League that all the International Brigade volunteers would be removed from the country in a matter of weeks in the hopes that Hitler and Mussolini would also do the honorable thing by removing their troops, thereby making the war a much more even match between Republicans and Nationalists, Spaniards all. But Hitler and Mussolini, sensing total victory, scoffed at Negrín's Faustian Bargain. The emboldened fascist dictators instead sent even more men and material to crush the crumbling Republic. Franco, who was close enough to touch the dictatorship he'd fantasized about since he was an adolescent, was not willing to negotiate, especially when total victory seemed inevitable.

A brief ceasefire was called so the International Brigades, the few who were lucky enough to still be alive, could march proudly together arm-in-arm in a parade through the heart of the city before being sent home. Stono, however, felt that America promised nothing but misery and terror for working class black men, especially those with the temerity to defy non-intervention neutrality. He had also fallen deeply in love with his bride, Azure, and the revolution she was fully willing to die for. So Stono, against Zapata's pleading, decided to stay in Catalonia and take his chances fighting fascists to the glorious or bitter end.

Zapata, conversely, jumped at the chance to catch the first boat back to France and ultimately to his wife and child in New York. For the first time in months, he donned his mud colored brigade uniform and insignia and blended neatly into the crowd of a few thousand volunteers from around the globe assembled in Turo Park. Dolores Ibárruri's, the stocky and aging salt-and-pepper haired Spanish woman who had become the oratory firebrand of the revolutionary movement in opposition to fascism, regaled the "volunteers for freedom" with a heartfelt farewell address. Her sorrow and despair contrasted sharply with Zapata's renewed sense of optimism:

"It is very difficult to say a few words in farewell to the heroes of the International Brigades, because of what they are and what they represent. A feeling of sorrow, an infinite grief catches our throat – sorrow for those who are going away, for the soldiers of the highest ideal of human redemption, exiles from their countries, persecuted by the tyrants of all peoples – grief for those who will stay here forever mingled with the Spanish soil, in the very depth of our heart, hallowed by our feeling of eternal gratitude.

From all peoples, from all races, you came to us like brothers, like sons of immortal Spain; and in the hardest days of the war, when the capital of the Spanish Republic was threatened, it was you, gallant comrades of the International Brigades, who helped save the city with your fighting enthusiasm, your heroism and your spirit of sacrifice. And Jarama and Guadalajara, Brunete and Belchite, Levante and the Ebro, in immortal verses sing of the courage, the sacrifice, the daring, and the discipline of the men of the International Brigades.

For the first time in the history of the peoples' struggles, there was the spectacle, breathtaking in its grandeur, of the formation of International Brigades to help save a threatened country's freedom and independence – the freedom and independence of our Spanish land.

Communists, Socialists, Anarchists, Republicans – men of different colors, differing ideology, antagonistic religions – yet all profoundly loving liberty and justice, they came and offered themselves to us unconditionally.

They gave us everything – their youth or their maturity; their science or their experience; their blood and their lives; their hopes and aspirations – and they asked us for nothing. But yes, it must be said, they did want a post in battle, they aspired to the honor of dying for us.

Banners of Spain! Salute these many heroes! Be lowered to honor so many martyrs!

Mothers! Women! When the years pass by and the wounds of war are staunched; when the memory of the sad and bloody days dissipates in a present of liberty, of peace and of wellbeing; when the rancor has died out and pride in a free country is felt equally by all Spaniards, speak to your children. Tell them of these men of the International Brigades.

Recount for them how, coming over seas and mountains, crossing frontiers bristling with bayonets, sought by raving dogs thirsting to tear their flesh, these men reached our country as crusaders for freedom, to fight and die for Spain's liberty and independence threatened by German and Italian fascism. They gave up everything – their loves, their countries, home and fortune, fathers, mothers, wives, brothers, sisters and children – and they came and said to us: `We are here. Your cause, Spain's cause, is ours. It is the cause of all advanced and progressive mankind.'

Today many are departing. Thousands remain, shrouded in Spanish earth, profoundly remembered by all Spaniards. Comrades of the International Brigades: Political reasons, reasons of state, the welfare of that very cause for which you offered your blood with boundless generosity, are sending you back, some to your own countries and others to forced exile. You can go proudly. You are history. You are legend. You are the heroic example of democracy's solidarity and universality in the face of the vile and accommodating spirit of those who interpret democratic principles with their eyes on hordes of wealth or corporate shares, which they want to safeguard from all risk.

We shall not forget you; and, when the olive tree of peace is in flower, entwined with the victory laurels of the Republic of Spain – return!

Return to our side for here you will find a homeland – those who have no country or friends, who must live deprived of friendship – all, all will have the affection and gratitude of the Spanish people who today and tomorrow will shout with enthusiasm – Long live the heroes of the International Brigades!"

Ibárruri's oration was so moving that for a moment, Zapata considered staying in Spain with Zapata and Azure to stay and fight to the glorious or bitter end. But Stono would not hear of it. "Go home," Stono pleaded, "you can't do anything for your family buried in the Spanish earth."

Zapata conceded. He bid Stono and Azure a heartfelt adieu and cautiously followed what was left of the decimated American battalion towards the docks, where they were expected to catch a liner bound for Marseille, and then onto New York. He was, for the first time since long before he went to Spain, beaming with a sense of joy, relief, optimism, and gratitude. When he first arrived in Spain, he was willing to trade his life for the cause. By the time of the cease fire and parade, he would have given anything just to spend one more fleeting moment with his wife and child. That wonderful dream of finally being reunited with the family he ached to see and touch so much seemed within reach as he bid Stono, Azure, and Albion – who decided to stay in Spain until the war concluded – adieu.

Zapata excitedly and quickly ascended the gangplank onto the overcrowded deck of the ship bound for Marseille. He turned around one last time and waved jovially goodbye to his friends. He, however, wondered worriedly why their demeanor suddenly seemed so concerned. They hollered inaudibly and flailed their hands, frantically remonstrating. Zapata quizzically shook he head, shrugged his shoulders, and held the palms of his hands skyward to ask, 'what's the matter?'

He was tackled from behind and pinned to the slick hardwood on the deck, handcuffed, and then dragged down the gangplank kicking and screaming by the henchman they had narrowly escaped at the monastery in March. They had been surreptitiously stalking Zapata and Stono since they arrived at Turo Park earlier in the afternoon. The henchmen first spotted Zapata marching behind the surviving Lincolns in the parade. The Soviets suspected many deserters would use the parade and promise of a trip home to come out of hiding. Many of the deserters with the temerity to march in the parade, Zapata included, were apprehended. Stono and Azure watched wide eyed, terrified, but ultimately helplessly as Zapata was dragged from the boat and shoved into the back of a packed paddy wagon stuffed full with dozens of deserters bound for Siberian gulags.

The Pyrenees, November 1937

By the time of the parade in Barcelona in September of 1937, the proverbial writing was on the wall for all combatants involved. The end of the war was nigh, and all but the most diehard or delusional knew the fascists would inevitably prevail. Stalin, who had already hatched a plan to assassinate Trotsky, who had fled to Mexico, was in the process of quietly pulling men and material out of Spain by the time Negrín had made his speech to the League of Nations. After his capture about the boat bound for France, Zapata and hundreds of other deserters were incarcerated along with dozens of anarchist prisoners of war at the monastery at Belchite. By October, the Nationalists had regained control of all of Iberia except Catalonia, the Basque Region, and Portugal, which was a dictatorship allied with Franco and the fascists ever since the start of the coup. The series of Nationalist military successes in the wake of Negrín's idealistic miscalculation finally forced Stalin's hand to the point that he decided to cut his losses and let Spain fall to Franco. By October of 1937, Stalin did not really care about Spain anymore anyway. He had successfully bought time to industrialize the Soviet Red Army in preparation for what he rightly believed was an inevitable invasion by Hitler's Wehrmacht.

The Soviets essentially inverted the network that smuggled volunteers into Spain in the first place in order to get Stalin's most prized advisors along with his most bitter enemies out of the county before the Republic caved in completely. Stalin's advisors and materials were to be shipped to France via boat or taken to the border, then to the "Red Express," and from there to Moscow or St. Petersburg. But Stalin also hatched a devious plan for deserters and anarchist captives, which he considered failures to *him* and *his* cause. The open secret in safe houses all across Barcelona was that the POWs and deserters who had been caught in Stalin's snare were to be marched like cattle over the Pyrenees, put on prison cars attached to the tail end of the "Red Express," and ultimately shipped to gulags deep in the dark heart of Siberia.

By the end of summer in 1937, Stalin's sadistic repression of dissenters – perceived or real – was common knowledge throughout most of Western Europe. Word of

Stalin's betrayal to volunteers thus came as little surprise to anyone but the most ideologically hardheaded, especially considering he did the bare minimum to feed, supply, and equip the International Brigades during their war with the fascists. It was thus no secret on the streets of Barcelona that from the first to the last days of the war, the volunteers lured to Spain by a mix of desperation, hope of restoring some semblance of manhood, and/or idealism were essentially intended to be lambs led to slaughter – fodder for geopolitics most of them could not even begin to adequately comprehend. It was also common knowledge amongst members of the Popular Front's underground resistance that Stalin would cut his losses and send the anarchist POWs and International Brigade volunteers who had deserted on a death march across the mountains when defeat seemed imminent. Those "fortunate" enough to survive the trek across the snow and ice covered peaks of the Pyrenees would be shipped like penned in pigs across the continent to labor camps where they would be worked to death or used as bargaining chips for Stalin to make Faustian deals with the governments of the countries the captives hailed from.

An unseasonal arctic storm had whipped down from the North Sea and dusted the Pyrenees with an early season snow. Hundreds of survivors, including Zapata, were huddled together, shivering as they trudge up to the peak of the range. The sun was dipping beyond the Spanish horizon as a thick and heavy fog set in.

From beginning to end, Stalin secretively funded the war on a shoestring budget. It should come as no great shock that there was only a handful of Soviets toting machineguns, one to every twenty-five prisoners on the march. The other captors were armed only with antique loading rifles similar to those the Union Army used in the American Civil War. The dusty and dilapidated rifles were hand-me downs from the Russian's war against the Japanese some thirty years earlier. Most could not even fire, though only a few of the captives suspected the guns were dysfunctional. Even the few skeptics who doubted the effectiveness of the weapons were too afraid to risk their lives to prove their hypothesis.

Had the prisoners not been so malnourished, cold, and disheartened, they could have very likely overpowered their captors with only a dozen or so casualties. But most of the deserters, Zapata included, went AWOL in the first place because they were simply so desperate to live a bit longer to see their loved ones again. Revolt at this point seemed highly unlikely.

Many of men on the forced march through the mountains were also somewhat optimistic they might be used as bargaining leverage and ultimately sent home at some point. By the war's end, most volunteers, especially Zapata, had suffered so much heartache and deprivation that they did not care if they had to face criminal charges, forfeit their passport, and even a prison sentence. Doing time in an American prison seemed a small matter compared to what he had already endured. All that really mattered to Zapata and most of the men on the arduous trek across the Pyrenees was making it home to their family and friends, no matter the cost.

The pack of captives were forced by their captors to stop a while at a thicket of forest a quarter mile beyond the French side of the mountains so the guards could relieve themselves, sip some vodka, smoke cigarettes, gossip, and rest awhile by a small fire before having to confront the last few miles of the march to the nearest train depot, where the prisoners would be processed and then loaded onto the "Red Express." The dozen guards cracked wise, cursed, and chuckled while passing around a cold bottle of Stolichnaya. Their calm and nonchalant demeanor contrasted starkly to the stark depression and despair inscribed on the gaunt faces of the shivering captives.

The foolhardy regaling and clustering of the guards proved to be their demise. A hollow, mysterious, and unseen shot rang out from deep inside the forest. The percussion caused birds to scatter and snow to shake and fall from tree limbs. The crystal-clear bottle of Stolichnaya shattered instantly in one of the guard's black leather gloved hands just as he was putting it to his lips. A bullet lodged in his eye socket. He dropped to the ground like a felled redwood. Timber.   The other guards were shocked and stood stock still and breathless as a volley of machinegun fire began mowing them down like grass. One-by-one, the guards fell. Steam emanated from the hot blood soaking into the pristine white snow collecting around their corpses.

Zapata and the other prisoners watched with bated breath, eyes wide and mouths agape, wondering what in the hell was happening. Most, Zapata included, assumed the Nationalists had intercepted them en route to the "Red

Express" and that they would all soon be dead too. One of the guards, who had been kneeling beside the fire, escaped being mowed down by machinegun and raced back towards the prisoners, many of whom were huddled around a small fire, petrified. He sprayed his gun into the mass of humanity, cutting down a dozen or so prisoners. Then, a shattering CRACK sound filled the forest and reverberated into the valley below. The surviving guard fell face first into the fire, which emolliated him.

Within three minutes, all the Soviets and a handful of prisoners were dead. Zapata and a few survivors had the good sense to instinctively pry the guns from some of the dead guards' hands, which was no easy task considering how rigor mortis caused the deceased to cling to their weapons with vice-like grips. There was a quiet and momentary lull that permitted some survivors, including Zapata, to scurry for cover into a nearby cave. Some, however, ran headlong and frantically down the mountain and into the valley. After a few moments, Zapata was somewhat confused to hear a familiar voice in the wilderness beckon. "Zapata?" His name echoed through the valley. He wondered if he were hallucinating.

"Zapata?" The voice again echoed through the forest.

"Stono?" Zapata said cautiously. "Is that you?"

"Yeah!" Stono grinned elatedly. "It's me! Come on out. I think it's safe. I'll cover you!"

Zapata cautiously crept out from the cave on his hands and knees and made his way back up the mountain a few hundred yards, back to the carnage of dead bodies and blood-soaked snow. The other survivors in the cave meanwhile, sensing their opportunity at freedom, raced towards the valley, chasing the other survivors.

"Where are you?" Zapata pleaded as he stood up. His weary yet excited eyes peered into the forest. Stono, who was toting a machinegun, and Azure, who was white-knuckling a sniper rifle, appeared like apparitions from behind a snow-covered thicket of pine trees. They had been planning to free their comrade ever since he was apprehended from the boat bound for Marseille a month earlier. Stono hotwired and stole a car, which the newlyweds had been living in the woods outside the monastery in Belchite, plotting Zapata's escape. They had originally planned to break him out of the monastery, which had been converted into a heavily fortified internment camp. The forced march into the mountains was fortuitous for the newlyweds because it finally provided a glorious opportunity to free Zapata.

"You didn't think we'd let you get to France without a proper goodbye, did you?" Stono said while slightly smiling. Zapata was relieved. He began sobbing as he hugged Stono tight around his neck, and then gave Azure, who was grinning graciously, a big kiss on her icy pink cheek. "You better get on down the mountain if you hope to make it to the depot by morning," Stono urged his friend. Zapata gazed a moment at the ragtag horde of prisoners trekking, trudging and stumbling through knee-high snow into the valley as fast as their frigid and exhausted legs could carry them.

"I'm not going," Zapata declared. "I'm going back to Barcelona."

"Don't be daft," Stono pleaded. "The endgame is to get to France, and then find a way to make it home to Maria and Versailles. Your nightmare begins to end just down that mountain." Stono pointed into the valley at the cadre of freed captives. Zapata gazed a long moment into the valley as a full moon began to rise over Spain.

"I'm going with you," Zapata said defiantly. "I'm going to stay and finish what we started."

"Please, man. I'm begging you,' Stono sighed. "Go home. There's nothing left for you here, if there was ever anything to begin with."

"Go on, Zapata," Azure pleaded. "Your wife and child need you more than the people of Spain."

"My wife and child are the people of Spain," Zapata declared as he proudly and determinedly marched towards the peak separating France from Spain. Azure and Stono shared a long sorrowful glance, and then reluctantly followed Zapata up the range towards Spain.

CHAPTER FIFTEEN

Barcelona, November 1937

A few days after Zapata's great escape from the Pyrenees, POUM vowed to retake the Barcelona telephone exchange. Part of the reason the anarchists were so initially successful repelling such a superior fighting force in the early stages of the war was because trade unionists, led by POUM, had control of the telephone exchange and could thus dictate what calls were transmitted in and out of Barcelona. As a result, those loyal or even sympathetic to the fascists had one hell of a time placing phone calls, which gave the revolutionaries a distinct strategic advantage. But the Nationalists were finally able to pry the building from the trade unionists in the days after the International Brigades disbanded and most had left the country. Once they possessed the exchange, the Nationalists were not about to relinquish it; it was too strategically important to winning the war. Whether the exchange stayed in the grasp of the Nationalists or was retaken by the revolutionaries could have potentially turned the tide of the war in the leftists' favor.

Albion, Zapata, Stono, Azure, and several other members of POUM, however, had serious misgivings about going into what seemed to be certain death by besieging what would be, due to the exchange's strategic importance to the outcome of the war, especially heavily guarded terrain. But all of those harboring reservations also felt bound by a kind of quixotic sense of honor and duty to each other to do anything in their power to take the exchange, even if it cost them their lives.

In the wee hours of Thanksgiving morning, 1937, Stono and Zapata hotwired a Fiat, which Azure stuffed full of 240 pounds of C4. At dawn, Albion plowed the Fiat turned mobile bomb into the telephone exchange. He jumped out of the car as it rolled into the entrance, hoping to escape with his life. Be he waited a half-second too long to exit the vehicle and was incinerated and killed instantly by the blast. Azure, who was serving as a sniper during the invasion of the telephone exchange mission, had a non-descript nest atop a seven-story apartment building across the street from the smoldering chasm in the exchange caused by the exploding Fiat.

A few frantic Nationalists hurried out of the building. Their arms covered their eyes and mouth in an attempt to ward off asphyxiation from the plumes of black smoke billowing from the building. Azure picked them off one-by-one as they scurried from the cauldron and into the street. Her days hunting rabbits with her father as a child was paying dividends in the warzone Barcelona had devolved into by 1937. Her sharpshooting provided necessary cover to three anarchists as they rushed into the burning building with fire extinguishers. Stono then led a dozen combatants, including Zapata, into the four-story fortress.

A fierce firefight ensued inside the exchange as Stono and his comrades cautiously inched up the stairs to the second floor. Stono lobbed a few Molotov cocktails into the stairwell leading to the third floor of the building. Fighting was far fiercer on the third floor. Nationalists took out half the POUM combatants with machine guns during a firefight lasting more than a quarter-hour. Running low on ammo, the Nationalists eventually retreated to the momentary reprieve provided by the fourth floor.

The fourth floor was the high-ground in the building, a battle ground. A machinegun strategically placed in the stairwell pinned down Stono, Zapata, and their comrades. POUM was determined to claim the building back. The goal of turning the tide of the war by regaining control of the exchange seemed a real possibility. One by one, the anarchists threw bodies at bullets, like the Lakota charging Custard and the Calvary. POUM's results were about as successful as Sitting Bull's Tribe. By the time the machinegun spewed its last bit of burning hot lead, only Stono and Zapata had survived the onslaught. Blood spewed from Stono's right eye socket, a terribly painful casualty caused by a jagged piece concrete and steel shrapnel that struck him during the firefight.

The last few surviving Nationalists were sans ammo and cornered on the roof by the time the sun was directly over Azure's snipers' nest on the seventh floor of the building across the street from the exchange. They had been trained and thus were prepared to fight the Americans hand-to-hand, if need be. That, however, was a moot point. Stono killed the last three surviving Nationalists cornered on the roof of the exchange with a perfectly thrown grenade he had been saving for just such a situation.

Zapata and Stono cautiously crept out onto the roof of the exchange. Stono waved up at Azure, who was gazing through her sniper scope from the top of the building across the street. She doffed her cap and smiled, then held her clenched fist victoriously high in the sky.

"No pasarán," she yelled elatedly.

The excited buzz caused by the sense of victory, however, dissipated in an instant. The feeling of pride she felt as a result of the notion that she had helped turned the tide of the war was replaced by dread and concern caused the rumbling buzz sound of a fighter plane's twin-engine fast approaching from behind. A Messerschmitt swooped down low, coasting within fifty feet of Azure's nest. The pilot let loose a chest full of tense breath as glanced back over his shoulder and unloaded the plane's payload, two tons of explosives, onto the roof. The massive blast of explosion killed Azure instantly, scattering her limbs and rubble on the street below. The seven-story building soon became a fiery inferno and collapsed.

Zapata hustled for cover on the roof of the exchange. Stono, however, was stunned, overcome, and heartbroken and thus could not move, though he tried. Moments after the plane dumped fiery death upon Azure's nest, two tanks barreled around the corner on both ends of the block and closed off the street. A division of Falangist infantry raced up the street towards the building, their boots click-clacking on the cobblestone street around the corner from the exchange. Stono and Zapata were boxed in.

"Come on," Zapata pleaded, "we've gotta get out of here,"

"I'm not going anywhere," Stono said dejectedly while wiping blood, puss, and tears from his eyes. "We've gotta hold the building until our reinforcements arrive."

"There are no reinforcements!" Zapata barked while peaking over the ledge at the troops closing in on the exchange. "There's nothing but fascists. Now please, come on." He hunched down next to Stono and tugged his arm.

"No," Stono said defiantly as he pried his arm free from Zapata's grasp. "You go, find a way to make it back to Maria and your little girl," he pleaded while shoving a grenade into his friend's trembling hand. "I'm not going anywhere. I'll cover you from up here. Now go!" Zapata reluctantly nodded his head and gave his friend a quick hug, hoping that some miracle would allow them to see each other again. Then he raced into the smoke-filled stairwell splattered with blood from scattered dead bodies. He inched past the smoldering Fiat, stepped over what was left of Albion's mangled corpse, and cautiously poked his head out from the blast crater. His frantic eyes quickly scanned both ends of the street.

The last Falangist infantry division had just rounded the corner when Zapata exited the building. From the roof, Stono sprayed a magazine of bullets in their direction, which caused them to stagger back around the corner, buying Zapata just enough time to sneak into a narrow cobblestoned alley adjacent to the exchange.

The tank at the north end of the street lobbed a massive artillery shell into the fourth story of the building. The explosion caused a searing chunk of shrapnel to rip into Stono's left arm and leg. He winced, wailed and grunted as he examined an artery on his arm that had been exposed and completely severed.

The infantry division regrouped quickly and made their way towards the gaping cavity leading into the exchange. Stono, whose now paralyzed arm was blood-soaked, dragged himself to his feet, leaned shakily over the ledge, lobbed a grenade over the side, and then haphazardly emptied what was left of his magazine of bullets, taking out seven enemy combatants as they tried to enter the building.

There was a prolonged hiatus before the Nationalists finally tried and enter the building again. They, however, assumed that entering the exchange was relatively safe due to the fact that Stono had resorted to dropping chunks of brick and mortar from the roof whenever combatants tried entering the building. Stono grew woozier and closer to death each moment. He listened intently as the sound of combat boots cautiously and slowly grew closer on the concrete steps from the third and then fourth floor until the Nationalists finally made their way to the roof.

Stono died just as the first wave of Nationalists appeared through the smoldering and smoky stairwell. A slight grin and sense of calm accomplishment washed over his face. "No pasarán," he said with his last breath. He clenched his fist and held it aloft as a final act of defiance. One of the infantrymen sprayed an entire magazine of bullets into Stono's body.

Zapata, meanwhile, had run nearly two miles in just over ten minutes, making his way through back allies, hoping to find the port, and ultimately a way to France. He finally found himself stuck behind a rundown restaurant and a dead end in the alley. He stayed there until the sun began to sink. He was paralyzed with fear and nervous exhaustion. The moon was high in the sky when he heard the boots of infantrymen marching in unison on a nearby street. He feared he would be captured. He thus reluctantly climbed into the dumpster behind the restaurant and closed the lid shut. The odious stench of rancid milk, meat, and dead rodents caused him to wretch reflexively. Though sick from the putrid smell mixed with the terror of being caught compelled him to endure the dumpster until just before daybreak.

Debilitating nausea finally trumped fear of being apprehended and compelled Zapata to crawl out of the dumpster. A beam of early morning light made his eyes sore. He squinted and took a deep breath as he brushed a piece of rancid chicken from his shoulder.

Hurried, though cautious, Zapata winded his way through the narrow alleys of the Ciutat Vella section of the city in the hopes of finding Port Vell Marina and potentially a boat that could escort him safely to France. Instead, he came upon a major thoroughfare bustling with laborers en route to factories, farmers on their way to market, and streetcars packed full with office workers whizzing up and down the street. He also saw a drowsy and somewhat hungover Falangist on the adjacent street corner gripping a machinegun between his hands.

Zapata dragged his tired and aching body aboard a streetcar as it buzzed by. He hoped he would go unnoticed. But his disheveled appearance and the horrid stench of rotten garbage emanating from him made it impossible for him to simply blend into the crowd. The streetcar conductor, fearing conflict and weary of being implicated in what he assumed was a convict's escape, quickly stopped the car and blew his whistle. A squadron of Falangist troops all donning powder blue shirts and khaki pants fast appeared at the front entrance of the streetcar. Zapata knew there was no escaping out of the front of the car, which was blocked by his would-be captors, so he shoved his way to the back as fast as he could. The hungover Falangist toting with the machinegun that was keeping watch on the block was, however, in hot pursuit behind the car.

Zapata lunged quickly through and open window, fell face first onto the slick asphalt, and then hobbled as fast as his sleep deprived body could carry him down a long, narrow, and winding street leading towards the sun soaked and glistening Mediterranean Sea. The hungover Falangist ordered him to stop. But Zapata was compelled by hope, fear and adrenalin to continue. And though he was terribly sick and exhausted from spending a godforsaken day battling fascists and watching his friends die, followed by a wretched night lying and breathing in rat infested trash, he made a mad dash into a narrow alley just a few blocks from the marina. The hungover Falangist was joined by a few of his comrades in pursuit of the fugitive. They gained ground fast.

Zapata darted left, back towards the bustling avenue the chase began. He snuck into a butcher's shop, which was the first door around the corner on the avenue, and ran through the back of the building and out towards Port Vell. *The Ciudad de Barcelona*, a small liner bound for Perpignan, left the port a few moments earlier. Zapata hobbled as hard as he could. His aching legs nearly gave out as he hurried along the hollow and somewhat wobbly boardwalk.

"Halt!" the hungover Falangist troop in pursuit demanded, "or I'll shoot!"

Zapata ignored the command and leapt headfirst into the frigid water. He was stunned by the initial shock of how frigid the water was. After what seemed to be an extended pause, he swam franticly after the boat, paddling with every modicum of strength left in his desperate body and soul. The hungover Falangist sprayed a round of hot lead, but the shot missed Zapata by less than three inches. A sympathetic crewman, a unionist that harbored anarchist sympathies equal to a hatred for fascism, was mopping the deck on board the *Ciudad de Barcelona*. He quickly dropped a lifesaver in the cold water. Zapata struggled mightily to grab onto it.

The hungover Falangist and one of his comrades fired rounds at Zapata just as he grabbed onto the lifesaver. A shot narrowly missed his leg. The bullets lodged in the side of the boats wooden hull. Zapata panted exhaustedly.

Though shivering, soaked in icy salt water, and nearing hypothermia, he felt a warm wave of elation as the boat steamed towards what he hoped would be the relative safety of open water between Spain and the South of France.

But, unfortunately for Zapata and the other 180 passengers aboard *The Ciudad de Barcelona,* as soon as the heroic crewman got Zapata to his feet and wrapped in a wool blanket, a long and menacing HIIISSSSSS sound, followed quickly by an earth-shattering explosion ripped into the starboard side of the boat. Passengers and deck furniture were thrown violently about in all directions and the vessel slowly began to sink.

Zapata and the heroic crewmen fell headlong over the railing of the deck, which was actually a lucky break compared to those trapped inside the ship that could not make it outside to a lifeboat. Many of them drowned in the hull of the boat, which was a tomb for hundreds of innocent bystanders unlucky to be on board *The Ciudad de Barcelona*. It plummeted in a matter of minutes to the floor of the harbor. The undertow of the sea swallowing the boat nearly pulled Zapata and the crewman under too. But they treaded water for nearly twenty minutes. The crewman finally lost his strength and bearings. His lungs filled with sea water and he finally sunk to the bottom of the sea. A few minutes after the crewman drowned, Zapata was overcome and lost consciousness. He bobbed on the surface of the water for a long moment, but finally began to sink. He was, however, fortune or not, fast approached by a tiny fishing boat that had been commandeered by the hungover

Falangist and a few of his comrades. They pried Zapata from the sea's death grip and then motored quickly towards shore.

CHAPTER SIXTEEN

Lower East Side, March 1938

Versailles, now a wobbly-legged toddler, leaned against the railing of her crib crying in the corner of a dim and musty room lit by a few half-melted red candles. Her gaping and tear-filled brown eyes gazed over the edge of the crib railing at her mother methodically massaging a middle-aged and somewhat dashing stockbroker who was a junior partner at a renowned brokerage firm a few blocks away from the parlor on Wall Street. The man, who was Yale educated and had grown up on Montague, had a tall and slender frame, long and lean hands, and slick-backed black hair with a few white streaks. He exhaled deeply, rolled over onto his back, and folded his hands like a pillow under the back of his head. His penis was erect and throbbing. "I'm in a rush, love," he said matter-of-factly. "Go ahead and finish me off." A wave of nausea crashed into Maria, who had already spent much of the day doubled over suffering crippling menstrual cramps. She inched away from the massage table and wiped the sticky coconut scented oil from her hands with a purple dishtowel. "I'm sorry, no," she said flatly. "My daughter is awake."

"I know she's awake," the broker sat up frustrated and he wrapped his thumb and forefinger around the base of his erection. "The goddamn kid's been crying the whole time I've been here. She's made it nearly impossible to relax. I won't pay you a dime for your time unless you finish me off." He gently wagged his dick, offering it to her.

253

"You sure as hell look relaxed to me," Maria said snidely as she chucked the towel over his groin.

"Stop wasting my time, you stupid guinea whore," the broker seethed while lurching from the massage table and on to his feet. "I didn't waste my entire lunch hour coming over to fucking Chinatown just so I could get some crumby back and shoulder rub. Time is money and I demand satisfaction— real satisfaction!"

"This is technically a massage parlor, sir, not a whorehouse," Maria said coldly. "Maybe some of the other girls might be willing to play hanky, but I'm not your readymade whore. I don't have to have sex with anyone I don't want to. I know my rights."

"Don't be daft with me, you silly whore," his voice vibrated with anger and embarrassment. "You might be just another idiot immigrant from the Old World, but you're not so dumb that you don't know goddamn well why men of means patronize places of ill repute, especially in China Town."

"I know my rights," she declared. "You came to a message parlor. You ordered a massage. I gave you a massage. You pay me for the massage!" She held her hand open waiting to be paid.

He lunged suddenly at her. She flinched and hurried to a small vanity next to Versailles' crib and grabbed a six-inch blade from the top drawer. She squeezed the butt of the knife tight inches from her assailant's scowling face. He snatched her wrist with the speed of a cobra strike. He squeezed her wrist with the force of a boa until the knife finally dropped from her hand.

The tip of the blade fell on his foot, gashing the soft flesh between his big and middle toes. The sudden sharp pain and sight of his own blood gushing from his foot pushed the broker into a blind rage. He belted her closed fist in the face. Her bottom lip split open. She fell back violently onto the massage table. A slight concussion caused her head to feel as though it was swaying to and fro. He pounced on her with the ferocity of a starving Bengal tiger.

His slender though sturdy hands wrapped all the way around her throat and neck. She clawed desperately at his face. The coconut oil stung his eyes a bit, but his grip did not loosen. It grew tighter the harder she struggled. She struggled with every ounce of might in her slight and underfed frame and tried to scream. But no air could get in or out of her lungs. Her screams were thus inaudible. Versailles' frantic crying kept the muffled sounds of Maria's distressed struggle from leaving the tiny dimly lit basement-level room.

Maria's bloodshot and tear-soaked eyes rolled back into her head. Her face turned lavender. She went completely limp. Her oil-sullied hands, which had been trying to pry the broker's long fingers from around her neck, dropped to her side as all life left in her had completely vanished from her diminutive body. One final gasp of air, the death rattle, escaped from her flaccid face. Her lifeless eyes gazed blankly at Versailles throwing a fit in her crib.

The broker, seemingly shocked by the site of Maria's limp and lifeless body, gasped as if he had an out-of-body experience and had only just regained his senses. He frantically shook her by the shoulders, hoping she might magically regain vital signs. Maria was, however, gone.

For a moment, the frantic broker thought of smothering Versailles to death to stop her from crying, but ultimately opted to hurry to get dressed and flee the crime scene quick as he could. He hurriedly pulled his navy-blue argyle dress socks onto his blood-covered feet. He then dressed quickly as could into his three-piece navy-blue pinstripe suit, and tied his recently polished black wingtips to his feet. He took a long, deep, and composed breath as he buttoned his waistcoat, slicked back his mussed hair with the palms of his trembling and aching hands, and then tried to look as nonchalant as possible as he fled the building through the nearby basement door down the hall from the parlor. The broker dashed up the small and dark staircase leading out to Ludlow Street. He cautiously scanned the sidewalk, fearful of seeing a beat cop making his rounds. But the sidewalk, which was covered in a layer of freshly fallen snow, was free of pedestrians.

The broker quickly headed west toward Wall Street. He glanced back over his shoulder at the crosswalk at Broadway. He was relieved that no one seemed to be following him. He was, however, terribly distressed that he was leaving a trail of warm merlot colored blood, which was seeping from his shoe, in the cold white now.

CHAPTER SEVENTEEN

Washington D.C, May 1938

The Republic of Spain finally collapsed in April 1939. The scholars and sundry other experts in such matters never expected the war to drag on for so long. The end of combat lead to widespread repression and festering wounds in Spain that have yet to completely heel. The end of the war also created a foreign policy crisis for countries such as the United States as a result of prisoners of war, such as Zapata, being held as bargaining chips by Franco.

In April 1939 – sixteen months after Zapata's internment in one of Franco's prisoner of war camps – the ever-irate J. Edgar Hoover was finally and begrudgingly summoned to President Franklin D. Roosevelt's Oval Office in the White House.

"I think we should let the bastards hang," Hoover said of Zapata and a few hundred other Americans wasting away from malnourishment, dysentery, and sundry other maladies in Spanish POW camps. President Roosevelt, who suffered from polio, rolled his wheelchair over to the window behind his desk. He lit a cigarette and gazed a long while upon the fresh morning dew that covered the west lawn. "Those traitors wantonly defied American neutrality laws," Hoover continued, "and I personally think they have committed treason. Let Franco deal with those turncoats however he sees fit. They're his problem now, far as I'm concerned."

"Look, Director Hoover," Roosevelt said somewhat defensively while exhaling a lungful of tobacco smoke, "I know those boys technically broke the law. But they are still Americans. You are a man of the law, so you of all people should understand best the vital importance of those men's right to due process, which they sure as hell won't get in Franco's dictatorship. Facing justice for their alleged crimes here in our court system, and not in some kangaroo court in a fascist country such as Spain, where they'd have no real chance of a fair shake, is a basic human right. Besides, Edgar, those boys had a courage and foresight none of us had. Hitler's Wehrmacht is rolling all over Europe while England and France stand idly by. Hell, it seems all but inevitable that there could be another world war any day now. Maybe, just maybe, our boys in Spain had it right all along and we, our blasted non-intervention agreements, got things all wrong."

"I respectfully disagree, sir," Hoover said while trying to conceal his animus for the president. "I still wholeheartedly believe Stalin and the Soviets are a far greater threat than Franco, Hitler, and Mussolini. At least we can do business with the fascists, which is a hell of a lot more than I can say for that madman Stalin. The fools rotting in Franco's camps went to fight for Stalin's interests and are therefore clear and present threats to the interests of the United States. My recommendation is to let them hang in Spain for their crimes. As far as I'm concerned, they forfeited the privilege of being American, including due process of American law, the moment they stepped foot on Spanish soil."

Roosevelt rolled his wheelchair from the window to his desk and glared pensively through a cloud of cigarette smoke up at Hoover, who was leaning forward with his palms flat on the president's desk. "Come on, Edgar. You know Henry Ford has a manufacturing plant in Russia. Besides, Chamberlain and Daladier cut a deal with the Germans," the president lamented. "If there's another world war, which seems all but inevitable, Stalin will, for good or ill, be our ally. We will have no choice but to do business with the Reds. So really, what does that say about all of us? If we are forced into a partnership with Stalin, aren't we – you and I – as bad, or just maybe as good, as those International Brigade fellas?"

"With all due respect, sir, Hoover tried to conceal his opprobrium, "I'm terribly afraid that war with the Russians is far more inevitable than war with the Germans is. The reason France and England cut deals with Hitler is so we all can avoid another world war. But Stalin is a madman. He can't be reasoned with. We're going to have to take him out sooner or later. I say, let Hitler deal with him."

"Look Edgar, you know damn well that I don't trust Stalin any more than you do," Roosevelt sighed. "But you're wrongheaded to think Hitler is a lesser form of evil than Stalin is. Any form of fascism, no matter what flag it is cloaked in, is equally insidious. Those American boys in Franco's prisons went to confront fascism. We need to bring them home. Besides, if there is in fact another world war, whether against the Russians, Germans, or Martians, we'll be all but desperate for men with the brand of courage, wisdom, and foresight – not to mention military experience – exhibited by those boys in Spain. Make the deal with Franco, Edgar. Bring our boys home. That's a direct order."

Spain, June 1939

The sun was just setting behind the watchtower overlooking the prison yard. Two drunk and embittered guards donning khaki shirts and trousers stumbled inside a barrack packed to the rafters with American, British, and Canadian prisoners of war. The stench inside the barracks, which was caused by the overcrowding of men into quarters that lacked proper sanitation and who were subsequently suffering from lice and dysentery, was inhumane. The first guard into the musty and dilapidated barrack stepped in a mound of feces left in the middle of the night by a hallucinating British prisoner dying of tuberculosis. "Goddamn these filthy swine!" the guard with the freshly soiled boot bemoaned.

The second guard winced and cupped his forearm over his nose and mouth while shining his flashlight in some inmates' gaunt, malnourished, and listless faces. The beam of light finally settled on Zapata. His head was shaved to the scalp, due to a recent lice outbreak amongst the prisoners. He was fevered so bundled in the fetal position, nearly shivering out of his stained and tattered britches. He was so sickly that his skin had a grayish taupe tint. His ribcage and collarbone were clearly defined. His aching and bloodshot eyes were sunken into his black and blue bruised face. "Here he is," the guard holding the flashlight said as the other scraped his soiled black boot on the wooden two-by-four board acting as the leg of a rickety readymade bunk bed, which was home to three British captives. The guards heaved Zapata up from his bunk. But his legs were too weak to stand and he collapsed to his knees, which banged the cold wood floor underneath so hard they began to bleed. The guards, who were reticent of touching Zapata, who was covered in filth, reluctantly dragged his listless body towards the egress of the barrack, including through the mound of feces left by the Brit with dysentery.

The stench caused the guards to cease breathing, which also made them struggle mightily to haul Zapata down three wobbly wooden steps outside the barrack. Once outside, the guards exhaled and took fresh breaths as they pulled Zapata's body into an open field soaked in late evening amber sunlight. The journey finally ceased fifty yards from the watchtower, at the steps of the makeshift chest-high gallows. Though Zapata had lost more than fifty pounds from an already slight frame since his capture by the Falangist in Barcelona sixteen months prior, the guards, who were spent from dragging him 100 yards from the barracks to the gallows, had great difficulty heaving the captive up the steps to the platform.

Zapata's legs were too weak to support enough weight to enable him to stand, which made placing the rope at the gallows around his neck especially difficult.

The guard with feces stuck in the grooves of his boot finally managed to string Zapata up. The prisoner's battered body dangled listlessly from his neck. His toes and bleeding knees barely touched the dusty wood of the platform underneath. His filthy bony hands, however, clenched tight to the rope. He put all the power left in his decrepit body into staying alive.

The second guard pulled the loose end of the rope with all his might as the other tried to pry Zapata's hands from the rope around his neck. The guard finally overpowered Zapata, who was literally fighting for his life. He tried to bind Zapata's hands behind the captive's lower back with twine. The knot caused the blood in Zapata's arms to cease flowing, which only made his struggle to stay alive that much more fiercely determined.

The guard with shit on his boot fought hard to hold the loose end of the rope. The force of gravity finally forced him to let it loose. Zapata dropped hard on his already bleeding knees. He coughed violently as he gasped for air. The annoyed guard meanwhile winced while inspecting the stinging pink and purple rope burns on the palms of his hands. "Fuck this!" he seethed. "Why don't we just shoot him instead?"

"To hell with that," the other guard said as he took the loose end of the noose into his hands. "The last time I shot one of these cock suckers, blood spurted all over my uniform. My wife had a hell of a time getting the stains out."

"Fine," the second guard lamented as he rolled his eyes and removed his Lugar from his holster. "You owe me one." He aimed the pistol squarely at some stubble on the back of Zapata's desiccated scalp, and then pulled the trigger. Zapata's eyes blinked frantically. The gun jammed.

The miffed guard confusedly inspected the dysfunctional hunk of metal in his hand. He jarred it a bit, blew hot breath hard into the barrel, cocked it once more, aimed it as Zapata's head, and then pulled the trigger. But the gun did not fire.

"Please," Zapata pleaded. "Whatever I did, I'm sorry. Please, I beg you. Don't kill me. I have a wife and child in America. They need me."

"Shut up,' the grizzled guard grunted as he smacked Zapata in the back of the head with the butt of the gun. "You should have considered your family before you came to Spain to fight a war that did not concern you or your family, you fucking murderer." He reluctantly holstered his defective weapon. "These fucking German handguns are such shit!" he seethed disappointedly to his compatriot. "Give me yours."

"Fine," his partner said begrudgingly while reluctantly handing over his weapon. "Try not to break this one too."

"Please, you don't have to do this," Zapata said through nearly inaudible sobs. "I never killed anyone. I came to Spain because just needed a job; I needed to provide for my family. That's the reason I came to Spain. Please, I just needed to provide for my family."

"Shush now," the guard said condescendingly and mercilessly as he cocked and aimed the pistol at Zapata's head. "Stop whimpering like a woman and die like a man."

Zapata sobbed as he dropped onto his belly and groveled. "Please," he begged. "I don't want to die. I don't want to die."

The guard's eager forefinger began to press the steel trigger down just as a loud and grating whistle from the watchtower cut through the humid evening air. Zapata and his assailants peered through the heavy rays of sun descending beyond the horizon and up at the guard station atop of the watchtower.

"Do not kill the American!" a shallow and muffled voice bellowed. "The Americans are not to be harmed anymore. Franco cut a deal to let them loose. We're in business with the Americans now." Zapata rolled onto his side and squinted up at the tower, afraid he was hallucinating.

"Fuck's sake!" the disappointed guard with feces on his boot lamented as he shoved the gun back into his partner's hand. His shoulders slumped forward dejectedly. "Fuck the Americans," he blurted. "Fuck Franco too."

"Dios Mio," the other guard's worried eyes were wide as he glanced up at the tower and then back to his partner, "watch what you say about the Generalissimo. You could easily end up in here with the rest of these swine." His nervous eyes cautiously glanced up towards the prisoner barracks. He quickly unbound Zapata's hands with the blade of a Swiss Army Knife, and then he hurried after his partner, who was storming across the open field towards the tower in hopes of gaining clarification.

CHAPTER EIGHTEEN

Port of New York, July 4, 1938

The boat ride past the Statue of Liberty along the Hudson River towards the Port of New York was especially emotional for Zapata. The red, white, and blue bunting, the old wooden boats plying the river, and the colorful fireworks exploding at sunset reminded him of his father's return from France after the "Great War." For the first time, Zapata was conscious of how emotionally and mentally his spirit had been transformed by war torn Spain.

Zapata spent most of the week crossing the Atlantic nervously pacing the neck, eagerly anticipating being reunited with his wife and child. He tried to wire Maria several times from the hospital, and also from the ship. He, however, never received any kind of response. He was especially worried that Versailles would have grown up and changed so much that he might not even recognize his own daughter. Worse yet, he was terrified at the thought that his daughter would harbor no memory of her father. Zapata was already underfed and very skinny when he left for Spain. He had lost another seventy pounds by the time he was freed from Franco's prison, but gained twenty of them back in the hospital. All told, he had shed fifty pounds and a lifetime of optimism and faith in there being any kind of inherent goodness remaining in human beings. He, however, hoped that some much-needed rest, relaxation, and quality time with his wife and child a world removed from a warzone would restore some modicum of his fleeting faith in the human race.

He quickly though cautiously navigated the gangplank of the ship to the dock hoping that the unanswered wires he had sent to his wife in the preceding weeks would have alerted her of his return. He prayed that Maria and Versailles would be waiting at the docks with big smiles and even bigger hugs. But the only people waiting for Zapata were two FBI agents donning fedoras, wingtips, and suit plucked from the bargain rack.

"Zapata Abrahams, I presume?" The bigger of the two agents said gruffly while flashing his badge. Zapata sighed deeply and reluctantly nodded his head, then handed over his passport as though anticipating apprehension by federal authorities upon his return. He glanced eagerly once more up and down the dock lining the Hudson River waterfront hoping to spot his wife's warm and smiling face. But she was nowhere to be seen. His heart sank as he was handcuffed, then led briskly towards a big black sedan idling on Ninth Avenue.

Local Precinct, Lower Manhattan, July 5 1939

After being apprised of his rights, a night of formulaic questioning, followed by a coerced loyalty oath he was made to sign, Zapata was finally permitted to make a phone call. He rang the apartment on Broome Street. But there was no answer. He expected Maria to be at work, and was thus not surprised that there was no answer. He was, however, terribly dismayed that the operator could not explain why the phone line had been disconnected.

His already heavy and breaking heart sank even deeper. He was overcome with angst when his public defender, a young Brandeis graduate who had only just passed the bar exam while Zapata was in the hospital, first came to visit him in his holding cell in lower Manhattan, just a few blocks from where Maria was murdered. "I've got to get out of here," Zapata pleaded with his lawyer. "I need to find my wife and child."

The young barrister, however, did not radiate optimism. "I'm sorry, Mr. Abrahams, he lamented. "The government has a pretty solid open and shut case against you and any of the other International Brigade volunteers that made it back. It was common knowledge the state department barred passage to Spain under threat of lengthy jail sentences and the potential of forfeiting citizenship. The Feds are, however, keen to cut deals and get this nonsense out of the papers as soon as possible."

"What kind of deal?" Zapata was suspicious.

"Plead guilty, serve three years in a federal penitentiary, but you get to keep your citizenship."

"Plead guilty?" Zapata seemed sickened. "I went to Spain to fight fascists, yet my government thinks I am the guilty party. What does that say about my government?"

The young lawyer, feigning interest in his client's not-so-hypothetical query shrugged his shoulders and surreptitiously glanced at his wristwatch, ever mindful of his next appointment. "Look, Mr. Abrahams, I see your point. But the quickest way to resume a somewhat normal life with your young family is to plead guilty, serve your time, and then close this chapter and put it behind you."

A deep and anxious sigh fled from Zapata's chest. He stared at the table separating he and his lawyer for what seemed to be an incredibly long and pensive moment.

"What's your decision," the impatient and overworked attorney prodded as he plucked his briefcase up from the floor next to his chair and plopped it into his lap. Zapata, however, was lost in his thoughts and did not seem to hear the question.

CHAPTER NINETEEN

Courthouse, Lower Manhattan, August 1938

In March 1939, Hitler and the Nazis invaded the Rhineland, Czechoslovakia. The joint occupation of Poland by the Nazis and Soviets seemed a foregone conclusion. Another world war seemed all but imminent by the time Zapata's trial for defying American neutrality laws began. In the weeks since returning to New York, Zapata had become a kind of cause célèbre. His internment in Spain and especially the federal government's prosecution of him and many other volunteers for the International Brigades grabbed headlines all through the summer, especially after Hitler began carving Europe into pieces.

By August, Zapata had become a kind of talisman celebrated by the city's progressives, many of whom came to think of him as a courageous man with the foresight and guts to confront fascism long before the U.S., England, and France were willing to. To conservatives such as Father Coughlin, J. Edgar Hoover, and Chancellor Cunningham, conversely, Zapata was anti-American and treasonous for openly defying American non-intervention laws.

During his hearing, the courtroom was packed full of people who supported him as well as those who prayed he would be convicted. Though Zapata, due in large part to Hoover's insistence, was charged by the federal government with treason and faced life in prison, he was far more consumed with the whereabouts of his wife and child, who he had yet to locate or contact since returning from Spain.

"Have you heard from Maria?" he whispered in his lawyer's ear while being led up the steps of the federal courthouse in lower Manhattan. His lawyer glumly shook his head. "Afraid not," he whispered. Zapata's heart sank. He had been featured in many newspapers stories since returning from Spain the previous month. He had hoped Maria would have seen at least one of the articles, and been able to track down his whereabouts.

Zapata, to his attorney's dismay, decided he could not in good conscience plead guilty. He also, fearing an unnecessarily drawn-out trial, waived his right to a jury trial, thereby leaving his fate in the hands of a federal judge. Judge Ochs, who was Harvard educated, and, like the defendant, grew up in the Bronx. There was a palpable buzz in the courtroom when Zapata and his lawyer entered the hearing room.

Ochs slammed his gavel many times until the crowd finally settled into reluctant and excited silence. Ochs wasted no time and pulled no punches.

"Mr. Abrahams," he said forcefully like a priest in a pulpit, "while I admire your courage to confront fascism in a foreign land, the fact of the matter is you confronted fascism in another land in violation of American neutrality laws. The laws were not created willy-nilly. They were designed to keep this country and its citizens from being tangled into matters that do not serve the interests of the average American. This country, the United States, suffered many thousands of casualties and many families were adversely affected by the violence and carnage of the 'Great War.' The neutrality laws passed in the wake of

"The Great War" were designed to protect average Americans like you, your family, as well as this great nation's treasure from being dragged into Europe's affairs and catastrophes. With that, do you care to address the court?" Zapata's lawyer nervously patted him gently on the shoulder as Zapata slowly stood and began to speak. Zapata scanned back over his shoulder, hoping to spot Maria's face in the audience. But no familiar face greeted his glance.

"Your honor," he said while clearing his throat, "I know I was technically in violation of federal law. But I felt that going to Spain in defense of their democratically elected government was a necessity in preserving principles fought for in the American, French, Haitian, and Russian Revolutions. These people," he motioned towards the polarized and charged audience assembled in pews behind him, "some of them think I'm a hero. Others think I'm a villain. The truth is I'm not a hero or villain. I'm neither guilty nor innocent. While I fully believed that those who went to the defense of the Republic of Spain were justified in their convictions and confrontation with Franco's coup and Hitler and Mussolini's forces, I did not want to leave my family to go to Spain. I much preferred to be with my family. But I was fired from my job at the Domino Sugar factory in the midst of a global economic depression and had no immediate way to earn a living for my family. The International Brigades seemed the only route available to making sure that my wife and child had a roof over their heads, coal in the furnace, and food on the table. The fact of the matter is, your honor, I am simply a working man who was desperate to find a way – any way – to provide for my family. If I'm guilty, so be it. I'll accept whatever punishment is deemed justice in the context of the United States' federal court system. But I plead with you for empathy and understanding of my situation and the pressure that forced me to make the decisions I made; to judge me not as a hero or a villain, but simply as a man who desired to do what was best for his family, by any means necessary."

Ochs, who was a proud Jew and a vociferous critic of Hitler since reading of the terrorism of Kristallnacht the previous year, was especially empathetic to Zapata. He was keen enough to know that the Great Depression had adversely affected tens of millions of New Yorkers, Americans, and working-class folks throughout the world. The Depression had forced people to confront impossible choices and obstacles. Most importantly, the judge understood all too well that people are shaped by their circumstances every bit as much as people have the agency to shape circumstances.

"Mr. Abrahams," he said while pushing his horn-rimmed glasses onto the bridge of his nose, "I think the federal government woefully exceeded its reach in charging you with treason. You did nothing to betray your country. In fact, I commend you for having the courage and foresight to fight in Spain, which in light of Hitler's recent invasion of Czechoslovakia, and his declaration of war on England and France, I now see as the first battles of what will, I fear, inevitably become a world war in which the U.S. will sadly be forced into. The fact is these neutrality laws almost certainly dissuaded England and France from intervening in the cause of the democratically elected

Popular Front government in Spain. The neutrality laws you technically violated were a key reason Hitler and Mussolini had the temerity to wage imperial campaigns in Africa and now in Europe. I find you not guilty of treason. I am, however, bound by law to find you guilty of violating neutrality laws. But I am suspending your sentence on time served. This court is adjourned."

A resounding murmur filled the chamber as the judge banged his gavel and then quickly exited the courtroom. Half the crowd cheered. The other half bemoaned the decision. Zapata's lawyer jollily slapped his client on the back. The media notoriety of the case, coupled with the positive outcome for his client, was a great victory and launching pad for the young public defender just starting his career. Zapata's reserved expression, however, did not budge an iota. He still had no idea where his wife and child were, and thus had no reason to show even a hint of joviality.

Zapata and his attorney descended the Romanesque steps outside the federal courthouse and waded through a throng of reporters towards the yellow cabs whooshing by on Pearl Street. Zapata's lawyer tried shielding his client from the swarm of reporters hurrying up the steps to confront them. The smattering of flash bulbs made Zapata feel a bit queasy, as did the bombardment of questions lobbed at him. He was now free and all he cared about was finding his young family. He was thus especially shocked and dismayed when callously asked by a reporter, "Mr. Abrahams, how long was your wife a prostitute?"

Zapata tried to speak but stammered confusedly before finally composing himself just enough to fumbled words from his mouth. "My wife was never a prostitute," Zapata said while glaring angrily at the reporter scribbling in a yellow notepad with pencil.

A second reporter held up the morning addition of *The New York Times*. The boldest headline read "Hitler and Stalin Cut Deal, Partition Poland." But it was the smaller and less distinct headline underneath that disintegrated Zapata's heart. "Arrest Made: Spain Volunteer's Wife Murdered in Chinatown Parlor," the headline read. Zapata was stunned and bewildered as he snatched the paper from the reporter's ink mussed hands. His panicked eyes scanned the content. His heart broke more with each word. He was nearly hyperventilating and his eyes were saturated with tears by the time he had read the fifth line of the story. He shoved his way through the fevered horde of reporters and pushed his way down the steps. He broke into a full sprint the moment the rubber soles of his Keds touched Pearl Street.

Zapata ran as hard as he could from Pearl Street to Broome Street. He ached for so long to finally return home. But now all he felt was fear as he rushed up the steps leading into brownstone. He twisted the handle of the door leading into the apartment, but the deadbolt was locked. His fist pounded the door. A frightened little Polish woman in her mid-fifties donning a stained red housedress nervously cracked open the door ever so slightly, just enough so one eye could peak into the hall. "Where's Maria?" Zapata demanded.

"Maria?" the bewildered Polish woman asked confusedly in a broken accent. "I know no Maria."

"She's my wife!" Zapata pleaded. "We live here! This is my apartment!"

"I'm sorry, but you are mistaken," the woman said cautiously, thinking Zapata had gone mad. "My family and I live here, now go," she said as she slammed the door shut and then dead-bolted the lock.

Zapata raced down to the super's basement floor apartment and banged on the door for more than a minute. The surly super finally cracked the door open ever so slightly. His bloodshot eyes grew wide. He was amazed Zapata was alive. "Where's Maria?" Zapata demanded.

"I'm not sure," the super said sheepishly as he ran his greasy fingers nervously across his scalp. "One of the tenants told me that she read in the morning edition that your wife was murdered in Chinatown. But I've not seen her since she moved out."

"Where's Versailles?" Zapata pleaded.

"Versailles?" the super seemed puzzled. "It's in France, I think?"

"Versailles is my daughter," Zapata seethed. "Where is she?"

"I'm sure I don't know," the increasingly nervous super said as he shrugged his shoulders with a dumbfounded expression plastered to his round and bloated face. "Maybe she was taken to an orphanage or something." He pushed the door shut and locked it. Zapata kicked the door as hard as he could. He nearly broke his ankle in the process, and then limped up the steps towards the front exit of the brownstone. He was in a daze, trying desperately to wake up from a bad dream, as he stumbled out of the building. His frantic eyes scanned Broome Street in both directions. His mind scrambled to think of where he had seen an orphanage. His mind was, however, too wound up to properly process information. Light rain began to fall. But he did not seem to notice. He stood inert, in a trance, for more than a minute.

A New York City policeman near the age of retirement with slick gray hair stuffed under his hat shuffled around the street corner with one hand on his radio and the other resting gently on the handle of his revolver. Zapata cut a suspicious figure standing motionless on the sidewalk. The cop assumed he was in a heroin stupor and cautiously approached the potential perp. "Hey pallie," the cop said in a thick East Brooklyn accent. "We got a dispatch from a lady who lives in this building," he explained. "Word is, a confused fella fitting your description was trying to force his way into her apartment."

"It's a terrible misunderstanding," Zapata said somewhat surprised, as though he had been suddenly woken up.

"Got any ID, pallie?"

"No," Zapata said. "I was incarcerated in Spain for several months. The FBI took my passport when I got back and have yet to return it."

"Spain?" The cop asked while squinting confusedly. "What's your name?"

Zapata reluctantly told the cop the truth. The cop radioed the name to headquarters. "Bring him in," a muffled voice blared through the receiver. "He's got a warrant for assault on employees at the Domino Sugar factory in Williamsburg."

The cop shoved his radio in the holster and began to unlatch his handcuffs from his belt. "Hands behind your back," he demanded.

Zapata shoved the cop with all the might he could muster and then raced around the corner of Broome Street as fast as his mangled ankle could carry him. The aging cop reluctantly chased his assailant a few blocks, begging him to "stop," lest he "shoot." But even hobbled by a sore ankle, Zapata was desperately running for his life, and thus much quicker than the cop, who had a foot in retirement. The ageing cop soon grew terribly tired of chasing an assailant more than half his age. He also had trouble removing his gun from his holder, fumbled it, and then dropped the weapon into the gutter, which permitted Zapata to flee the scene.

The confrontation and subsequent great escape from Broome Street helped jog Zapata's memory. He ran as fast as his sprained ankle would allow to the orphanage on Houston Street, which was the closest he could think of. He was panting and rain and sweat soaked by the time he entered the dilapidated Victorian mansion that had been converted into an orphanage in the 1920s. He placed his hands on his knees and panted as rain and sweat dripped from his nose onto the warped hardwood floor beneath his scuffed Keds. A somewhat bewildered but pretty and young Protestant woman with scarlet lipstick and bleached blond hair sitting at the reception desk carefully watched Zapata, who doubled over and struggling to catch his breath. "Can I help you, sir?" she finally asked in a nervous tone.

"I'm looking for my daughter," Zapata panted. "His mother was murdered in Chinatown while I was in Spain. Is she here, my daughter?"

"What's her name?" the woman asked determinedly as she opened the registry atop the reception desk.

"Her name is Versailles," Zapata panted, "Versailles Abrahams." I'm afraid I don't really know what she looks like anymore. She must have grown and changed so much since I last saw her." The woman had a befuddled and confused expression pasted to her cherubic face. Zapata tried hard to clarify. "I have not seen my daughter in many months, you see," he stammered. "She was very young when I left for Spain. She must be a toddler now. I doubt she'd recognize me at all."

The young woman began to be frightened that Zapata was unhinged and thus a potential threat to both of them. She thus proceeded with extreme caution. "What color is your daughter's hair, her eyes?" she asked timidly.

"She has brown eyes, and I imagine dark hair like me and her mother. The mother is Italian, and I am of Jewish ancestry, so dark features."

"Well," she said in the hopes he would abandon his search and leave before anyone was hurt. "We haven't received a child that quite fits that description for quite a while now. We got a little Negro in last week, but no Jews or Italians for some time now. Tell you what, if you leave your name and contact information, we can contact you if a child fitting the description of your daughter is brought in."

"I don't have any contact information," he said dejectedly. "I'm currently homeless and so I don't have a mailing address or phone."

"Well then," she said somewhat distressed as a concerned sigh escaped her being, "perhaps you should contact the department of child services, or perhaps check some of the other orphanages in the city. There are several new ones since the Depression hit. More and more people can take less and less care of their children. It's tragic."

Zapata nodded disconsolately, and then hurried out of the Victorian and down the steps to Houston Street. He raced towards the telephone booth outside a dingy hourly motel across the street from the orphanage. He frantically thumbed through the phonebook quick as he could in search of the address for child services. After searching for nearly a minute, he found the number. He dug deep into the pockets of his trousers hoping to find a nickel to call child services. His pockets were, however, empty. He tore the sheet with child services' address out of the phonebook, shoved it into his pocket, and then sprinted across the street and around the corner onto Canal Street, which was packed vendors hocking and hustling wares.

Back inside the orphanage, a young Protestant couple that had had a great deal of difficulty conceiving a child during their first two and a half years of marriage entered the reception area. The young wife had sandy blond hair and hazel eyes. The husband had a head full of red hair and blue eyes. They were greeted warmly by the girl with bleached blond hair and scarlet lips, and then led into the back-office area, where they were met by an aging patrician woman from the Upper West Side with silver hair and a slight case of kyphosis, causing her to hunch forward a bit. The old woman winced a bit while shaking the young husband's hand. The wife, meanwhile, made a beeline for the toddler sitting calmly in a crib in the corner of the office.

"Is this her?" the wife asked excitedly. She drank the child's calm mien in with wide and tender eyes, and then scooped the toddler into her arms.

"That's your new daughter," the patrician matron exclaimed through a refined Central Park West accent.

"She looks a tad Jewish," the father said, barely attempting to conceal his disappointment.

"Yes, she is of Jewish stock, I'm afraid," the matron lamented. "But the mother was also half Italian. The child has Roman blood coursing through her veins."

"That's a relief," the young mother said as she kissed the somewhat bewildered child on her pudgy and slightly pouting cheek. "To be perfectly honest," she continued, "I don't care if she's a Martian. She's positively precious."

"You both will be such a godsend to this little one," the matron explained. "She's had a terribly rough go of it of late. Her mother was murdered in Chinatown while his father was fighting for the Communists in Spain."

"My dear," the husband was aghast. "Where's the father now?"

"Last I heard, he was reported as missing in action," she explained. "Apparently he deserted his unit and was never heard from again."

"You see, honey," the husband assuaged his wife, "I told you it might be a blessing that we couldn't conceive. Perhaps it is God almighty's plan to be providence to this little one." He tenderly shook the child's pudgy little hand.

The woman gently pressed the child's cheek to hers and warmly snuggled her. "Perhaps you're right, dear," the wife beamed, "perhaps you're right. I can't wait to get this little one to the farm. She'll have an absolute ball living in Westchester, away from this dirty city. This awful jungle is no place for a child to be raised."

"Any ideas what you might call the child?" the matron asked.

"Victoria," the young wife proudly declared, "after Queen Victoria."

CHAPTER TWENTY

Downtown New York City, August 1938

Zapata was covered in sweat and rain by the time he arrived at Child Services on Fourteenth Street and Third Avenue. He could hardly breath or form words through frantic breaths, and appeared properly psychotic to the girls working the reception desk in the lobby.

His blood pressure finally lowered just enough for him to explain that his wife had been murdered and that his daughter might have been made a ward of the state while he was incarcerated in Spain.

The girls at the counter were incredibly warm and sympathetic to Zapata, who was clearly coming unraveled. A lovely young black girl promised to do all in her power to find an answer for the heartbroken and frightened father desperate to locate his daughter. The girl spent a quarter hour digging through file cabinets in the basement archive. Each minute felt like a lifetime to Zapata, who paced relentlessly back in forth in the cramped waiting room white knuckling the morning edition of the New York Times, reading and rereading the article about the stockbroker who had confessed to murdering Maria in a Chinatown parlor because she refused to sexually gratify the insistent broker.

The girl finally returned from the basement archive with a manila folder tucked under her arm. Her face expressed a strange mix of accomplishment and confusion.

"Versailles Abrahams," the girl spoke in a confident and smoky tone. "Here's her file."

Zapata snatched the file from the girl's hand. His eyes guzzled the information faster than his frantic mind could process it. His heart ached that the picture of the little girl in the file photo looked so much older than the child he remembered. 'She's done so much living without me,' he silently lamented.

"I don't understand," his voice quaked and quivered. "She's was taken to the orphanage on Houston Street last month?" He was baffled. She's at the orphanage on Houston?"

"If that's what the file says," she nervously nodded her head while shrugging her shoulders.

He reflexively raced for the egress leading out to Fourteenth Street with both the morning edition and file tucked tightly under his arm. "Excuse me, sir," the girl called after him, "you can't take the file. It's state property!"

Zapata did not pause. Even if he had heard her, he would not have relinquished the file, especially the snapshot of his daughter.

The sight of Zapata manically sprinting up the rain-slicked steps through the French doors of the Victorian made the cherubic faced blonde's stomach clench in knots. She had wished the young Protestant couple the best of luck with their new daughter Victoria, who the girl knew damn well was named Versailles. "Where's my daughter?" Zapata forced from his lungs through thick and heavy breaths.

"I'm sorry, sir, I'm quite sure I don't have a clue what you're talking about," she assured him. "I already told you that we had not received any children fitting her description in quite some time."

"Bullshit," Zapata growled while holding the manila folder aloft. "I went to child services; I know she's here. Now, where is she?" His darting eyes quickly scanned the premises. He located a grand staircase attached to the foyer. "She's up there, isn't she?" He moved quickly towards the staircase as the concerned matron appeared from the first-floor office.

"What's the source of all this commotion?" she demanded.

The blonde's fear filled eyes pointed to Zapata who was stalking towards the staircase, which alerted the patrician matron. "I'm terribly sorry, sir," she said forcefully, "You are not permitted upstairs."

"My daughter is up there," he said matter-of-factly while fast ascending the steps.

"What's the meaning of this?" the matron demanded of the frightened blond.

"It's the little Jew girl's father," the blond explained.

"He's alive?" the matron seemed astonished.

"Apparently so," the blond slightly nodded.

Upstairs, Zapata pushed his way into the nursery and quickly scanned the faces of a dozen children. None were familiar. He poked his head into a few other doors, but he saw no sign of Versailles. He hurried back downstairs.

"I need a policeman at the orphanage on Houston Street as quickly as possible," the blond whispered into the telephone as the matron rushed into the foyer, hoping to usher the manic father towards the exit. Zapata snatched the matron's sagging throat and pinned her against the wall.

"Where is she," he demanded. The matron feinted. The weight of her body was too great and Zapata was forced to let loose of her neck. She slid to the floor. The terrified blond feared her boss might be dead. Her trembling hand hung up the phone. Zapata made a beeline for her. "Tell me where my daughter is, or I will kill you." The blond frantically nodded her head and quickly, though cautiously, crept into the matron's office. Her mind was scrambled, so she had trouble unlocking the file cabinet and fingering through the folders. "Hurry up," Zapata screamed. Her entire body quivered and she wet herself before finally locating Versailles' file.

"Here," her hands quaked as she held it towards him. He snatched it from her. "The name and address of her adopted parents are in here. Now, please, just go."

"Her adopted parents?" Zapata was befuddled. He peered into the blonde's hoping she could elaborate. Her terrified eyes seemed to soften ever so slightly as they darted towards the French doors leading into the Victorian. The very same cop Zapata had tussled with on Broome Street was cautiously ascending the steps from the street with his gun drawn. Zapata tucked both files and the soggy and smeared morning edition under his arm and made a beeline for the exit. Zapata shoved the ageing cop, who fumbled his pistol as he stumbled back down the steps. The dazed cop scrambled to retrieve his weapon, but Zapata got to it first. The elderly officer climbed to his haunches and watched helplessly as Zapata rounded the corner.

He ran and ran, fueled by mania and adrenalin until his legs finally gave out in alphabet city. His sprained ankle throbbed, but he was too consumed by emotional agony to pay the physical pain too much attention. He rested a while on a park bench next to a basketball court on Avenue C. He thumbed through the files taken from the orphanage and discovered, to his great dismay, that a family living in Westchester, Pennsylvania had adopted his daughter. He was so deeply engrossed in the file that he momentarily forgot he was a fugitive who was almost certainly being hunted by every on-duty member of the New York City Police Department who had access to the police radio within the preceding half hour. The incessant sound of several cars pinned in behind an incredibly rude motorist who had left his Buick sedan idling on the one-way avenue as he attended to a pressing matter inside one of the brownstones. Zapata watched half-interestedly as car after car piled up, each with peeved motorists blaring their horns in the hopes that the owner of the Buick would return and move the car out of the way. Zapata, as if in a dream, floated over to the car and looked inside. The keys were plugged into the ignition. He scanned up and down the avenue, and then finally opened the driver side door. He plopped the files and morning edition in the passenger seat. The owner of the Buick hurried out of a nearby building just in time to see Zapata hop in the driver seat. "Hey!" the owner of the Pontiac screamed as Zapata put the car into drive. "Stop," he pleaded as the Pontiac rounded the corner, "that's my car!"

CHAPTER TWENTY-ONE

Westchester, Pennsylvania, August 1938

Zapata was amazed that the farm in Westchester was so eerily similar to the one he had dreamed of one day buying for Maria and Versailles. It was as though the young Protestant couple had stolen his daughter and his dreams for the future. He was scared the entire time he staked out the residence. He hunched low in the Buick until well after midnight. He wrestled internally for hours debating whether he should attempt to take her, or let the court system sort the mess out. He was, however, afraid that since he was technically a convicted felon that the state might side with the adopting parents over him. He was not willing to risk it. The even greater fear that seemed to paralyze Zapata was getting caught kidnapping the child and thereby forfeiting his newfound freedom and his daughter in one fell swoop. "They never found the guy who took Lindbergh's baby," he repeated under his breath over and over as he pried the screen off the bay window leading into the living room.

He crept as softly as his sprained ankle would permit up the narrow wooden staircase. His eyes had adjusted somewhat to the dark by the time he made it to the second floor of the house. He poked his head into the master bedroom. His heart paused and his breath seemed especially heavy and loud as the young woman rolled over and draped her arm around her husband's heaving chest. Zapata's art pounded so hollow that he was sure it would wake the young couple up, so he inched further down the hall.

The door leading into Versailles' room creaked ever so slightly as he entered. It sounded loud as an avalanche to Zapata, who was fully on edge the moment his psychotically determined eyes made contact with Versailles. She was wide-awake, gazing up at the jungle animals on the mobile dangling over her crib. She smiled at her father. "She recognizes me," the words quickly and quietly slipped from Zapata's lips. He nearly cried as he scooped her into his arms.

She cooed slightly as he crept past the couple's bedroom towards the staircase. The woman sensed a presence and sat up in bed and trained her ear towards the darkness outside the room. She wondered if it was merely her imagination that sensed something methodically descending the staircase. The phone rang the moment Zapata's scuffed Ked made contact with the foyer floor.

The young wife shook her husband awake. "What is it?" He groggily queried. "Who could be calling at this hour?" He yawned as he slowly pulled his bathrobe over his broad shoulders and slid his slippers onto his feet.

The sound of the phone and stirring up stairs sent a wave of terror through Zapata. His hands trembled so violently that he feared he might drop Versailles as he struggled to unlatch the deadbolt lock on the front door. Zapata squeezed the front door shut behind him just as the young husband was beginning to descend the staircase. He, fearing, he would lose the call, rushed down the steps and into the foyer and plucked the receiver. "Hello," his voice was quiet and gravelly. His attention, however, seemed to grow laser focused with each word he heard. His tired eyes quickly transformed into worried determination. "I see," he blurted. "Hang on one moment." He left the receiver dangling as he raced up the stairs two at a time.

"What is it?" the young wife's voice was frantic as her husband raced by the room and hurried down the hall into Versailles' room. His distraught eyes quickly scanned the room. "She's gone," he stammered as his wife rushed into the room. He ran back down the stairs and plucked the receiver up. "She's gone," he screamed into the phone, "she's gone." He hung up the phone and, compelled by instinct, walked out onto the front porch to see the taillights of a Buick speeding west, kicking up dirt behind it.

CHAPTER TWENTY-TWO

Route 66, Amarillo, Texas, September 1938

Zapata's weary eyes stared lifelessly at the yellow lines on the highway, which were illuminated by a new moon over head, flash by on Route-66 just west of Amarillo, Texas. He had been driving for more than 30-hours straight with no game plan or set destination. He just knew he had to get as far away from New York and Westchester as fast as he possibly could, lest he risk losing his freedom and, worse yet, his daughter. The car radio blared a hokey episode of *Amos 'n' Andy* in which Kingfish duped his brothers in the Mystic Knights of the Sea Lodge. Zapata, however, paid the program little mind. The only reason he kept the radio on was to help him avoid dosing off and veering into a tree. His tired mind was far more occupied by Versailles crying profusely in the back seat than it was with the adventures of Amos & Andy.

All four windows of the Buick were rolled completely down in an unsuccessful attempt to air out the smell of the child's soiled diaper. The needle on the dashboard that gauges whether the car has a full or empty tank of gas was all the way right of the E. Zapata knew the car would break down any moment if he did not get gas very soon. He was also as desperate for diapers and he was gas. He, unfortunately, was penniless.

He had had modest success filling up the tank and simply speeding away without paying from a several unfortunate gas stations between Pennsylvania and Texas. But by the time they had zoomed through Amarillo, he desperately needed provisions for his fussy toddler, as well as a full tank of fuel. Normally, he would have had few qualms about robbing a store to get essentials to living. But having Versailles to look after complicated things. Zapata glanced in the rearview mirror. Versailles was plopped atop the vinyl backseat and wrapped in a dirty diaper. She was fidgeting and crying profusely. Zapata's face was contorted. The stench made him gag. He saw no alternative to risking an armed robbery.

The car skidded to a halt at an all-but-abandoned Texaco station on the side of the lonely highway. Zapata left the pump plugged into the tank filling the car with gas while he tried to act as nonchalant as possible as he entered the service station. The bells fastened to the entrance of the store alerted the adolescent girl with a head full of sandy blond hair flipping through the newest edition of *The Saturday Evening Post,* the cover of which had a quaint Norman Rockwell drawing depicting a little black girl waving an American flag. She was no older than 18 years old, and seemed unconcerned that a peculiar stranger had entered the establishment.

Zapata made his way to the rear of the store, where he found a small shelf with a modest selection of provisions for young children, including Pampers disposable diapers, and carrot flavored Gerber baby food. He wedged the diapers under his arm, then stacked a few jars of carrot flavored gelatinous gruel on top of them. He then walked as calm as he could to the front counter, where the young girl was flipping through the magazine and chewing a mouthful of chewing gum.

"Anything else?" the girl mumbled a thick Texas panhandle twang through a garbled mouth full of gum.

"Let me have one of those Snickers bars too," he replied while noticing a copy of *The Dallas Morning Star* with a startling headline that read: 'Hitler and Stalin Partition Poland.' His heart sank as he lamented all he had lost in the failed attempt to stop the spread of fascism. "I'll take this newspaper too," he said somberly.

The young Texan turned around on the heel of boot to fetch the candy bar as Zapata wedged the newspaper between the diapers and his elbow. She tossed the candy bar on the counter, then flinched and took a quick and hard step back.

"I'm sorry," Zapata was as apologetic as an armed robber could be while aiming the pistol he took from the elderly cop in Manhattan. "I don't have any money. I'm sorry about having to rob you. I don't want to hurt you. But I am a desperate man and I will hurt you if I have to. Don't do anything stupid. Now, empty out the cash register."

"Please mister," the girl sneered, "I only took this job to save for a prom dress. My daddy will never let me go to the dance if I let the store get robbed."

"I guess times are tough for damn near everyone now and days," he lamented while glancing out at Versailles standing in the backseat and looking frightfully out the window of the Buick. "Empty it, fast" he cocked back the hammer of his pistol and motioned towards the cash register.

The girl begrudgingly emptied the register and slid forty-seven dollars and thirty-three cents across the counter. Zapata stuffed the pistol into the waistband of his BVDs, then the cash into the pocket of his Levi's. He left the Snickers bar sitting atop the counter as he backed cautiously but quickly towards the store exit. He pushed open the door with his tailbone, which caused one of the jars of Gerber to shatter on the concrete slab just outside the store.

Versailles was still balling at the top of her lungs as her father hurriedly tossed the diapers and food into the passenger seat, and then jumped into the driver's seat. Zapata floored the gas pedal. The car, however, had a bit of trouble exiting the station because Zapata neglected to remove the gas pump handle from the car, which pulled the entire pump over onto its side.

The incensed teenager raced out of the store clutching a double-barrel shotgun that was half her size. She fired a round, which nearly knocked her over. A bit of buckshot lodged in the trunk, bumper, and also busted the rear-right taillight of the Buick as the car sped west on Route-66. Zapata peered concernedly in the rearview mirror at Versailles, who continued to sob disconsolately.

Route 66, Kingman, Arizona

An incredible meteor shower cascaded across the gaping western sky as dawn finally broke over Arizona's high dessert. Zapata, however, was too exhausted to admire how majestic the picture around him was. He had not eaten or slept in more than forty-two consecutive hours. His weary eyes stared lifelessly at the highway, but glanced up into the rearview mirror every so often to check on Versailles. She had calmed soon after Zapata changed her diaper and fed her carrot-flavored gruel, and eventually fell asleep. Zapata's eyes seemed slightly calmer and more focused each time he looked at his young daughter, who was curled quietly as she snoozed atop the backseat of the Buick.

The car zoomed by a massive field full of lush red strawberries soaking in early morning sunlight and dew, which were being diligently harvested by a small army of migrant workers. Zapata was amazed by the fact that the newly built Hoover Dam and government sponsored irrigation projects and roads had so quickly transformed such a vast and inhospitable dessert into some of the world's most fertile soil, which attracted migrant workers from all over the world, especially south of the border. He sardonically wondered why the government could alter and transform billions of years of ecological development, yet could not demolish the class system that kept the harvesters who slaved away in those fields from sunup to sundown mired in lives defined by abject poverty.

His pensive lamentation was, however, disrupted suddenly by a hollow bang and popping noise caused by the sound of a metal rod deep inside the Buick's engine snapping in half. It was so loud, that many of the pickers in the field flinched, thinking it was the sound of a shotgun. Versailles woke suddenly and seemed a bit dazed and out of sorts. Fumes spewed from the Buick's engine and the car gradually slowed until it came to a complete stop on the side of the highway, which ran adjacent to the to the strawberry fields. Zapata inspected the engine as best as he could. But his automotive expertise was terribly limited.

Versailles grew fussier with each degree hotter the dessert got. It was well past four in the afternoon and much hotter than one hundred and ten degrees by the time Zapata figured it best to try and hitchhike to the next town in the limited hope of getting the car repaired. He changed Versailles' diaper, fed her a few bites of Gerber gruel, and then headed west directly into the hot and heavy setting sun. He held Versailles in his arms for quite a while. But she was blistering hot and thus terribly upset the entire time her father held her. They watched dozens of cars speed by on the highway, but none stopped to offer the disheveled father and his young daughter assistance.

Sleep deprivation and heat exhaustion began to get the best of Zapata who, by sundown, was as irate as he was famished. Versailles had finally dozed off, so Zapata took the opportunity to sit a spell next to a massive cactus adjacent to the highway. It was dusk and getting dim quick by the time he spied a late model Ford truck slowly approaching in the distance. He was, however, too tired and demoralized to hold his thumb aloft. He had already suffered enough rejection.

Luckily the truck, which was packed full of weary and sun stroked laborers who had been picking strawberries since before dawn, slowed to a halt on the side of the road a few hundred yards from the idled Buick. A handsome, albeit dirt covered young worker no older than the girl

Zapata had robbed at the Texaco outside Amarillo smiled as he beckoned Zapata towards the bed of the truck.

"What's the trouble"" the young man asked.

"My car broke down," Zapata said as he gazed back behind him at the disabled Buick off in the distance.

The young man hollered at the driver in Spanish. The driver, who was nearly twice as old as Zapata, hollered back. "We can give you a tow," the young man smiled. "My uncle… he can fix anything. He says he will give you a tow and fix your car."

"That would be incredible," Zapata exclaimed. His weary eyes grew wide. He was shocked by the graciousness and generosity provided. "Are you serious?"

"Of course," the young man grinned and waived Zapata onto the truck. "It's no trouble."

He lowered the lift gate leading up to the truck bed and helped steady Zapata as he, with Versailles tucked tight to his sweat soaked chest, climbed on board. All of the bushed workers stuffed onto the truck bed were enervated from a full day of backbreaking labor. None, however, expressed the slightest hint of resentment as the truck raced back towards the debilitated Buick broke down next to the strawberry fields.

"Philberto," the young man offered his calloused and dirt covered hand to Zapata, who gladly shook it. Philberto was surprised and interested in learning the origin of Zapata's name. "Your parents named you after a hero of the Mexican Revolution?" he prodded.

"My father escaped from Russia during the Pogroms," Zapata explained. "The old man was always fascinated by the American, French, Haitian, Mexican, and Russian Revolutions. He regretted not being able to take part in the Russian Revolution, especially since it was against the very same royal family that he had to flee from when he was a kid."

Philberto seemed genuinely interested. Zapata was impressed with the teenager's sense of curiosity and the emotional intelligence. Most of all, he was especially thankful for Philberto's and his uncle's magnanimity.

Zapata stood next to a cactus clutching tight to Versailles, who had finally nodded off as Philberto quickly secured a rope from the back bumper of the Ford and attached to the front end of the Buick.

The moon was high in the sky by the time the Ford full of workers made it to a humble but jovial collection of canvas tents on the outskirts of Kingman – just across the Arizona-California border from Barstow. Zapata was especially struck by the sense of community he witnessed in the humble tent city assembled. People played festive music, shared delicious foods with each other, guzzled beer, danced joyously, and sang merrily as though they did not notice that they were mired in slave like conditions. Zapata, whose war-weary spirit had been broken too many times to count, was particularly impressed by how full of love and life the workers seemed to be after a day of soul crushing labor. He wished he possessed such a durable soul.

Early the next morning, which was a Sunday, Philberto, who seemed somewhat dismayed, cautiously waked Zapata, who was in a deep slumber next to Versailles atop a second-hand cot covered with a dusty wool blanket. "I'm sorry," Philberto lamented, "but Tio Carlos said your car... it blew a rod. He will have to order the part from Los Angeles.

"I see," Zapata said as he wiped some crust from his sleep-deprived eyes. "How long will it take for the part to get here?"

"It could take a few days," Philberto shrugged his shoulders slightly, "maybe a week or two. Mail is usually pretty slow out here. You are welcomed to stay with us until your car is fixed, if you want."

"I don't want to be a bother."

"It's no bother, really. You can stay as long as you like."

"How much is the part?"

"Ten, maybe twenty bucks."

"Okay," Zapata dug deep into his pocket and pulled out the forty-seven dollars and thirty-three cents. Philberto was impressed by what he considered an ample amount of money. Zapata handed two ten-dollar bills to Philberto, who hurried from the tent with the cash in hand. Zapata softly kissed his daughter on her forehead and pulled the wool blanket snugly over them both. For a fleeting moment, he felt as though he may have found a home.

Although Philberto seemed impressed with forty-seven dollars and forty-seven cents, Zapata knew he would be hard pressed to raise his daughter unless he soon found work. He was a fugitive with no job prospects, and was stranded in the far west with no means of transportation. His primary concern was providing for his daughter. But he had no idea how he would be able to raise a healthy child while on the lam.

He eloquently expressed his concerns about locating employment to Philberto at the sundown dinner enjoyed by the workers on the Catholic Sabbath. "Work with the rest of us," Philberto urged his new friend. "We don't get paid anything near what we deserve and the conditions are terrible. But a gringo such as yourself could maybe be able to stick with it a while – at least until your car is fixed."

"Whom do I speak to about gaining employment?" Zapata, who had been through trench warfare and was thus undaunted by the idea of picking strawberries, prodded.

"You need to speak to Mr. Rush," Philberto's voice lowered an octave, "He owns the land. His son Edgar, he's the guy who oversees the operation. Both are assholes. But they are always looking for new field hands because they are always losing field hands."

"Why are they always losing workers?" Zapata was curious.

"All kinds of reasons," Philberto shrugged his shoulders slightly. "Sometimes people just can't take anymore and the leave. It's tough, soul crushing work. Lots of people can only do it so long before they break."

The next evening after the workers returned from the field, Zapata left Versailles with Alejandra, Philberto's cousin. She stayed at tent city with a few other young ladies to look after the children as the others toiled the fields. Philberto borrowed his uncle's truck and escorted Zapata three miles east on Route-66 until they came upon a compound that housed the proud owners of the strawberry fields on which the migrants labored six days a week from sunup to sundown.

Mr. Rush was a gangly man in his late-fifties with gaunt and grayish facial features. He originally hailed from Oklahoma. He chain-smoked cigarettes and had a half-grapefruit and full glass of Wild Turkey straight bourbon whiskey each morning for breakfast. He was plastered by the time Zapata nervously crept into the makeshift office. He glared suspiciously across the wobbly card table used as a desk as Zapata slunk into the foldout chair.

"Edgar tells me you're interested in working with our beaners?"

"That's right," Zapata proceeded, "I'm hoping to work some hours and make some cash while my car is being repaired."

"Uh huh," Mr. Rush exhaled a deep lungful of tobacco smoke. "And where ya headed when your car is fixed?"

"I'm headed west, to California."

"What's waitin' for ya in Cal-i-for-ni-a?"

"I'm not quite sure just yet," Zapata shrugged slightly. "I just felt it was time to get out of New York. California seems like a better place to raise my daughter than the city."

"I'm not quite sure this place is the right for ya," Mr. Rush said matter-of-factly while spewing smoke from his tattered lungs. "I need a gringo from back east fillin' the bean eaters' heads full of European ideas like I need a second asshole."

"Look," Zapata tried to assure the landowner, "I'm no labor organizer. I'm just a father who's stranded and needs to find a way to make ends meet until my car is fixed and I can keep on heading west. Simple as that."

"You see, son, the real problem out here is, the beaners are illegal aliens, which means we can pay them under the table. They don't make a minimum wage, which they don't mind so much because we still pay em a helluva lot more than the caudillos across the border ever would. But to a while fella such as yourself, we can't pay you a minimum wage, which thanks to goddamn FDR, means we'd be breakin' federal law. You bein' an American complicates things, ya see."

"Well…" Zapata suggested while smiling wryly, "just pretend I'm not an American. I do it all the time." He chuckled.

Mr. Rush glared hard a moment at Zapata as though his quip was blasphemous. A nervous knock outside the landowner's quarters, however, diverted his attention. "Yeah," his brusque voice beckoned the overseers' son, Edgar, who was in his early twenties, into the office. He nervously whispered into his father's ear. Mr. Rush did not welcome the news. Rush nodded and motioned for his son to excuse himself while putting out his cigarette in the ashtray atop the wobbly card table.

"Guess it's your lucky day," Mr. Rush sneered, "if you could call it that. We had some defectors today and are a few hands short. Looks like we might have a bit of work for you until we can get a new crop of beaners across the border. Rest up. You start first thing in the morning."

A wave of relief washed over Zapata. He stood fast and offered his hand across the card table for Mr. Rush to shake. The landowner, who preferred not to think of workers in his employ as human beings, gazed condescendingly at Zapata's hand a moment before giving it a quick and tepid shake.

Zapata and several other workers were already covered in sweat by the time the sun peaked over the mountainous horizon behind them. Mr. Rush's son, Edgar, and the half-dozen other overseers toted shotguns and rode horses up and down the hedgerows as they sipped coffee from canteens. Edgar patrolled the hedgerow where Zapata and Philberto diligently harvested strawberries.

"I need to think of some way to thank your cousin for babysitting Versailles all day," Zapata whispered in Philberto's direction.

"You don't need to get Alejandra anything. She loves kids, especially Versailles."

"Why does she like Versailles so much?" Zapata was curious. "All she can really do is eat, poop, and cry. It's got to grate Alejandra's nerves after a while, especially considering she looks after so many of the other workers' kids too."

"I think Alejandra likes Versailles so much because she has a crush on you," he smiled, thrilled that he was making his friend blush a bit. The lighthearted moment was, however, made heavy by Edgar's presence. "Y'all don't get paid to talk," he barked.

"Come on Jefe," Philberto smiled wryly as he retorted, "maybe we work better when we can talk. It distracts us from how lousy you pay us. Ever think of that?"

Edgar hopped of his mare and charged Philberto. He wrapped his arm around Philberto's neck and choked him from behind, lifting the boy off the ground. Philberto choked as he tried to wriggle free from Edgar's crowbar-like grasp. Zapata, along with all the other workers, were stunned still during the sudden assault.

"You talk when I tell you to talk and you shut the hell up when I say so!" Edgar hollered as loud as he could, so that all the workers in the field could hear him. Life was fast escaping Philberto. His legs went from frantic kicking to completely limp. His eyes rolled back in his head. Edgar finally – mercifully – let loose with him.

"From sunup to sundown Monday through Saturday you are the company's property! You eat and shit when I tell you! You talk when I tell you! You shut the fuck up when I tell you!" His shrill voice reverberated through the strawberry fields. "Now all you lollygagging beaners get back to work!" He cast his forefinger at Philberto, who was doubled over on his hands and knees, desperately trying to pull air into his lungs. "This lippy asshole just cost all y'all a water break!" He shoved a wedge of Red Man chewing tobacco behind his bottom lip.

Zapata held his hand out to Philberto in order to help his friend to his feet. But Philberto, who was both dazed as a result of the assault and smarting from embarrassment, refused assistance as he struggled to regain his balance and footing. The other workers dutifully continued working, as though nothing untoward had occurred. Zapata, however, had greater difficulty ignoring the outrage.

Dusk had descended over the strawberry fields. Zapata, whose mind was cluttered and whose heart was heavily distressed, was the only worker wide awake in the back of Carlos' Ford truck while being shuttled back to the tent city on the outskirts of Kingman. The other workers were bushed and hoping to catch a few winks of desperately needed rest after an especially long and hot day of harvesting. Zapata sat silently a while, gazing the fields fly by and the moon rise over the horizon. As the tent city came into view on the near horizon, Zapata felt emboldened to nudge Philberto awake with a slight rap of the elbow into his friend's ribs.

"Why did everyone ignore what happened today?"

"What do you mean?" Philberto, who was a bit groggy, seemed slightly confused.

"That asshole nearly killed you," Zapata lamented. "Nobody even seemed bothered by Edgar's attack."

"Edgar and the others rough us up all the time," Philberto said. "He was right; they don't pay us to talk. He was just doing his job."

"But you have a basic human right to not be abused by your employer, especially for something as trivial as chatting while you work," Zapata, who was beyond disheveled, blurted.

"Look," Philberto explained, "we're illegals. We don't have 'basic human rights.'" He looked at Zapata as if he were an ignorant child woefully out of his depth. "Workers go missing all the time for much less than ignoring an order. I'm lucky they didn't bury me out in the desert with the others."

"Why do you let them treat you like this?" Zapata's respect for his friend was slightly wavering.

"What choice do we have?" Philberto chuckled. "Besides, even when at their worse, things here are still better than back home."

"It's not better for those buried in the desert," Zapata shook his head dejectedly as he gazed at tent city, hoping to catch a glimpse of Alejandra and Versailles.

"I'm not buried in the desert," Philberto smiled as the truck rolled to a stop. "I'm here, with you. Let's grab a cerveza and forget today ever happened." He seemed completely undaunted as he hopped over the side of the truck bed and made his way quickly towards the scent of cooking chicken wafting from a barbeque grill somewhere on the premises.

The vibe at the tent city was far less tense than it was in the bed of the pickup. "Look," Carlos said to Zapata as the two followed Philberto," the only way to do this job is to let the day go when it ends and start fresh in the morning. Go give Versailles a hug and kiss, get some food, have a beer, get a good night sleep, and forget about today. Put it behind you and move forward. Today was just a figment of your imagination. Start fresh in the morning." He patted Zapata gently on the back.

CHAPTER TWENTY-THREE

Kingman, Arizona, September 1939

Zapata quickly integrated into the community and was glad to feel part of something bigger than himself. Living in tent city and harvesting strawberries from sunup to sundown six days a week in a strange and distant land was far from the dream of buying a farm for Maria and Versailles which had helped him endure so many terrifying and soul crushing moments in Spain. But still, he wholeheartedly believed that Versailles stood a far better chance of living a more sustainable existence in a rural community such as the tent city in the Arizona high desert than in a place as inhospitable as New York City was during the Great Depression.

More than a week went by without incident. Zapata did as Philberto suggested and kept his head down and mouth shut during days slaving away on the Rush family's strawberry fields, and then he learned to leave the adversity and travail of the day behind him in the evening, so as to genuinely enjoy quality time with his daughter for the first time in either's lives. It was, for a time, a workable system.

The last Sabbath in September 1939, Tio Carlos sneaked into Zapata's tent just after sunrise. Zapata was bundled under a wool blanket atop a cot. Versailles was sleeping snugly in a crib Tio Carlos had made for Zapata the previous Sunday. Carlos gently nudged Zapata awake. Carlos smiled diffidently as he dangled the ignition key of the Buick in front of Zapata's groggy face.

"Your car is finally ready," he said in a tone attempting to mask his sense of pride in the accomplishment.

"Carlos, you're a genius," Zapata gushed as he dug his hand into the pocket of his Levi's. "I can't thank you enough."

"There's no need to thank me," Carlos grinned as he set the key next to the cot. "I like to fix things. It's my passion. I even fixed your busted taillight just for fun. What was that, buckshot?" He flashed a suspicious grin at Zapata, who remembered how terrified he was that the young shotgun-toting Texan at the Texaco station outside of Amarillo might inadvertently shoot Versailles as the Buick sped west on Route-66.

"Yeah, uh," Zapata stammered as he grasped for an alibi, "it was a hunting accident." The words tumbled clumsily from his mouth.

Tio Carlos chuckled to communicate, 'I know you're lying, but it doesn't matter anyway.'

"Please, take this" Zapata insisted while holding a handful of crisp but crumpled bills he stole from the cash register at the Texaco in Texas, which he retrieved from the pocket of his dusty blue jeans. He held the handful of crumpled bills in front of Carlos, "I'm sorry that I can't afford to give you more."

"No, please Zapata," the graceful pride emanating from Carlos was fast replaced by awkward uneasiness. "I don't want any of your money. You already paid for the rod, which took more than a week to get here. Please, just consider the labor as a gift from an amigo to his new friend." He gently kissed Zapata on the cheek and patted him softly on the shoulder as he stood to exit the tent. "Just make sure to say goodbye to me, Alejandra, and Philberto before you go." He hurried from Zapata's tent, bound for the smell of freshly made coffee wafting from another tent.

Zapata sat up at the edge of his cot squeezed the key to the Buick tight as if it were a totem, then shoved it and the crisp billfolds into the pocket of his blue jeans. Versailles stirred awake and smiled up at her father as he kissed her chubby cheek and brushed a curl that reminded him of Superman's from her forehead.

The other workers were surprised to see Zapata climb onto the bed of Carlos' pickup truck at the crack of dawn Monday morning. Everyone expected that the gringo and his little girl would have left the moment Carlos had finished fixing the Buick. Zapata, however, felt as though he had become part of the community. He felt as though they genuinely cared about his wellbeing. He certainly cared about many of them, especially Philberto, Carlo, and Alejancra. They helped distract him from the agony he felt about losing Maria.

Zapata had originally planned to leave for California the very same Sunday afternoon the car was repaired. But he had so much difficulty bidding adieu to his new friends, that he decided the postpone departure until the next morning. By Monday morning, he had decided to stay a while longer in order to raise a bit more money before heading into the great unknown.

The sunrise truck ride to the Rush's strawberry fields from tent city was somewhat jovial. The other workers razzed Zapata, saying things like, "you wish you were Mexican," and, "once you go beaner you never go back," and other self-deprecatingly off-color remarks that helped alleviate the normal somber Monday morning blues sentiment that was most common on the first ride of the week out to the fields.

The sense of light-heartedness evident on the ride from tent city was a distant and fleeting memory by noon. The Indian summer sun was directly overhead and blistering. The thermometer read one hundred and twenty-one degrees. The few jugs of water that were designated for the dozens of workers to revive themselves had already been tapped out by ten in the morning. Productivity was slowed drastically as a result of the onset of dehydration and heatstroke several of the workers were battling through as they harvested berries. The diminished work rate made Edgar and the other overseers increasingly irate. They, all of whom rode horseback and had perpetually full canteens, assumed the workers were hung-over or, worse yet, simply being the lazy and shiftless stereotypes they were already preconceived to believe. The overseers were, like the pickers, certainly made extra uncomfortable by the intensity of the heat. But their canteens runneth over with water as they patrolled the rows of crops on horseback. They thus did not really understand the suffering endured by the workers in the Rush's employ.

Zapata and Philberto's waning focus was interrupted further by a stark commotion transpiring in the southwest quadrant of the Rush's property, which was quite near the highway. Both Zapata and Philberto tried to ignore the fracas for fear of being punished. But the commotion grew so persistent and dragged on so that their curiosity soon subsumed their inhibitions. They dropped their canvas sacks half-full of berries and hurried towards the highway. They saw Edgar hop down from his mare and race over to someone laying face flat in the dirt. "Philberto!" a shrill voice screamed. "Philberto, hurry, it's your Tio!"

The mix of curiosity and confusion on Philberto's face was instantly replaced by concern as he hurried across the fields towards Carlos. Zapata chased after him.

"Get up!" Edgar hollered into Carlos' contorted face after rolling him onto his side. Carlos, who had been struck down by sunstroke, was suffering a violent seizure and choking on a mouthful of dirt. Edgar was not sympathetic. "Stop your goddamn lollygagging!" He barked, then plowed the toe of his snakeskin boot into Carlos' thigh.

Philberto was as furious as he was frightened. He charged at Edgar, but was stopped dead in his tracks as the overseer aimed his rifle squarely at his chest. "Gettin' kilt ain't gunna save your uncle, boy." Edgar explained.

"Please," Zapata pleaded, "Somebody needs to call an ambulance!"

"They won't call an ambulance," Philberto seethed dejectedly, begrudgingly accepting his uncle's fate. "The Rush family risks getting in trouble if one of us illegals dies on their land while picking their crops. That's why so many of us are buried in the desert. Man, Tio is as good as dead." He knelt down next to his uncle and caressed his sweat soaked face with the back of his dirt-covered hand.

Zapata cautiously crept towards Carlos and dropped to his knees in the hopes of somehow reviving him. He pressed his chest and tried to give him mouth-to-mouth resuscitation, like he had seen someone do in a movie before. But Carlos did not survive the seizure.

A few of the other overseers dragged Carlos' corpse away and plopped it onto the back of his truck. "Look on the bright side," Edgar said callously and with malice as he tossed a set of keys at Philberto, "you inherited his truck." Philberto charged at Edgar, but was quickly restrained by Zapata and a few other pickers.

"Where are you taking him," Zapata demanded. "His family and friends have a right to give the man a proper burial and memorial. You can't just dump him in the fucking desert."

"You want the body?" Edgar seemed unfazed, "take it. So help me God, if anyone involved in law enforcement learns of this, you'll all have unholy hell to pay. The rest of y'all get to work unless you went to be on the next truck back across the border." He spit out a mouthful of tobacco residue.

Philberto was despondent and silent as he drove the truck back to tent city as the conclusion of the workday. Carlos' body was prone in the bed of the truck and surrounded by several of his friends, including Zapata. They were all evidently heartbroken, but lacked a sense of outrage that Zapata felt was both rational and requisite. "What the hell is the matter with you?" he chastised his comrades. "How can you let people treat you like this? If you let people treat you like this they always will. Wouldn't you rather die on your feet than live on your knees?" None responded. They all kept their eyes cast low, lost in their thoughts and paralyzed by fear and anguish.

Zapata scooped his daughter up from Alejandra's tent and exited without saying a word. Alejandra had never seen Zapata so irate before, which inspired concern. He fast gathered all his belonging and hurried towards the Buick, which was parked at the front of the tent city. He tossed his belongings into the front passenger seat, and then plopped Versailles in the back seat. He hopped in the driver's seat, furiously rolled down the window, and revved the engine. Alejandra hurried from the collection of tents and stood directly in front of the Buick's fender just as Zapata put the car into drive.

"Where are you going?" she demanded. "You're going to leave like this, without saying goodbye?"

"I've had it with you people," Zapata grunted as he begrudgingly put the car back into park.

"What do you mean, us 'people'?" she was equal parts confused and offended.

"They all just stood by and watched Carlos die," he began to cry. "We outnumber the overseers twenty-to-one, yet they can abuse us with impunity. I've fucking had it."

"Please," she said as she reached into the window and turned the car off. "You don't understand what it's like. We have no choice but to take abuse. We're not spineless, like you may think. We are just poor. What choice do we have? We know how unfairly we are treated. But life is not fair. That's a fact. But an unfair life is still better than no life at all."

"A life full of tyranny and misery is no life at all," Zapata snapped back.

"Our lives are not 'filled with misery,'" she explained. "We can find moments worth living here and there – in the simple pleasures. In a strange way, the bad times only serve to make the good times that much better. You know that old cliché – whatever doesn't kill us just makes us stronger – it's true."

"What about your father?" his voice quaked. "He's not getting any stronger now that he's dead."

"My father is in a much better place now that he is dead," she said matter-of-factly. "He's finally in a place where there is equality. My father once told me; life is like a game of chess. There are kings and there are rooks. But after the game, they all end up in the same box."

"You really believe that hocus pocus?" Zapata chortled condescendingly.

"Of course, I do," she beamed. "What choice do I have? Now please, come pay your respects to my father with the others. He really cared about you and would want you to stay a while longer. We're going to have small service and fiesta in his honor. At least stay until after you pay your respects."

A deep and sorrowful sigh escaped Zapata as he reluctantly opened the door. Alejandra took Versailles from the backseat of the car and snuggled her tightly as she led Zapata back towards the collection of tents.

Philberto, who was driving Carlos' truck, stared straight ahead and did not say a word. He was pensive and nervous. Zapata and the others, who were huddled on the bed of the truck, were likewise mum. A heavy tension was evident amongst the workers because they knew conflict with the overseers was a very likely possibility once they arrived at the Rush's property.

Edgar, who was riding on horseback with canteen full of water around his neck and a loaded 12-guage shotgun at his side, whistle as loud as he could in order to officially signal the start of the workday. The laborers, however, refused to harvest. They instead stayed near Carlos' pickup truck and the water jugs with their arms locked together, forming a unified wall.

"What in the holy hell do you idiots think you're doing?" Edgar flashed a wry smile that masked throbbing anger.

"We won't harvest until you meet our demands," Philberto said timidly. Edgar glared a long and tense moment at Philberto and the other workers linked arm-in-arm. His eyes eventually settled a moment on Zapata, who he regarded as the true source of his problem with the workers and thus regretted ever letting toil his father's fields. He then gazed long and hard at his fellow overseers, each of them on horseback and toting loaded shotguns and canteens full of cool water. They all suddenly began to laugh hysterically in unison. The workers seemed confused.

"Alright, little beaner boy," Edgar tried to compose himself as he spit out of mouthful of tobacco residue, "let's hear your 'demands.'"

Philberto's hands trembled as he unfolded a small piece of paper. He took a quick breath to compose himself. "We demand a water break every hour on the hour. We also demand a half workday Saturday. We also demand $250 so that my tio can be buried with his family in San Luis, and also so his children have a bit of inheritance to soften the blow of losing their father."

"Boy," Edgar rebutted, "for $250 I could fire and hire a whole new crop of beaners."

"The hell you can," Philberto's anger and confidence grew simultaneously, as though both emotions fed the other. "You'd lose thousands of dollars today alone if we all collectively decided not to work today. Who'd pick the berries, you and your boys?" Philberto chuckled condescending as he flashed a quick glance at the privileged overseers keeping watch of the workers. "Paying the $250, which is far more than fair, would be nothing compared to having to explain to your father that you lost him thousands of dollars' worth of profit in a single day."

Edgar glared down a moment at Philberto as he quickly crunched the numbers in his mind, ultimately calculating that it would be far more cost effective to relent to Philberto's demands. He gazed over at another overseer, who reluctantly nodded his head ever so slightly, as if to say, 'he's got you there... checkmate.'

"Alright then," it pained Edgar to say, "I'll get you your $250 by the end of the Sabbath so you can send your uncle back across the border. And you got your hourly water breaks. But there is no way in all of god's earth that my daddy is gunna agree tuh let y'all take half of Saturday off. He'd sooner kill the lot of y'all and me too than let you cheat a half a day a week from him."

Philberto's beseeching eyes glanced down the line of workers locked arm-in-arm until they settled on Zapata. He slightly shrugged his shoulders and nodded his head. The reassurance emboldened Philberto.

"Okay," Philberto broke ranks with the other workers linked arm-in-arm and approached Edgar. "We have a deal." He was beaming with a sense of elated pride and accomplishment as he boldly held his hand aloft for Edgar to shake. Edgar did not like thinking of the workers as human any more than his father did. He was thus reticent to shake hands with Philberto, but finally did.

"Now get to work!" Edgar demanded. "We're losing daylight."

Philberto glanced up at the sun directly overhead, then nodded and smiled as the other workers, including Zapata, hurried to make up for time lost harvesting. Edgar shoved a fresh wad of Red Man into his bottom lip, wiped his chin clean with his sleeve, and stewed bitterly over losing a faceoff for concessions with what he felt was an inferior people and terribly ungrateful workforce.

Mr. Rush had been drinking whisky since lunchtime. He had eagerly awaited the arrival of his son, Edgar, since getting word of the workers' revolt earlier in the day. It was well after dark when Edgar was beckoned into his father's office. Mr. Rush was carving a fourteen-ounce T-bone steak into bite size pieces, yet seemingly had no appetite. He was too concerned about how to proceed to savor the meat. He shoved the plate to the side as Edgar sat across the wobbly card table doubling as a desk.

"Well, daddy," Edgar asked pusillanimously, "what'd ya think we ought a do?"

"Hell, we can't just get rid of all of em," he huffed, "it'd be too expensive to send them all back. It'd be cheaper to kill em all. But the last thing we need is some engine findin' a mass grave out in the dessert and the law connectin' back to us. That might be the one way to turn the law against us."

"I say we just pay them the goddamn $250," Edgar seemed slightly squeamish, "and then put this damn nightmare behind us."

"You're getting' soft, boy," Mr. Rush gazed upon his son with air of disappointment and disgust, which deeply wounded his son. "We can't pay $250," the elder Rush enlightened Edgar. "Paying those uppity beaners $250 would be admitting guilt and could set a precedent that might reverberate through the entire valley. Hell, before you know it, the beaners all through the valley will be submitting their list demands and striking if we don't bend to their will. There's no way in all of god's creation I'm about tuh let a bunch of beaners tell me how to run my business."

"Well,' Edgar's voice lowered an octave, "what in the hell can we do? We can't send them back and we can't kill them all."

"We had a real garden of here, didn't we boy?" Mr. Rush chafed. "What ruins a garden?"

"I'm quite sure I don't know what you're gettin' at daddy," Edgar bewilderedly shook his head and slightly shrugged his shoulders.

"We got us a weed in our garden, boy," Mr. Rush elaborated. "We need to pluck it out before it destroys the whole garden." His heavy and weary eyes gazed intensely into his son's tattered soul. Edgar exhaled a deep and tense sigh as he nodded. Mr. Rush, whose appetite had suddenly returned, pulled his plate of meat back in front of him and shoveled a hunk of especially rare steak into his mouth.

The moon was high in the sky. Zapata, ever the insomniac, stared at the ceiling of the canvas tent overhead. Rustling and footsteps cautiously approaching the tent alerted him. He sat up on his cot and listened hard to the darkness. "Who's there?" he whispered frightened. He received no response. He perched on the edge of the cot. A murky and mysterious figure appeared at the entrance of the tent. "Who is it?" he whispered once more.

"Alejandra," she whispered softly. Alejandra, wearing an ivory colored linen nightgown, inched towards the cot, climbed underneath the wool blanket, and pressed her torso against his. "I'm so cold and sad," she confessed.

"I'm so sorry you lost your father," he said. "I know how hard it can be to lose someone you love."

"You do?" Her doughy eyes gazed at him. "How do you know?"

"My wife," he was reluctant to elaborate details. "She passed away when I was in Spain."

"Oh Zapata," she nuzzled her nose into the nape of his neck. "I'm so sorry for your loss. But I'm very glad that we can comfort each other."

The two warmly cuddled closer, thereby providing much needed human contact, as well as emotional and spiritual support to the other, if only for a few fleeting moments. But cuddling turned quickly into heavy petting. Heavy petting soon became kissing. Coital intimacy seemed inevitable. Then, Versailles began to fidget a bit in her crib, which seemed to sober Zapata. "I'm sorry," he whispered in Alejandra's ear. "I think you are wonderful; any man would be so beyond lucky to be intimate with you, but I can't. It's too soon. If we're intimate at this vulnerable stage, there's a good chance I will fall in love with you. I'm just not ready for that. I've got lots of thinking and heeling to do before I could be in a healthy relationship. I don't want us to end up hating each other because we jumped into the deep end while we're both in such emotionally vulnerable places."

"I agree," she sighed and smiled sweetly as she gave him a quick peck on his cheek. "Let's just get some sleep. Both of us have full days ahead." She curled tightly against him for warmth, closed her big brown eyes tight, and exhaled a deep and soothing breath.

Not much talking and even less listening was done on the truck ride from tent city to the Rush's strawberry fields the morning after Zapata and Alejandra shared a cot and covers. She stayed behind at tent city to look after the children. Zapata, Philberto, and the others dutifully showed for work at the crack of dawn, even though Edgar had yet to pay the $50 promised, which was earmarked for sending Uncle Carlos' body back to Mexico so he could be buried in his hometown. Philberto waited with great anticipation all through the day to be paid. Dusk finally settled over the valley, but Philberto still had not been paid, which made for a tense situation.

"I'm sorry to be a nag," Philberto said hesitantly to Edgar as the others were loading onto the trucks at the close of the workday, "but my tio is rapidly decomposing and we need to get his body back home as soon as possible."

"Sorry," Edgar flashed a half-grin knowing full well Philberto and the others were sans bank accounts. "I forgot my checkbook. "Tell you what, I'll give you the $50 in cash Saturday, when I pay you for the whole week."

"If we wait until Saturday," there won't be anything left of him to send home."

"Goddamn it, boy," Edgar said after spitting a mouthful of tobacco residue a few feet from Philberto, "I said Saturday. Now you can take it or leave it." His hand surreptitiously caressed the oaken butt of his rifle.

The end of Saturday – payday – was the biggest reason Zapata and Versailles remained in Arizona. Sure, Zapata was tempted by Alejandra. He was also terribly attracted to her. But the reasoning behind in his rebuff of her advance the previous night was genuine. He was deeply scarred by the death of his parents and friends in Spain, and especially damaged by the death of his wife, which he felt largely responsible for. He was afraid that if he were to fall into an intimate relationship with Alejandra that one if not both of them could be destroyed in the process. He also feared that his presence amongst the pickers was ultimately causing more trouble than good. Carlos' death and the controversy swirling around it, coupled with the tension over Philberto being paid $50 to bury his uncle in Mexico seemed to exacerbate the fact that Zapata was exposing his newfound friends to inevitable risk and reprisal by the Rush's. He was thus desperate to leave. But he had to wait until after the close of the workweek – Saturday at sunset – to be paid the money he had already earned and desperately needed to start a new life.

"Hey King Gringo," Rush hollered to Zapata as he climbed aboard the truck bed at the end of the workday. "Why don't you take a ride with us?" The other overseers, all six of who were on horseback, surrounded the truck.

Philberto flashed a concerned glance at his friend before furtively shaking his head in the hopes of convincing Zapata not to go with Edgar and the other overseers.

"What the hell for?" Zapata insisted.

"Not sure," Edgar responded plaintively. "Daddy said he'd like a word with you. That's all I know."

"Don't go," Philberto grunted under his breath, "or you're dead."

"Ain't like ya got a choice in the matter," Edgar grinned as he lowered the barrel of his shotgun. Zapata took a deep breath in the hopes of composing himself, and then slowly climbed over the side of the truck bed.

Edgar, who was still toting his twelve-gauge, followed Zapata into his father's office. "Care for a whisky?" Mr. Rush pushed a glass full of Wild Turkey across the card table used as a desk. He then downed full glass, and wiped a bit of whisky from his moustache with his hand. Edgar put his hand on Zapata's shoulder and guided him into the seat across the table from Mr. Rush.

"Let's just get to it," Zapata insisted.

"Man of action," Mr. Rush smiled as he slid the glass of whisky earmarked for Zapata back across the table. He took a quick gulp, then slid a photograph across the table for Zapata to peruse. "What's that?" Mr. Rush prodded.

"A license plate?" Zapata said finally after closely examining the picture.

"Yes," Mr. Rush smiled, "but whose license plate is it?"

"I don't quite understand what you're getting at," Zapata shook his head as he shrugged.

"That's the license plate on your car," Mr. Rush grinned. "Only problem is, Edgar here had a buddy of his at the Sherriff's office run your plates trough the FBI database. Turns out, your car actually belongs to a Charles Chesterfield of New York, New York."

"Yeah," Zapata explained, "Old Charlie, he's a pal of mine. He sold me the car for a good price after I got back from Spain."

Edgar and his father glanced at each other and chuckled. "Our man in the sheriff's office said the car was reported stolen a couple of weeks back."

"That can't be," Zapata stammered. "There's got to be some kind of mistake."

"Tell you what," Mr. Rush continued, "all you gotta do is get the hell out of Arizona tonight and don't ever come back. If you ain't gone by sunup, we're gunna have tuh let the sheriff sort out who the rightful owner of the car is. Those are the best terms you gunna get, boy. Tell you what though, my hunch is that you stole that Buick. If it is stolen, you stand to lose an awful lot, most especially that precious little girl of yours," he slurped down the rest of the glass of Wild Turkey. Now, I tell you what, Edgar's gunna be so kind as to run you over the Beanerville so you can mosey on out of here as soon as possible. Boy, don't let that Arizona sun rise on you, or so help me god." He signaled for his son to lead Zapata towards the door.

Edgar followed Zapata out of the office. Zapata was concerned, but also glad he would never have to speak with the drunkard Rush again. "Walk three miles that way," Edgar said as he cast his index finger west, "you'll find your beaner friends."

"Your dad said you were taking me back to tent city," Zapata said.

"Yeah, well…" Edgar scratched his chin, "I ain't." He climbed into his Chevy pickup and fired up the engine.

"What about the money you owe me?"

"I don't owe you shit, boy," Edgar revved the engine. "Get out of Arizona tonight or there's gunna be all kind of hell to pay, not just for you but the beaners too. He floored the gas pedal. The back tires kicked up dirt, which enveloped Zapata as he watched the truck speed east on Route-66. Zapata finally headed west with his thumb wagging in the warm wind, hopeful that someone would be gracious enough to pick him up and escort him to tent city.

Zapata was exhausted by the time he dragged himself into the tent city outside Kingman. It was well after midnight. Most of the workers were sound asleep. But Alejandra was wide-awake, and looking after Versailles, who was asleep. Alejandra cooked Zapata some scrambled eggs and refried beans, then tucked him in bed, promising to wake him long before sunup.

Zapata, who had suffered from insomnia ever since he traveled to Washington D.C. in the summer of 1932 with his father, was so terribly tired that he fell asleep the moment his head touched his musty pillow. Unfortunately for Zapata, he dreamed of heartbreaking memories that had been repressed since he was an adolescent. His subconscious exposed him to aching memories of tens of thousands of World War I veterans assembled in the nation's capital to demand that President Herbert Hoover and the federal government pay them their desperately needed bonuses for their service during the "Great War," which technically was not owed until 1945. Many veterans were, however, pulled into poverty as a result of the stock market crash and were living hand to mouth. They were thus especially desperate for the payout.

Zapata actually enjoyed the Amtrak ride from the Penn Station to Washington. It was a much-needed bonding experience between the son and his father, who had gradually retreated more and more inside himself since returning from France in 1918, and especially since the market crash of 1929. Zapata was proud to guide his father, who was donning his Army uniform, through train station in his wheelchair. He was even more proud to escort his father on a march from the White House on Pennsylvania Avenue to the Lincoln Memorial. He also had fun camping with thousands of other protesters and their families on the tent city they had constructed on the grand lawn next to the Smithsonian, one of which taught Zapata to drive his rickety Model-T. Zapata and his father were best friends that fateful summer in the nation's capital. The son even began to feel as though he understood his father more intimately than ever, which made him care for and respect him to a degree he never had before. Zapata had never seen his father so charming and charismatic, so determined, and so courageous as he did those six weeks camping out and protesting with working class people from all across the country.

The experience was, for a time, a kind of therapeutic heeling for many of the veterans assembled in

Washington D.C. in the summer of 1932. That sentiment was, however, shattered in July when President Hoover demanded that the protesters be removed from government property. The protesters, many of whom considered themselves to be carrying on the legacy established by the continental army, which pulled a similar stunt in order to be paid their bonuses earlier than scheduled back in the eighteenth century when the republic was in its infancy, were to be expelled from government property. "Many protesters championed refrains such as, "We the people are the government! Government property is the people's property!"

Hoover was, however, preoccupied with a reelection campaign and thus determined to get the protesters, who were a terrible public relations problem, off the front-page of the newspapers. But he never considered paying them their bonuses early, which would have helped him save face. Dispensing the bonuses early would, Hoover and his cabinet believed, set a nasty precedent in which the federal government could be beholden to mob rule. In July, Hoover reluctantly ordered his attorney general, William D. Mitchell, to do all in his power to convince the veterans to leave government property with all due haste. Mitchell kicked the order down the chain of command to the local police. Mitchell hoped that if a riot ensued, it would be the metro police, rather than the federal government would take the blame, thereby insulating the president from further controversy.

A riot did in fact ensue when the Capital Police Department stormed the lawn next to the Smithsonian.

Thousands of protesters were injured in a melee, and two police officers were shot. Hoover's poll numbers dipped precipitously. He was backed into a corner and thus felt compelled to order over to Army Chief of Staff, Douglass MacArthur, to remove the rest of the veterans.

MacArthur was a military man. He did not think in terms of reelection campaigns, public relations, egalitarianism, et cetera; he only thought in terms of either gaining or losing objectives. His objective was to remove the rabble from government property. He did not care how politicians on Capitol Hill or newspaper reporters were to perceive his methods. He was given an order, and thus considered the veterans potential enemy combatants. He also believed many, if not most, were, whether they were conscious of it or not, doing the work of Bolsheviks. He thus had no qualms about employing violence to force the veterans – American citizens all – and their families from government property. MacArthur deployed an entire infantry, including six tanks, against the ragtag protesters.

The campsite was ultimately razed, which sent thousands of frantic protestors and their families fleeing government property for their lives. Zapata tried to rush his father from the flames engulfing the campsite. The wheelchair, however, moved especially slowly and clumsily on concrete, never mind a grassy hillside encampment. Leopold and Zapata were attacked with impunity. A few troops, none of who was older than twenty-two, tossed Leopold from his wheelchair and beat he and his son savagely with the butts of their rifles. Zapata struggled to aid his father, who tried to claw his way to safety. He wailed and cried from the physical pain, but even more so from the emasculating fact that he was powerless to defend his son from assault at the hands of his own government, a system he had literally given limbs to preserve. As battered as his body was, it did not even begin to compare to how shattered he was spiritually after the attack.

The assailants finally ceased assaulting Leopold and his son in order to peruse other protesters fleeing the flames. Leopold, whose face was covered in blood as a result of a flesh wound on his scalp, sobbed disconsolately as his son wrapped him in his arms and swayed him back and forth. Zapata, who had long revered and feared his father, never saw him through the same eyes again. Sure, he still loved and cared for his father. But the son always saw his father as pathetic, helpless, and broken after the summer of 1932. Their relationship would forever be tainted because both forever harbored the awkward discomfort of the submerged memory of being completely overpowered, injured, and humiliated by their own federal government. The son and his father could never even manage to look the other squarely in the eyes ever again.

Zapata woke suddenly. He pulled a deep and hollow breath of air into his lungs. Versailles was standing wobbly legged at the edge of her crib staring at her father and crying. He wiped crust from his eyes and hurried over to Versailles. He plucked her up, held her tightly to his chest, and rocked her soothingly back and forth. He could see day breaking through the egress of the tent.

"What in God's name?" Edgar, who was riding his mare and sipping his canteen muttered. He was dumbfounded to see Zapata hop over the side of the truck bed and approach the fields with dozens of other workers. He had heard his father order Zapata to leave town less than twelve hours prior. The consequences of Zapata staying in Arizona were, Mr. Rush assured, dire. Edgar watched with bewildered amazement for more than an hour, observing Zapata, who, along with the others, worked as diligently as usual.

The sun rose high in the sky and the temperature skyrocketed. Edgar eventually blew his whistle, signaling a water break. Edgar approached Zapata as he was waiting to take a sip from the water jug.

"What in god's name are you doing here?" Edgar demanded.

"Getting some water," Zapata said matter-of-factly.

"No, dummy," Edgar's patience was waning fast. "What in the hell are you still doing in Arizona?"

Philberto cast a long glance at Zapata, who, although desperate for every penny owed, was unbowed. "I'm not leaving until I'm paid what I'm owed for services rendered. I'll leave Arizona the moment I'm paid me for the money I earned and you pay my associates the $50 promised to send Tio Carlos back across the border."

Edgar's eyes settled momentarily on a fellow overseer, who was riding a beautifully shiny black gelding. He grinned and nodded slightly. Zapata inferred that delaying payment and letting Tio Carlos' body decompose to the point that there would be nothing left to bury in Mexico was their plan all along. He called their bluff. Edgar aimed his rifle squarely at Zapata's chest.

"Why you makin' me do this, boy?" Edgar grimaced. "Look around you," he added. "This is Arizona. This state doesn't have much. But it does have seemingly endless horizons of places to dump a dead body. You been nothin' but trouble for us since the minute you got here. You made your daughter an orphan." He cocked the rifle and steadied it. Philberto, followed by a dozen other workers stepped in front of Zapata to shield him.

"You'll have to kill us all," Philberto's voice was steady. More workers crowded around Zapata, creating a human wall.

"This don't concern y'all," Edgar was grunted. "Y'all get back to work, or so help me god, my daddy will send every last one of you back across that godforsaken border and will make sure not one of you ever makes it back."

"We're not working until you pay my friend the wages he is owed," Philberto's courage grew precipitously, "and not until you pay me $50 cash."

Edgar cast a long and inquisitive glance at the overseer atop the gelding. He seemed gob-struck as he shook his head and shrugged his shoulders. "Get back to work right this minute, god damnit!" Edgar was coming undone.

"Come on," Philberto's confident voice reverberated through the fields, "let's take the rest of the day off to give Mr. Edgar some time to consider how valuable we are to him and his family!" Philberto, followed by the others, strode determinedly towards the trucks parked along Route-66. The other workers stayed close to Zapata in an attempt to insulate him from potential harm.

The overseer atop the gelding reeked of concern as the workers boarded the trucks in unison. Edgar was suffering a terrible conundrum. He understood better than anyone besides perhaps his grizzled father that the company stood to lose thousands of dollars for each day his workforce was on strike. It would, in the interim, be much more cost effective, in fact, to pay the $50 to send Carlos back across the border and the payment owed to Zapata. But Edgar feared that establishing a precedent in which he cowed to the workers' demands would let a genie out of the bottle that could never be put back in. He stewed angrily but sat stock-still atop his mare and watched helplessly as his entire workforce quickly crammed onto trucks and headed west on Route-66 bound for the tent city outside Kingman.

Night had settled over tent city, which enhanced the sense of tense insecurity. Nights in tent city were normally festive and filled with joviality. But the uncertainty of the future as a result of the workers walking off the job earlier in the day unsettled things.

Philberto, Zapata, and a few other workers, all of whom had their mouths and noses wrapped with red bandannas in attempt to ward off the stench of rapidly rotting flesh, lugged Tio Carlos' corpse from a tent secluded far from the others, out by the roost where the free-range chickens roamed. They plunked the pine box Philberto fashioned as a receptacle for his uncle's body down in the dirt. It instantly attracted fruit flies. Philberto was banging the final nail into the top of the makeshift coffin with his hammer when he was alerted to a pickup truck speeding along the dirt road that ran perpendicular to Route-66, which led directly into tent city. Philberto, Zapata, and many of the other workers hurried towards the front of tent city. He was hopefully Edgar had come to cede to the workers' demands, and ultimately offer reconciliation in the interest of creating a more harmonious working environment for everyone.

The workers gathered around Philberto and Zapata. They all ached for good news. Edgar, who was flanked by five of his most trusted overseers, men he had gone to school with when they were boys. Each was white-knuckling fully loaded Remington Rifles – the gun that won the west. The show of force made the workers – most of whom were desperately hoping for a resolution that would allow them to back to work in the morning – terribly uneasy. Zapata, who had engaged in savage battle with employers before, was especially distressed by the animus exuded by Edgar, who was clutching a shiny chrome Colt-45, as he strode towards the uneasy workers.

"You've gone and done it now," Edgar seethed. "I've never seen daddy so upset. Why in the hell didn't you just go like you was told? If you'd a just left Arizona like daddy said neither of us'd be in this goddamned pickle!"

"Look, all you gotta do is pay us the money that you owe us and all of this mess goes away!" Zapata pleaded. "It'll be like it never happened."

"Nah," Edgar lamented. "The dye has been cast. Word of you and your beaners' strike has already spread through the valley. The other farmers are afraid of a general strike, a goddamn revolution. The only way to get the genie back in the bottle is by getting rid of you." He cocked and aimed the chrome Colt-45 at Zapata's head. Zapata did not blink. He would not give Edgar the satisfaction of flinching. A frantic murmur rippled through the crowd of workers. Several onlookers, including Alejandra, who was holding tight to Versailles, nervously hurried from the scene and sought shelter in a tent towards the back of the community.

"Please," Philberto pleaded, "you don't have to do this! Just pay us the money rightfully owed and all of this goes away. Why risk a murder charge over a few hundred dollars?"

"It's not about money, boy," Edgar enlightened the young migrant worker. "You don't quite understand how things work up here in Arizona. Your pinko friend from New York here came out here to our land and filled you ignorant beaners' heads with pie in the sky ideas of equality. Truth is, there ain't never been no kinda equality in this world. There have always been brainworkers and mudsills. We're the brainworkers," he motioned towards the overseers, all of whom were white men. "Y'all are the mudsills," he motioned towards the workers gathered around Zapata and Philberto. "You start meddlin' with God's design, and tragedy like this is the inevitable result. That's how nature works." He squeezed the trigger of his Colt-45.

The gun barrel flashed white-hot light. A solitary bullet lodged in Zapata's forehead. Blood spewed down his nose, lips and chin. He stared forward with an oddly appeased expression on his face. He stood on his feet for what seemed like a few seconds, then finally fell prone and motionless. Blood splattered on Philberto's dusty Converse high-tops. He and the other workers grossly outnumbered the overseers, but were far too stunned and heartbroken to redress the murder. Their dejected brown eyes cast long gazes at the crimson earth beneath their feet. "The rest of y'all be sure to get a good night sleep," Edgar callously bellowed. His voice reverberated through the fields – his birthright. "Anyone of you dumb enough not to be harvesting by the time the sun comes up in the morning will be on the first truck back to San Luis. Ya hear?" He wiped a bit of blood from his snakeskin boots, shoved his gun into the waistline of his Fruit-of-the-Looms, and then walked calmly and confidently back towards his pickup truck as though order in the universe had been restored.

It was close to midnight by the time Philberto had finished fabricating another coffin for his nearly dead friend. He and a few other workers plopped Zapata's blood-soaked body into the box, which was next to Tio Carlos' fly covered coffin. Three police cars with lights and sirens blaring on the dirt road perpendicular to Route-66 fast approaching the tent city diverted Philberto's attention. He and several other workers nervously navigated their way through the mass of tents towards the front of the community, where the patrol cars skidded to a halt. A young deputy, a former school chum of Edgar's, cautiously approached the fearful migrant workers. Alejandra, whose eyes were bloodshot from crying all night, continued to hold Versailles tight as she cautiously approached the commotion. The deputy and the other seven law enforcement agents backing him up all had their guns drawn and seemed ready to do battle. They cut an especially menacing figure compared to the heartbroken and frightened migrants.

"Which one of you is named Philberto?" the deputy demanded. None of workers responded. "One of you beaners better cop to," the deputy's frustration was already at a crest, "or, so help me god, I'll get INS out here and you'll all be back across the border by lunchtime." A long and tense moment ensued. "Alright then," the frustrated deputy plucked his radio from the holster on his hip, "y'all leave me no other option." He pressed the button on his radio. "Hey there Sheila," he spoke into the device, "can you get me INS on the horn." Philberto reluctantly stepped forward. "Scratch that, Sheila," the deputy spoke into the receiver, then holstered it. "Okay, fella, hands behind your back, boy," he ordered Philberto.

"What the for?" Philberto's voice betrayed the fact that he was terrified.

"Murder," the deputy said as he clamped chrome cuffs around Philberto's trembling wrists.

"Murder?" Philberto was bewildered. "I've never killed anyone!"

"We got an anonymous tip from a source that said if we were to search the premises here, we'd surely find at least two dead bodies."

"My uncle and my amigo's body are boxed up in the back," the words fumbled from Philberto's frantic mouth, "but I didn't kill anyone."

"Yeah, well," the deputy said as he guided Zapata into the backseat of his patrol car, "you can tell your story to the judge and jury."

The deputy hopped in his cruiser and aimed it towards Route-66. The other deputies, all of whom were nervous and had their guns drawn, made their way cautiously towards the back of the community in search of the dead bodies that had been reported. One of the younger workers, a boy who considered Philberto a mentor, hurled a rock at a deputy, which caused the cop to open fire. The other officers also fired rounds into the crowd. A panic followed by a riot ensued. A kerosene lamp was mistakenly kicked over in the melee. Fire spread rapidly through the tent city. Versailles, who was being held by Alejandra as she ran as hard as she could towards the highway, wailed at the top of her lungs. Zapata, who was but a few breaths from being completely brain dead, could hear his daughter crying far in the distance. The sound gradually grew fainter and more distant until it was completely inaudible.

Zapata rose to his feet and stepped out of the blood-filled pine box and walked calmly across an open pasture as the orange sun was setting, casting purple, pink, and yellow hues across a lavender sky. Versailles, who was now old enough to be in grade school, and Maria, who looked more unburdened and beautiful than he had ever seen her before, sat at a wooden picnic table next to a charming hillside house and barn, both of which were situated at the corner of sprawling dairy farm. Maria and Versailles seemed to be having the time of their lives as they swirled sparklers in their hands. Zapata looked down to see a sumptuous butter cream and chocolate cake in his hands. It read "Happy 4th of July" in blue and red frosting. A soothing wave of serenity washed over him. Then everything went black and completely silent.

www.ingramcontent.com/pod-product-compliance
Lightning Source LLC
Chambersburg PA
CBHW020532020726
47494CB00006B/1733